Mistletoe and Mayhem

The Little Red Truck Mysteries

Book Three

Mistletoe and Mayhem

JANICE THOMPSON

BARBOUR
PUBLISHING

Print ISBN 979-8-89151-172-9
Adobe Digital Edition (.epub) 979-8-89151-173-6

Cover illustration by Victor McLindon

Published by Barbour Publishing, Inc., 1810 Barbour Drive, Uhrichsville, Ohio 44683, www.barbourbooks.com

Our mission is to inspire the world with the life-changing message of the Bible.

Printed in the United States of America.

"Do not fear, for I have redeemed you; I have summoned you by name; you are mine. When you pass through the waters, I will be with you; and when you pass through the rivers, they will not sweep over you. When you walk through the fire, you will not be burned; the flames will not set you ablaze. For I am the LORD *your God, the Holy One of Israel, your Savior."*

ISAIAH 43:1–3

CHAPTER ONE

"Mom, please don't cry." I settled into the spot next to my mother on the sofa and rested my palm on her shoulder.

"But. . .you're moving away." She turned to face me, tears welling in her soft blue eyes. "I never thought it would actually happen, RaeLyn. It's just taking me a minute to get used to the idea that you won't be here much longer, that's all."

I released a lingering sigh.

"Nothing will be the same."

And that, of course, was what had her most upset. Change didn't come easily to my mother.

To any of us, actually. I'd always pictured myself living on the Hadley family property forever, even raising a family here on the sweeping sixty-three acres that had framed my life. I felt sure my one-day children would settle easily on the land and keep the traditions going. But my sweet fiancé had other plans. Big plans, apparently, though I hadn't been able to weasel the details out of him just yet. And for now, at least in this very moment, the idea of doing something brave and adventurous with him felt good. Felt right. No matter how much it pained my mother.

"What if he's moving you off to Timbuktu?" Mom dabbed at her eyes with her stained floral apron. "What then?"

My heart quickened at the very idea. Then, just as quickly, it settled back down. "Mason would never do that." I spoke the words with confidence. "He knows my heart is here, in Mabank. I've got my column at the paper. And my work at Trinkets and Treasures. I love that store. Besides, he knows I could never move far away from my family."

I adjusted my position on the large leather sofa in our spacious living room, the one I'd spent every day of my life in for the past twenty-seven years. Leaving would be so hard, for all of us. But I wasn't going far. I hoped.

"You're sure?" Her expression told me that she was not convinced.

"Very. Mason wouldn't take me away from all of that, so please don't fret."

"But he's got all that money now." Mom sniffled, as if my fiancé's income was some sort of curse instead of a blessing. "He could take you away to an exotic new life in some place exciting, far away from Mabank, Texas."

"Again, he would never do that," I countered, my heart now firmly affixed to my throat. "And we both know Mason would trade every penny of that settlement to have his daddy back."

A pained look filled her eyes, and I could tell she felt remorse for her words. "I'm sorry I mentioned the settlement. I'm just saying you'll have everything your heart could desire now that money's no object. I don't know why that scares me a little, but it does."

"Mom, look at me." I gazed at her with greater intensity than before. "I've *always* had my heart's desire. This life you and Dad have provided for me all these years has been the best any girl could ask for."

I pushed back the lump that rose in my throat as I spoke those words. Growing up on the Hadley acreage was idyllic. I wouldn't trade a moment. But things were different now. With the wedding coming up, Mason and I would need our own lives, our own space.

"Then why. . ."

"Mason and I are going to be honeymooners." I cleared my throat as I felt heat warm my cheeks. "We'll need privacy."

Her eyes lit with a spark of excitement. "I promise never to bother you if you take your aunt Bessie Mae's room."

Oh boy. This was my cue to refill my coffee cup. I headed into the kitchen to do just that. Mom tagged along behind me.

"Now that she's moved out it's just sitting there empty," my mother explained. "It's nice and big, with its own bathroom and closet. A nice closet, plenty spacious enough for you and Mason."

"I know, Mom." I did my best not to sigh aloud again. She'd only mentioned this possibility hundreds of times. But I needed time away with Mason to start our new lives together. And I couldn't imagine anything more awkward than living the first few months of my married life in the room my eighty-three-year-old aunt had occupied for the past several years.

"I understand." My mother's sigh felt a bit exaggerated. "And, to be honest, your dad has this bright idea that he and I should move in there. It's bigger than the master."

Well, this was a delightful idea! "I think that's the perfect plan. You two deserve your own honeymoon. Maybe you could even redecorate." Should I mention that her 1980s decor in the current master was woefully out of date? And it would be fun to see Bessie Mae's old room decorated in anything other than John Wayne posters.

"If you help, sure. You've always had a better eye for things like that than me." Mom's nose wrinkled. "Of course, you'll be really busy, so I doubt you'll have time."

"I'll still be around after the honeymoon. You know I'll be here at least four days a week, manning the store."

"Right."

"And I'm excited to see what Mason has planned." I settled in at the breakfast table and set my cup down. "This all feels like a big adventure. Hopefully Mason will tell me what he's been up to over the past few weeks." With only a week until our big day, he'd better get a move on.

"Any ideas?" Mom walked to the coffee maker and filled her mug.

I fingered the handle on my coffee cup. "I heard Wyatt Jackson's place was up for rent, so I'm thinking that's it. He mentioned it in passing one day and we even drove by there a time or two. So I'm guessing he's already got a contract on it."

Mom wrinkled her nose as she took the seat next to me. "That place is pretty run-down. I was there about six months ago delivering a meal and noticed how rough it looks. And besides, it's only four acres. Mason has to know you would want more land than that."

"Mom, I would live in the apartment above his car shop if he asked me to."

My mother fanned herself with her hand. "Heavens. Let's hope it doesn't come to that."

I knew better, of course. Mason's tiny apartment above his auto repair shop wasn't exactly honeymoon material, and we both knew it. I wouldn't be able to wash the scent of motor oil out of my hair, no matter how hard I tried. I suspected he had something far greater in mind. If only he would fill me in.

"Things are going to be hard enough with Bessie Mae married and living over at Bob's place now." Mom rested against the back of her chair and reached for her coffee mug. "I'm not used to doing all of the cooking for this crew. That's going to take some getting used to."

It was strange, knowing that Aunt Bessie Mae would no longer be here as well. But if anyone deserved a happily ever after with her childhood sweetheart, it was my sweet elderly aunt.

"Get the twins to help you. Dallas and Gage can cook."

Mom snorted. "As if."

Okay, so my twin brothers weren't always the most helpful inside the home, especially with their new jobs. But Dallas could definitely cook. He and Tasha had been working side by side at her family's seafood restaurant for months now. And both of the boys were handy around the property, as were my older, married brothers, Logan and Jake, who both lived in their own homes on the Hadley property.

"I know transitions aren't easy, but soon you and Dad will have the house to yourself."

I had a feeling Dallas was going to be proposing to my BFF Tasha any day now, but this probably wasn't the day to share that news with my mother. She seemed distraught enough already. And now that Gage had a steady girlfriend, his attention had shifted too. And I dared not mention my brother Logan, who lived in the trailer on the back of the property. His recent elopement to his fiancée, Meghan, had pretty much sent my mom over the edge. Not that I blamed her. Our most responsible family member running off and getting married without our involvement was a knife to the heart, and a bit of a shock, to be honest.

The back door opened, and my father came in. He stomped his feet on the mat and then took several steps toward the coffeepot.

"Welp, that was the last run to Bessie Mae's new place." He slumped into his usual spot at the end of the table and pulled off his worn farm cap. "I think we got everything from her list." Dad swiped his hand over his wavy hair and pressed the cap back on.

"So she's all settled in over there?" Mom asked. "That's nice."

"I'm not sure *settled* is the right word," my dad said. "She was carrying on about Bob's kitchen. Apparently, it's not a baker's kitchen, whatever that means. And I guess she's not keen on the size of his pantry. Oh, and he doesn't have a second fridge in his utility room like we do. So that had her worked up. I'm thinking this move will take some adjustment."

"For all of us." Mom sighed. "But I'll text her and let her know that she can always come back home and bake her pies here. Just because she's married now doesn't mean she has to spend every waking moment with the man."

My dad gave her an odd look. "Flora, they're honeymooners."

With a wave of a hand, Mom appeared to dismiss this idea. "Chuck, honestly. They're in their eighties. I would imagine they're both happy just to abide under the same roof."

"We'll see. Last I saw, she was removing his old mismatched dishes and silverware from the kitchen and putting her stuff in their place. I'm not sure Bob knew what to make of it all, but he seemed to be playing along."

"Once she fries up a chicken-fried steak for the man, he won't complain," I said. "And I know she feels very strongly about those dishes. They've been in the family as long as I can remember."

"Yes, they have." Mom's eyes narrowed. "And she just walked right off with them, like they belonged to her."

"Mom!"

"Okay, they *do* belong to her. They were her mother's dishes. But I got used to them too, so they felt like mine all of these years. I know we've got our old set, but it's chipped and worn."

"If it's new dishes you want, then dishes you shall have." My father rose and stretched his back. "Pick out some new ones next time you're at Walmart. My treat."

"Good grief." My mother groaned. "Thank you for your generosity."

"I've been trying to convince her to redecorate the new master bedroom too," I chimed in.

My dad's eyes lit up. "Does this mean we're moving into Bessie Mae's room, Flora?"

Mom shrugged. "If RaeLyn is absolutely sure she doesn't need it. I was kind of hoping. . ." Her words drifted off.

"As soon as I get back from my honeymoon we'll go shopping for your new bedding and decor," I promised. "We'll make a day out of it. Maybe even a few days, depending on how much you want to buy."

My father rested his hand on the counter. "Hey, I said I'd spring for new dishes, not new bedding."

"Speaking of. . ." Mom's eyes took on a faraway look. "Maybe we should look at getting new bedroom furniture. We've had that same old set since we got married a million years ago."

"Before dinosaurs roamed the earth, apparently," my father muttered. "Now I'm regretting this whole idea. I'm fine with my current bed in my current room, thanks."

"I don't think you're getting off that easily, Dad." I offered him a warm smile.

The back door opened and my brother Gage stepped inside, a brisk gush of cold air coming with him. Tall and lanky, he seemed to tower above the rest of us as he drew close.

"The temperature dropped overnight." Gage crossed the room to grab a coffee cup out of the cupboard. He filled it and then took a swig. "This might end up being the driest December on record." His gaze shot my way, and I knew why. With my wedding coming up in a few days, the weather was bound to be a factor. "It's like a tinderbox out there. The chief told us to be on high alert."

His new job at the Henderson County Fire Department was pretty much all we heard about these days. Not that I blamed Gage for being concerned about the dry fields. Our sixty-three acres were in rough shape. The land was so parched one spark could set the whole thing ablaze. The very idea sent a shiver down my spine.

"I should check the weather app to see what this coming week looks like." I reached for my phone from my pocket.

"RaeLyn, it's too soon for that." Mom clucked her tongue at me. "Don't fret. The wedding is still almost a week away."

"Yeah." I set the phone down on the table. Still, I couldn't help but worry a little. After weeks of drought, the whole county was praying for rain. But me? With only seven days till the big day, I prayed any rain showers would come and go quickly. I couldn't imagine a soggy field on my wedding day.

"You sure you still want to get married outside. . .in December?" Dad took another swig of his coffee and gave me a pensive look. "It's not too late to change your mind."

"About getting married, or having the ceremony outdoors?" I pushed my phone aside after seeing that the weatherman predicted dry but cold weather for the next several days. "Because I'm definitely getting married."

"You've got the church on standby for an indoor ceremony, right?" My dad rested his palms around his coffee cup. "Folks would understand if you changed it."

"They might even appreciate it," my brother added. "Not everyone will be comfortable outdoors."

"In December." My dad rose.

This wasn't the first time they'd debated me on my wedding plan. Getting married in a field with bales of hay for seating might not be everyone's dream, but it was mine. I'd been planning for this event since I was seven.

Okay, so I had always pictured it happening in the springtime, with bluebonnets springing up around us. I'd never once considered a winter wedding. But waiting until spring seemed impossible now that I'd given my heart to Mason Fredericks.

I would become his bride, and the sooner, the better.

CHAPTER TWO

"Dad, I've been dreaming of getting married on our property since I was seven," I reminded him as he settled down at the kitchen table after refilling his coffee cup. "Besides, what's a little hypothermia between friends?"

"I guess you're right," he countered. "So, it's cold on your wedding day. So what? Our tears of joy will just turn into little icicles. No problem."

"Dad."

"At least the cake won't melt," he added. "Gotta look for the silver linings, right?"

"We'll have goose bumps bigger than that diamond on your ring," Mom chimed in. "But it will be worth it."

My parents were really on a roll today.

"I've been thinking about buying thermal blankets for the guests," Dad said. "Otherwise they might just freeze in place and look like statues."

"Are you serious?" I paused to think this through, though I had a feeling he was just joking around. "We would need so many."

He shrugged. "Just mulling it over. If we don't keep them warm, folks are going to send me their doctor bills afterward. I can't afford that and a wedding too."

"Very funny." He might have been joking, but there was a layer of truth to his words. He was fronting a lot of money for this wedding, and everything needed to go smoothly.

The back door opened, and my oldest brother, Jake, stepped inside. The door slammed closed behind him, suctioned by the wind. As it did, the glass window shook.

"Heavens!" Mom walked over to check the window to make sure it hadn't broken. "Must be rough out there."

"Winds are high. Hopefully they'll die down overnight."

I breathed a sigh of relief, hoping his presence would distract everyone from the conversation about my outdoor wedding. But when he looked my way, I could tell something was up.

"Just wanted you to know that Annalisa has a cold. Carrie's worried it's about to turn into an upper respiratory infection, so she's taking her in to the pediatrician in Athens just to make sure she's okay."

"Oh no!"

This was terrible news. My tiny niece wasn't even a year old, but I'd chosen her to be the flower girl on my big day. We planned for her mom to pull her down the aisle in a red Radio Flyer wagon, all decked out in a frilly ensemble we'd chosen from a baby boutique in Tyler, complete with a ruffled pink sweater.

"I'll be praying she's okay," I said. And not just because of the wedding. That little girl meant everything to me. To all of us.

"You sure you don't want to move this wedding indoors?" he asked. "Temperatures are going to drop this week. We'll have to figure out a backup plan for the baby if it's too cold."

Good grief. Was this a coordinated attack?

Mom dove into a discussion about the home remedies Jake and Carrie should try with Annalisa. Before long, she was scurrying around the kitchen looking for ingredients to make some sort of medicinal concoction that Carrie would surely never give her baby.

Before I could mention that, the door opened again and my brother Logan stepped inside with his new bride, Meghan. His wavy hair jutted up in wild tufts, as if he'd been doing battle with the wind.

Meghan and Logan were deep in conversation about something, and it looked pretty intense, judging from her furrowed brow. This wasn't a side of my easygoing sister-in-law I'd seen before, so it intrigued me.

"Hey, y'all." Logan offered a faint smile, but it disappeared pretty quickly.

"Everything okay?" I shifted my attention to Meghan, who looked a little off.

"Yeah." Her nose wrinkled, and she fussed with her dark, messy curls. "Fine."

It was that kind of "fine" that convinced me things were not, indeed, fine. But at least the attention diverted to her and away from me.

"Better tell her, Meghan," Logan said.

She looked my way and released a loud sigh. "Remember I told you that my bridesmaid dress was too big?"

"Yes."

"Well, I had it altered—I found a great place in Athens—only, now it's snug. Miserable, in fact."

"Oh my."

"It's okay. I'll just hold my breath."

"For the whole night?" Logan asked.

Meghan shrugged. "Hey, we do what we have to do. Right, ladies?" Her gaze shifted back and forth between Mom and me.

Mom shook her head but remained silent.

Poor Meghan. She'd spent the last five months trying to impress my mother, to no avail. Running off and eloping with my brother had sealed her fate as an interloper. Mom wasn't one to let go of things easily, especially this. Until recently, Mom had privately referred to Meghan as "the one we don't speak of."

Only, now Mom was ready to speak, judging from the look on her face. "I wish you'd come to me, Meghan," she said. "I'm pretty handy with a sewing machine. Would you like me to take a look at it? Maybe I can take it out a little."

Go, Mom!

"Would you?" The relief on Meghan's face was evident. "That would be great."

Dad rose from the table and carried his coffee mug to the sink. "Anyone seen Dallas? I need his help with something in the barn."

"I sent him into town to pick up some pizzas," Mom explained.

"Pizzas?" My father's eyes widened. "Bessie Mae moves out, and now we're having pizza for dinner instead of real food?"

"Let the fireworks begin," Meghan whispered.

"Only because it's been such a busy day," my mother explained. "I'm not setting a precedent or anything."

Truth be told, we were all wondering how Mom would fare without Bessie Mae in the house to do most of the cooking. My mother could cook. She just preferred not to.

"Pizza is real food, Chuck," Mom said. "All of the food groups in one handy bite. And we can use paper plates."

"Bessie Mae is gone, and we've already entered the realm of paper plates and pizza at the Hadley estate." My father sighed. "I wondered if things might end up here."

"If it's such a big deal, then feel free to grab some meat from the freezer and cook it up yourself, Chuck," Mom said. "There's a grill out back, if you've got a hankering for a home-cooked meal."

Thank goodness, that conversation never went any further. Dallas arrived with the four large pizzas. As the back door opened, the howling wind seemed to propel him inside, almost causing him to drop the boxes and sending a definitive chill into the room.

My father grumbled. . .until Dallas opened the box with the meat lover's pizza inside. Then he grabbed a couple of slices and took his usual spot at the table. I opted for a couple of slices of pepperoni and extra cheese. Then we all joined him at the table moments later, and the conversation shifted in more positive directions.

Dallas settled into the spot beside me and offered a wide smile. "I stopped by Tasha's place earlier, and she's really excited about hosting your brunch on Tuesday. She's already hard at work on the house." He took a big bite of his slice of pizza, and a contented look came over him.

I couldn't help but smile as he mentioned my best friend. Tasha had really outdone herself as my maid of honor. And not one rude comment about my outdoor ceremony. They could all take some lessons from her.

"She's a great maid of honor." I dabbed at my lips with my napkin. The pepperonis on my slice were a little on the greasy side.

"She *is* a little panicked about the weather," he added. "Something about how her hair doesn't do well in cold? I dunno." He shoveled the rest of his slice into his mouth in one swoop.

Good grief.

Gage glanced my way. "Hey, I need to get out to the barn to check on Delilah, so I thought I'd go ahead and count the bales of hay while I'm out there."

I smiled as he mentioned the name of one of my favorite mares. Delilah was set to foal any day now.

"How many hay bales did you say we'll need?" Gage gave me an inquisitive look.

"I'm thinking at least sixty," I countered. "We can seat three people per bale, right? Roughly?"

"Depends on the width of the backsides," Dad chimed in.

"We've got RSVPs for 170, maybe more. I really need to get Mason to give me his final numbers." I took another nibble of my slice of pepperoni pizza, savoring the delicious crunch of that crispy crust.

My fiancé had been noticeably absent this week. Usually he got back with me ASAP when I texted, but nearly every text over the past three days had gone unanswered until later in the day.

An odd feeling of concern washed over me, but I did my best to push it away. Mason loved me. No doubt he was just distracted with our housing situation. My sweetheart was very detail oriented and was likely up to his eyeballs in contracts and such.

The conversation about hay bales made a natural progression to a chat about the quilts that would cover each of the sixty bales. By then we'd finished up the pizza, and I rose to help my mom with the cleanup.

"How are you coming with the quilts, Mom?" I asked. She had agreed to take on this project from the get-go, and I knew she wouldn't let me down.

"Bessie Mae has four, we've got six, Dot has five, and Melody Burchfield has been gathering them from the ladies at church. There are over forty of them there. She said we can pick them up tomorrow."

"Perfect. I know that Tasha has a couple," I said. "And Summer has one as well."

Mentioning Gage's girlfriend, Summer, sent the conversation in a different direction. Summer's son, Colt, was going to be our ring bearer and—from what Gage was now telling me—had a suspicious rash on his neck.

Perfect.

We wrapped up our meal, and Gage offered to walk with me out to the barn to address the bales of hay.

We were greeted by my beautiful cattle dog, Riley, who was bouncing up and down with excitement at the cold weather. As we walked together, the brittle grass crackled underfoot, and a brisk cold breeze ribboned its way around us, offering up the familiar scent of hay. I loved that smell.

"This dog was born to live on a ranch," I said. Which made me wonder how she would make the transition to wherever I happened to be moving. Was it really fair of me to pull her from the only place she'd ever known and take her to. . .I wasn't sure where. I patted her on the head and paused, my gaze shifting to the skies above.

"I saw lightning earlier," Gage said. I could hear the concern in his voice.

I decided to offer a little encouragement. "Weather app says no rain."

"Right. This was dry lightning. I know you're worried about the field, but personally I wish it would go ahead and pour right now, days out from the wedding. With this stupid drought, we could really use the rain, and the land will dry up in no time. It's so parched."

I released a sigh. "Tell me about it. I was hoping for a pretty backdrop for the wedding, but everything is as dry as a bone."

"You know me." He paused for a moment and appeared to be thinking. "Just hoping we don't end up with any brush fires."

"That would be awful."

"There's a burn ban going on, so hopefully folks will heed the warnings."

"Surely they will."

I shifted my gaze and tried to envision the pasture on the far side of the property fully decked out with those lovely rectangular bales of hay. Hopefully we had enough.

Gage and I went into the barn and did a quick count. Turned out we had more than enough. There were over seventy-five bales in total, and most looked to be in great shape. My dad joined us as we talked through the plan for how and when the bales would be set into place. We settled on Friday, just one day before the wedding. I hated to cut it close, but put them out too early and they might get soaked by rain. . .or snow.

I tried to press my concerns aside as and we headed back to the house. The wind howled through the pecan trees behind us and sent a rustling across the dry grass under my feet. Even the land was crying out for rain. Or snow. Anything to moisten the ground. But as much as I loved a white Christmas, this definitely wasn't the year for it.

CHAPTER THREE

Out of the corner of my eye I caught a glimpse of an old beat-up truck pulling up to our family's antique store on the far side of our property. I couldn't quite make out the driver as I squinted against the afternoon sunlight that streamed across the driveway, casting a warm, golden glow.

"Someone didn't get the memo that Trinkets and Treasures closed early today." Dad glanced my way. "Want me to see who it is?"

I agreed to go with him. Curiosity had the better of me.

Gage headed back toward the house, but I walked with my father over to the family's antique shop and watched as an older man climbed out of the driver's side of the truck. It took me a minute to recognize him as Buck Adler, a distant neighbor who had once attended our church. We didn't see a lot of Buck these days. Hardly ever, in fact. He had really aged. Wow. I did my best not to stare at the deep wrinkles in his face and the hunched-over way he held himself.

"You folks closed up already?" he asked as we approached, his deep, gravelly voice catching my attention right away. His truck door slammed shut with a resounding thud that echoed across the space between us.

The older man's worn boots kicked up a puff of dust as he shuffled across the gravel drive in our direction.

Something else caught my attention too. Mr. Adler reeked of smoke. That wasn't unusual in these parts, but during a drought? Definitely not something locals would do.

"Yup. Today was moving day for Bessie Mae," my father explained. "We're beat."

"Ah. Heard she and Bob Reeves got married." The weathered older man spit onto the parking lot, the scent of chewing tobacco now permeating the air around us. Lovely. He stretched his shoulders and attempted to stand straighter but winced in pain.

"We've actually shut down the store for the whole week," I explained. "Partly because of the holidays but also because I'm in wedding-prep mode."

"Oh?" He reached into his pocket and pulled out a tin of chewing tobacco. "Gettin' hitched?"

"Yes, Mason Fredericks and I are getting married on Saturday, just two days after Christmas."

"Fredericks." His brow furrowed. "That the one whose old man was killed in that horrible crash last year?"

"Yes." But I was glad Mason wasn't here to hear his father described as his old man. Ugh.

"Well, congratulations to you. Glad to see someone has something to celebrate." Buck muttered something under his breath as he rolled a wad of the stinky tobacco. Fine lines formed between his eyes, and for a moment I wondered if he might be angry about something. Just as quickly he shook it off and swiped at his nose with the back of his hand.

"How are things out by your place, Buck?" my father asked.

"Dry as a bone, just like here." The older man pressed the wad of tobacco into his cheek. "Every day I look up at the sky hoping we'll have a deluge, but so far. . .nothing. Driest December on record so far."

"It'll come," my father said. "It always does, in due season."

"Can't come soon enough for me." As he shoved the tobacco container back into his pocket, Buck grumbled something about how his property was at higher risk than most. I only heard about half of what he said. Honestly? My mind was on other things, like the streak of lightning that flashed across the sky on the far side of the property.

"Whoa."

"Dry lightning," he said. "I've been keeping my eye on it."

I nodded, my gaze fixed to the skies. "Yeah, that's what Gage said."

"Gage?" This name seemed to confuse him.

"One of my youngest," Dad said. "I've got twin boys—Dallas and Gage."

"Oh, right." His gaze shifted to his truck. "Well, if you're closed I don't want to bother you. I just came by to ask if you folks would take this old Frasier Oil sign off my hands. I don't want anything to do with 'em anymore."

"Why's that?" Dad asked.

"There was a time I could live comfortably off the money my place brought in from mineral rights from Frasier. But these days, there's barely enough each month to cover the light bill."

"I hear you on that." My dad's bright smile faded.

"It's really fallen off. And don't get me started on how Frasier Oil tried to rip me off. I had to hire a lawyer. Their lies run deep."

"I heard some folks ended up hiring attorneys," Dad said. "Sorry to hear you were forced to do that."

"They didn't give me any choice. And those lawyers cost a pretty penny, money I didn't have."

"I'm sorry."

"Welp, I'll keep on fighting till the well runs dry." He kicked the toe of his boot into the gravel driveway, stirring up dust. "Your father would have understood. He wasn't a fan of Frasier either. Liars, all of 'em."

"He never really shared the details of why he didn't trust them," Dad said.

"Too much to tell in one conversation." Buck spit again. "I'll tell you this—I'd sooner burn my place to the ground than lose it to the likes of Frasier Oil. They will never get their hands on it. Trust me when I say that's their endgame here, and they don't appear to be slowing down anytime soon."

"Are you saying Frasier is trying to take possession of your land, Buck?" My father's words were tight with concern over this news.

"According to the attorney, it's possible. You don't even want to know what they've put me through. I'm telling you, they're all a pack of liars and manipulators."

"I hear you on the mineral rights," my dad countered. "They've really dropped off."

"That's why we opened the resale shop," I explained. "We were looking for a way to make up for some of that loss."

"Well, if you think of anything I could do, let me know. Right now I'm barely scraping by. But I'm sure as shootin' not hanging on to any memorabilia from Frasier Oil, so if you want that sign—"

"Let's see it," my father interrupted and then glanced down at his watch. I knew he was worried about the time. He still had to tend to the animals and make sure Delilah had everything she needed.

Buck walked to the back of his truck and pulled down the sign, nearly knocking over a large red gas can in the process. He hefted the heavy can upright once again, then pulled out the sign.

My father and I gasped in unison as it came into view. The huge sign—which had to be at least three foot by four, was in mint condition. I walked over and ran my finger along the edges, looking for rust.

Nothing.

Not a flaw on it.

Buck ran his hand along the edge of the sign. "I took good care of it, as you can see. Kept it in the game room by my pool table. My wife always hated it. I guess she'd be happy to see it gone."

"I heard she passed away last year," Dad chimed in. "I was sorry to hear that. She was always so nice."

I remembered Mrs. Adler. She'd once taught my Sunday school class, back in the day.

"Thank you." Buck's face softened at the kind words about his wife. "Anyway, she'd be glad and I'm ready to be rid of it, so if you want to make me an offer, go ahead. Or we could list it on consignment. I don't know how you do things in that antique store of yours, but I'm game for whatever. Just don't want to think about Frasier Oil again."

No doubt we could get a pretty penny for it. We might even be able to sell it back to Frasier for their museum, which they'd set up at the front of their plant in Malakoff.

Dad offered him a fair price—$300—and Buck took it, and then I headed into the shop to grab the checkbook to pay him. Minutes later, he got back in his old truck and backed out just as the sun dropped off in the sky to our west.

Dad and I put the sign in the storeroom of the store, wedging it into the perfect spot. I gave it one last look, my heart overwhelmed with all sorts of feelings the sign brought up. Memories of my grandfather.

I ran my fingers along the lettering one last time before flipping off the light. The sign felt like a piece of Mabank's history, and I felt sure it carried untold stories.

We locked up the shop and headed back to the house.

"He seemed pretty worked up," I said as we made our way to the back patio.

"Yeah, Buck's always had a temper, but I get it. These oil companies don't always play fair. They always find ways not to pay up. It's hard to get to your sixties or seventies and not have the income you were counting on."

My father sighed, and I realized we weren't talking about Buck Adler anymore.

A wave of guilt washed over me. My parents had really struggled over the past year. I'd done my best not to be a financial drain. Mason and I had covered most of the costs of the wedding. Still, I would have loved to be able to wipe the look of concern off my father's face just then.

I slipped my arm around his ample waist and leaned against him. "In case I haven't said it, thank you for everything, Dad. You and Mom are the best."

"I don't know about all that." He shuffled alongside me, the toe of his boot kicking up dirt from the dry ground below.

"No, you are. And just for the record, I know you're sad that I'm leaving, but I promise I'll see you all the time."

"Well, sure you will." He pressed a kiss into my hair. "Someone's gotta keep the shop running. Your mom's gonna have her hands full trying to feed us all, now that Bessie Mae's gone."

"Gone, my eye."

A voice sounded from a distance, and I looked up to discover my elderly aunt standing on our back porch, pie container in hand.

"Bessie Mae, aren't you supposed to be setting up house?" I glanced into those twinkling blue eyes framed by soft crinkles in that beautiful skin.

"Yep. But I needed to try out that ridiculous oven over at Bob's place, so I baked up a pie." Her nose wrinkled as she shifted the pie container in her arms, nearly dropping it in the process. I reached to take it from her. As I did, the sweet aroma wafted up from the warm container in my hands, which only served to tease my senses.

"Bessie Mae!" I sniffed the air in dramatic fashion. "Seriously?"

"Bob has an electric oven. I'm used to gas. It's going to take some getting used to, but I suppose the pie isn't too bad. It's cherry, by the way." She glanced my way. "I know you love cherry, RaeLyn. Figured you probably needed a boost of energy for all that work you've got ahead of you this week."

"Aw, thank you. But where's your hubby?"

"Back at his place, setting up that new air fryer that Tasha gave us as a wedding gift."

"Don't you mean *your* place?" my dad asked.

"Right." She shrugged and her gaze shifted longingly to our back door, the one that led straight to the kitchen she'd always loved. "That might take some getting used to. Same with the air fryer. No idea what I'm supposed to do with a contraption like that."

"Air fryers are all the rage," I explained. "They do all kinds of things, especially the newer ones."

Mom stuck her head out of the back door, and her face lit up the moment she saw my aunt. "Bessie Mae! You've come home to us!"

"Only to drop off a pie," my aunt said. "But I'll stay for a slice, if you don't mind."

"Mind?" Mom practically dragged her into the house. "Of course we don't mind. Let me pull out some Blue Bell Golden Vanilla to go with that pie. It'll be just like old times!"

And at that, all the Hadleys were home again, at least for a few minutes.

CHAPTER FOUR

Sunday morning dawned bright. . .and dry. Still not a cloud in the sky. I could tell my dad was upset by this, especially as more dry lightning streaked across the skies. The poor man was probably weary with praying for rain.

I entered the kitchen, drawn by the tantalizing aroma of coffee and bacon. Mom had been hard at work this morning. I found her at the sink, dishes clattering as she washed them by hand.

Gage couldn't seem to look away from his phone as we ate our breakfast. From what I could gather, all his coworkers were stirred up about something.

Still, off to church we went, just a typical Sunday morning for the Hadley family. Unless you counted the part where I was getting married in six days. Woot!

As we walked out to the car, high winds caught me off guard. We loaded into Mom's car, the wind providing plenty of comedic relief as it pulled us to and fro.

"Whoa." I grabbed hold of my jacket as the wind threatened to pull it off me. I quickly zipped it up to lessen the risk of losing it.

The bright sunlight overhead caused me to blink. Or maybe it was the dust whipped up by the wind. It made my eyes sting. By the time we got to the driveway, my throat was feeling unusually scratchy and dry. I swallowed a couple of times to wash away the dry sensation. What a mess. All of this raised a host of concerns about next Saturday. Maybe Dad was right. Maybe I should go ahead and switch the ceremony to the church now, while I still had adequate time to make the necessary adjustments.

Of course, that meant I'd probably have to switch the reception from the tent on our property to the fellowship hall. Where we couldn't dance.

Decisions.

Mom usually drove her own car, but today Dad offered to take the wheel. Good thing too, because the winds made the drive to church unusually difficult. Mom was a nervous wreck as we approached the bridge just before town. "Hope we don't get blown into the lake." She gripped the door as if her life depended on it.

As we passed over Cedar Creek Lake, I couldn't help but notice how the bright winter sun reflected off the rippling waters below. They captivated me, as always. One thing could be said about the four seasons in Mabank, Texas. They all came with their own beauty. . .and peril.

We managed to make it to the church with no trouble, but when we got there we noticed several others struggling with the wind as they made their way into the foyer of the church. Poor Mrs. Oberdeen looked wobbly on her feet, so I rushed her way and slipped my arm through hers to steady her up the steps and into the foyer, where we were greeted in the usual enthusiastic manner.

I looked for Mason but didn't see him, so I headed to the ladies' room to check my hair. Sure enough, the wind had done a number on it. I looked like something the cat dragged in. I reached into my purse to grab my brush and then did my best to fix the mess.

Bessie Mae came in a couple of minutes later looking disheveled. She fussed at her reflection in the bathroom mirror. Her short white curls frizzled outward in multiple directions at once. And her bright floral jacket seemed to be suffering from a severe case of static cling as well. Oh my.

"Between this wind and my hair spray, I'm basically a tumbleweed waiting to happen this morning! Can you fix me up, RaeLyn?"

I did my best, but all that hair spray made my job tough. Her hair resembled a bird's nest today. And the bathroom's fluorescent lighting wasn't helping one bit.

"Bob is going to think he's married to a lion with an unruly mane."

She patted her stiff, chaotic hair and then shrugged. "Oh well. He's already stuck with me now."

"Stuck with you?" I laughed. "He's lucky to have you, Bessie Mae!"

"No." She turned to face me, and tears sprang to brim her lashes. "I'm the lucky one. I'm so blessed to have this chance after all these years."

I slipped my arm over her shoulders and pulled her into a gentle hug.

"Even if the man's oven leaves something to be desired." She sighed. Loudly.

An echo of voices from the hallway outside clued us in to the fact that the morning service was about to begin. We made our way to the back of the sanctuary, where I waved at a couple of golden-years folks passing by. I gave—and received—hugs. Lots and lots of hugs. The biggest one came from Melody Burchfield, our pastor's wife. I returned the embrace, so grateful to have her nearby. She'd been so valuable over the past few weeks, a big help with wedding plans. The woman had a gift.

"Hey, before you go today, I've got all those quilts I collected," she said. "They're in the fellowship hall."

"Oh!" Bessie Mae startled to attention. "That reminds me, I've got a handful of quilts for you too, RaeLyn. Be sure to get them on Tuesday after the brunch."

I nodded at both of the women, then turned my attention back to Melody. "I'll ask Mason to grab the ones you've gathered to put in his truck after service. I don't know that we have room in Mom's car, and Tilly is out of commission right now. She's stalled out in the parking lot of Trinkets and Treasures. Hasn't been moved in days."

I sighed as I mentioned my sweet little red truck, Tilly. What a terrible time for her to break down.

"Oh no. What's wrong with Tilly?" Melody asked.

I offered a little shrug. "Mason thinks it's the carburetor. Hopefully he'll get it all fixed up before the wedding. We plan to use her as a prop. And we'll drive off in her when the reception ends. If he gets her fixed, I mean."

"I pray it all works out." She rested her hand on my arm. "In the meantime, I'll see if I can get a bunch of the guys to help Mason load up all those quilts into his truck after church. Sound good?"

"Absolutely." Anything she could do to lessen my load would be good.

I made my way up the center aisle and found Bessie Mae's new hubby, Bob, seated in his usual spot, visiting with several of the men in his age group. No doubt they were all welcoming him back from his honeymoon, judging from the playful slaps on his back. The poor man looked more embarrassed than a hound dog in a tutu.

I sat next to Mason and filled him in on the quilts. He nodded, but he seemed a little distracted this morning. In fact, when Pastor Burchfield asked everyone to sit after the final song, I had to tug on Mason's hand to stir him to action. Weird. And he was usually more attentive to the people around us before and after service, but today he seemed off.

Meghan and Logan left as soon as service ended, headed out to the grocery store to pick up some things that Mom needed for Tueday's brunch. My dad had a board meeting. Gage was distracted by a phone call.

We caught up with Jake just before he rushed out to get home to Carrie and little Annalisa.

"What did the doctor say?" I asked.

He glanced back my way before reaching the door. "Negative for RSV and flu. Lungs are clear. It's all in the upper airway, which is good news."

"That's a relief."

Still, judging from the look on his face, Jake was anxious to get home to his girls. I didn't blame him.

Mason pointed himself toward the fellowship hall to collect the quilts. I offered to help, but Dallas and Tasha stepped up, ready to help him load up.

"Go visit with your friends, RaeLyn," Mason said. "Take a breather."

And so I did.

I headed out to the foyer, just like I did every Sunday morning. I always seemed to land in this familiar space. It had that "welcome to the family" feel about it, with its polished tile, flowers, and soft lighting. This was where true fellowship took place, and I loved it.

Today I found myself surrounded by friends and loved ones offering congratulations for my upcoming wedding.

My friend Annie James approached, all smiles. "I took my camera in to be serviced," she said. "I'm ready to go for the big day."

"I'm already looking forward to the pictures you're going to take." I gave her a warm hug.

"Hopefully we'll catch that sunset perfectly. If so, it's going to be amazing!"

She headed off to talk to her husband, Landon. I gave him a little wave, and he responded with a warm, "See you at the rehearsal!"

Landon would play the role of deejay on our big day, and I knew he would do a great job.

The hum of conversation carried on all around me, balanced against the strains of a familiar worship song, still playing in the adjoining sanctuary. I glanced around and saw Mom and Bessie Mae standing near the foyer doors, with many of their friends gathered around them in conversation. I took several steps in their direction but almost found myself toppling when one of the ushers opened the door to let someone out and a gush of wind swept through.

"Whoa."

"It's sure crazy out there today." These words came from the elderly Mrs. Oberdeen as she took quick steps toward the open door. "I feel like I might get blown off to Oz."

"Hopefully not!" I said.

"If I do, just look for the gal wearing the ruby slippers!"

"Do you need help getting to your car?" I asked.

Before I could assist, one of the other ladies reached for her arm, and off they went, into the windy abyss.

The doors closed again, and I attempted to rub the goose bumps off my arms.

I joined Mom and Bessie Mae and listened in as the ladies exchanged quick updates on family and community events.

As folks passed by, I welcomed a few more hugs, most of them from our church's seniors. I'd gotten used to being embraced by folks of all ages. That's how we did things here in Mabank. A hug could solve a thousand problems, especially one from a church friend.

Only, one friend was noticeably absent today.

"It seems so strange, coming to service without Dot here." These words came from Iva Gabriel, one of Mom's friends. What Iva lacked in height she more than made up for in fashion, as was apparent from her bright pink coat and wild floral scarf.

Twin sister Eva was more conservative in appearance but not personality. "That woman pretty much runs the town," Eva said. "So it is odd not to have her here. But I'm so glad she got to go on that amazing trip with her sisters. A cruise sounds divine." She turned to her sister, eyes wide. "We should do that, Iva! Let's take a cruise to the Caribbean!"

"Who would man the tea shop while we're gone?" Iva pulled a lipstick tube from her faux Gucci bag. "We can't afford to shut down."

"Summer could do it. Or we could hire someone temporarily. What do you say?"

Iva swiped on some lipstick and then pursed her lips. She seemed lost in thought for a few seconds. "I saw a documentary about a woman whose body disappeared off the side of a cruise ship. She was never seen or heard from again." Iva tucked her lipstick container back into her bag.

"The husband did it," Eva chimed in.

To which Iva responded, "It's always the husband. Which makes both of us perfectly safe, since we're single, Eva!"

A thoughtful look crossed Mom's face. "Then Dot's safe too."

Iva nodded with enthusiasm. "True! She's the strongest self-made Southern gal I've ever known."

"Life has given her no choice." Mom paused and appeared to lose herself to her thoughts. "She lost her husband at such a young age, poor thing. Raised the kids on her own, but they're grown and gone now, so she's become one tough cookie. Life has offered her no other option."

You wouldn't know it by watching Dot, that was sure and certain. If she grieved the past, she didn't let it show. Maybe staying so busy was just a way of coping.

"True." Eva nodded. "If a fella ever tried to shove Dot off a ship, she'd karate chop him."

"And then convince him to join the chamber of commerce," Iva threw in. "She's really persuasive."

She was, indeed.

I looked back and forth between Iva and Eva, taking in their petite statures and rounded physiques. "You two aren't allowed to go anywhere until after my wedding. I need you too much."

"Oh, honey, we're ready." Iva's eyes sparkled with delight. "The food at this wedding is going to be off the chain!"

"I believe the expression is off the charts, Iva," Eva said.

"Chain. Charts. It's going to be amazing." Iva rested her hand on my arm. "Just you wait and see."

"Well, anyway, I'm so glad Dot had this opportunity to get away for a while," Melody said. "If anyone deserves a break, she does. She worked so hard on our Thanksgiving food drive."

"And the Christmas toy drive too," Mom added.

"And the town's tree lighting ceremony," I said. "She has that down to a science."

"Dot threw the loveliest little brunch for the chamber of commerce members a couple of weeks back," Iva said. "The woman is a wonder, an absolute wonder."

Mom nodded. "Truth be told, Dot is a whirlwind, the busiest woman I know. But I never met anyone with a better head on her shoulders."

Boy, that was the truth if I'd ever heard it. My mom's best friend was the most loyal, solid, unwavering soul in town. She'd more than proven her dedication—to the Cedar Creek area and to us—over the many, many years we'd known her. And it did feel mighty weird to attend church without Dot in her usual pew near the front. But if anyone needed—and deserved—time away on a cruise, she did.

"Is Dot going to be back in time for the wedding?" Aunt Bessie Mae's words interrupted my ponderings.

Mom answered with a nod of her head. "Yep. She's coming back in town tonight." My mother glanced down at her watch. "Actually, the ship has already docked in Galveston, but she still has to drive back up. I believe she's dropping off one sister in Corsicana and another in Malakoff. This was a sisters cruise, one she's looked forward to for months."

I couldn't even imagine my big day without our town's biggest cheerleader. Dot was a fixture, a rock. Without her nothing made sense.

My thoughts shifted to Mom. Maybe she felt the same way, now that Bessie Mae and I were both leaving the Hadley house at the same time. Maybe nothing made sense to her right now.

"Are you and Mason taking a cruise for your honeymoon?" This question came from Iva, who gazed at me intently with a smile on her face. "Sounds so romantic."

"Nope. I didn't want to spend my honeymoon seasick," I explained. "The only time I went on a boat that size I ended up sick as a dog."

"That would never do." Iva's nose wrinkled.

"And Mason had a good point. He said a cruise would be really crowded. We'd be jam-packed with other people all around us. So we settled on an all-inclusive resort in Playa Del Carmen with all sorts of amenities. We're flying down there the morning after our wedding. Our flight leaves Dallas at 1:00 p.m. one week from today."

"Playa Del Carmen?" Melody asked. "Great name. Sounds so. . .exotic."

From what I'd been able to discover from photos and videos online, we were in for a real treat. I reached for my phone to show her pictures of the resort.

"It's right on the water. Just wait till you see the pictures of the beach." I flipped the phone around, and before long she was bug-eyed at the scenic pictures.

It seemed impossible, really. But one week from today, I would be Mrs. Mason Fredericks.

A delicious shiver ran down my spine at the thought of just how amazing our life together was going to be.

CHAPTER FIVE

"Earth to RaeLyn!" Eva jabbed me with her elbow. "Did we lose you, honey?"

"Oh." I felt my cheeks grow warm as my gaze shifted back to the photos on my phone. "Just thinking about the wedding."

"No you weren't, silly." Eva laughed. "You were thinking about the *honeymoon*. Ooh-la-la!"

Okay, now the heat in my face was harder to hide.

They all laughed, and I shifted my gaze to Bessie Mae's new husband, who had chosen that very moment to join us.

He looked back and forth between the ladies and asked the obvious question: "What are we talking about, folks?"

"Honeymoons," Eva responded, her thinly plucked brows arching.

"Oh." He cleared his throat and his gaze shifted to the floor. Then he looked back up with a smile. "Bessie Mae and I had a wonderful little road trip to Fredericksburg. Other than the part where my arthritis flared up and her diverticulitis kicked in, we had a great time."

Bessie Mae shot him a warning look. "That's TMI, Bob."

"TMI?"

"Too. Much. Information." Bessie Mae jabbed him with her elbow.

"You don't have to tell all of our secrets to the masses."

"This ain't the masses." He looked around from woman to woman, a smile lighting his soft face. " 'Sides, there's probably nuthin' these folks don't already know. My arthritis has made the prayer list more times than I can count, and don't even get me started on your diverticulitis."

Bessie Mae smacked herself on the forehead. "Good grief."

"RaeLyn and Mason are going to Playa Del Carmen," Iva chimed in. "Hopefully they won't have to deal with any of that at their age."

"Playa Del. . .what?" He put his hand to his ear, and I remembered his hearing loss.

"Carmen!" I said, my voice elevated above the noise in the foyer.

"Like Carmen Miranda?" he shouted back. "She was very popular, back in my day. Wore a fruit basket on her head."

"No, Bob. *Playa* Del Carmen." Bessie Mae turned to face me. "Show Bob the pictures, RaeLyn."

So I showed them all over again, this time to a very compliant Bob Reeves, who probably didn't care one iota about my honeymoon plans but who played along to make his new bride happy.

"Nice," he managed as I showed him a picture of a gorgeous palm-tree-lined beach. "But that would never work for me. My doctor told me to stay out of the sun. Skin cancer. Had three removed just last month." He rolled up the sleeve of his plaid shirt to show me a jagged scar above a crusty elbow. Lovely.

"Well, this is a very romantic conversation." Bessie Mae rolled her eyes. "I never dreamed married life would be so thrilling."

Bob reached over and gave her a kiss on the cheek. "How's that?"

"Better. For a fellow with arthritis you're still pretty limber." She gave him a smooch on the lips and several passersby applauded, including Pastor Burchfield, who encouraged Bob to keep up the good work.

Bessie Mae came up for air and hollered, "Hey, I was the one doing the work that time!" which caused Bob's cheeks to flame a crazy shade of speckled red. He quickly rolled down his sleeve and shuffled off to talk to the men. I didn't blame him one bit.

"A Caribbean resort sounds amazing, whether it's by plane or by cruise," Eva said. "One day we really can go, Iva. What do you say?"

Her sister's nose wrinkled. "I'll think about it. But right now, the only thing I'm thinking about is the grocery list for the wedding. We need to get going on that."

"Yep. We still have a wedding to get through before there can be a honeymoon," I responded.

"Absolutely." Iva turned my way. "If you have some free time tomorrow, could we have a phone call? Or maybe even a meeting in person? I've got some questions about the appetizers. I need to finalize the list before we make our grocery purchases. And if you have a final head count, I'll need that too. It's important we don't run short on anything."

"Agreed. And please let me know if we need to increase the budget." I lowered my voice, not wanting to draw attention. "Mason said it's no problem if we do."

"Honey, you're going to have a king's feast on a pauper's salary. If there's one thing Eva and I know how to do, it's how to make budget-friendly foods look fancy." Iva messed with her flamboyant scarf.

They did, indeed. They managed to do so at our local tearoom regularly. And I had no doubt they would pull off a miracle on my big day, wowing the crowd with their tasty and beautiful dishes.

"Speaking of the wedding, where's your groom?" Iva peered off through the crowd. "I thought I saw him earlier, but I've lost track of him."

"You and me both." I would have expected him to join us by now. I looked around but didn't see Mason anywhere. "Probably still loading up quilts."

"Actually, I think he's done with the quilts," Melody said. "I just saw him in the side hallway talking to Nadine Henderson. They had a pretty intense conversation going."

"Oh." That made sense. "He's working on one of her cars, the one she got in the divorce." My mind reeled back to the chaos of that divorce and the pain it had caused not just our dear friend but the whole town. Nadine's ex was a scoundrel.

I excused myself from the conversation and wove my way through the crowd to the side hallway, where I found Mason and Nadine deep in conversation.

Nadine finally looked my way and grinned. "Here's our bride now! How are you, honey?"

"Good. Just searching for my groom."

"I kidnapped him—sorry." She shrugged. "I've been bending his ear."

About what, she didn't say. Not that I was worried about Mason visiting with Nadine Henderson. She was a dear friend and had never so much as batted an eyelash at my fiancé.

Tasha walked up, and before long the four of us were in a discussion about lunch plans. We often went to Fish Tales, Tasha's family's restaurant, especially with Dallas working there now. I wasn't sure what the plan was for today, though.

"You missed a lively conversation about the honeymoon," I said to Mason.

"Oh?" He looked my way. "Why are folks talking about our honeymoon? We haven't even had the wedding yet."

"Which reminds me, did you ever find that track for the song we're dancing to? Landon needs it to add to his playlist. He wants to make sure we've got the right version."

The blank expression on Mason's face told me that he'd forgotten about it.

"Mason Fredericks!" Tasha gave him a stern look. "Does the maid of honor have to do everything? You can't download a simple copy of 'I Will Always Love You'?"

"I will, I promise. I've just been so busy. I'm juggling a lot."

Nadine's phone rang, and she reached for it. "Sorry, y'all. Gotta take this. I'll see you ladies on Tuesday at the brunch!" At that, she disappeared through the crowd.

Mason gave me an apologetic look. "I'm sorry, RaeLyn. I promise, I will get a copy of that song to Landon."

I smiled as he mentioned the name of our Sunday school teacher and good friend. "It's okay. This is his first time playing the role of deejay, and I want to make it as easy on him as possible."

"Right." Mason paused. "By the way, did you want the Whitney Houston version or the Dolly Parton version?"

This stopped me cold. Surely the man knew I would prefer Dolly's version. Did he not know me at all?

Before I could respond, Tasha said, "Dolly. Duh."

He gave me a thumbs-up and reached for his phone. "I'll buy it right now and share it with Landon. Give me a minute." Mason stepped away from us.

"He okay?" Tasha asked.

I shrugged. "Girl, you tell me. I sure hope he's not getting cold feet."

"Mason?" Her eyes widened. "Getting cold feet? Are you serious? He's loved you since you were in junior high, remember. There's a zero percent chance he's going to bail, I promise you."

"Something's up with him. Hope it's not wedding jitters."

"It's not." She patted my hand. "I suspect it's something else entirely. Something that will work out beautifully for you in the end."

I nodded, realizing she must be talking about my housing situation.

"God has bigger plans for us than we have for ourselves." She turned her attention to Dallas, who joined us at that very moment.

"You guys seen Gage?" Dallas asked. "He took off in a hurry."

Before I could respond, Gage's girlfriend, Summer, joined us. I could see the concern etched on that beautiful face of hers. She held tightly to her son's hand, and I thought for a moment something must've happened to him.

"You okay?" I lowered my voice to say, "I heard Colt had some sort of rash?"

"Yeah." She leaned down to straighten his collar. "I took him to urgent care. They said it's an allergic reaction. Probably my laundry detergent. Nothing big."

"Oh, wow. Well, I guess that's good?"

"Yes." She brushed a loose hair out of her face as the doors opened again. "I'm just worried about Gage. Have any of you seen him?"

"I was just asking that same question," Dallas said. "He took off pretty fast and looked worried."

Summer glanced toward the door. "Yeah, he shot out of the service at the end when he got a call. Not sure what's up, but something happened."

That didn't sound good. Still, I wanted to put forth a positive front, so I offered a cheerful, "I'm sure he's fine."

Tasha and Dallas started talking about the high winds outside, but I could tell Summer had something else on her mind. She asked if she could speak to me privately, and when I agreed, she led me to a quieter spot in the hallway.

"I just wanted to say thank you. That's all."

"For what, Summer?"

"For asking me to be a bridesmaid in your wedding. Gage and I have only been dating a few months, but you Hadleys are the closest thing I've had to family in a long time. I can't tell you what that means to me."

"Well, I feel the same about you." I slipped my arms around her neck and gave her a sisterly hug. "It's almost like you've been here all along."

"Thanks for welcoming me. . .and Colt." She reached down and scooped the little boy into her arms. Only now did I see the rash on his neck, which he scratched at. "I can't tell you how excited he is to be the ring bearer in your wedding." She pulled his little hand away from his neck to stop the scratching. "It's an honor, one he'll never forget."

Hopefully for all the right reasons. I'd once attended a wedding where the ring bearer spent the entire ceremony tossing the pillow in the air and catching it in his hands.

Still, I couldn't say that, so instead I smiled and said, "I think it's only fitting that my brothers' wives and girlfriends stand up with us, and I'm happy to include you."

I meant it too. Having Summer in the wedding just made sense. I had a feeling she would be around for the long haul. And with my BFF and sisters-in-law taking their positions as bridesmaids, I knew she would fit right into the pack. The Hadley family was blossoming into a thing of beauty.

Aw, who was I kidding? We'd always been a thing of beauty, even going back several generations. God had smiled on our little clan and we were blessed, indeed.

"Just let me know if there's anything I can do." Summer squeezed my hand. "I've been a bridesmaid four times before, and I know the drill."

Before I could respond, something caught my eye. Or rather, someone.

My brother Gage. Rushing toward us, the wind from the open door at his back. He swept our way, pressing through the throng of people, concern etched on his brow.

My parents must have noticed him from across the foyer because they both rushed to join us, as did Tasha and Dallas.

I barely got out the words, "What's wrong?" before Gage offered an explanation.

"There's a wildfire. Big one. Started at Purtis Creek State Park, and the wind's blowing it south, straight toward our place."

CHAPTER SIX

"Wait. . .a fire?" I felt my blood pressure rise at once as a throbbing sensation started in my ears. "Are you sure?"

He nodded, his pensive gaze telling me all I needed to know. This was bad.

"I can't think of a worse possible time for a fire," Mom interrupted, her words strained. "Everything is so dry."

"And the winds are way too high today," Gage added. "Which is why they haven't been able to get it stopped at Purtis Creek. It took off fast, headed due south."

"That's awful, Gage." I rubbed at my ears.

"I know. We're looking at a worst-case scenario here." He slipped his phone into his back pocket and shot a glance at Summer. "They're calling all of us in. I've got to go. Sorry."

She reached over and gave him a quick hug, then gripped Colt's hand.

"But it's not your shift, son," my mother argued as he moved away from us. "Can't someone else—"

Gage glanced back. "Have to go. Y'all be careful."

"No, *you* be careful, Gage," I countered. "And please text if there's anything we need to be concerned with. We'll be praying."

He paused at the door, and I could read the concern in his eyes. "I can tell you that the winds are moving at a high rate of speed, which is driving the fire across the dry pastures at a rapid clip. Last I heard, it was headed straight for 175 just north of our place."

"Ugh." Surely they could stop it there, before it crossed over. These firefighters knew what they were doing. This wasn't their first rodeo.

Gage shot another look our way before heading out. "Take care of things at home. Make sure the animals are all together, in case they need to be transported quickly. And water everything down around the perimeter of the house. Make sure it's nice and saturated all the way around. Promise?"

We promised to do that and then watched as he shot out the expansive double doors.

My dad approached, all business. "We need to get straight home to get the animals rounded up in the barn, just in case they need to be moved off property. Delilah's gonna be tough to move, in her condition, but we've got to keep her safe." He reached into his pocket for his keys and headed toward the double doors with Mom on his heels.

"I don't know what to do with myself." Bessie Mae looked back and forth between us and Bob. "I feel like I should be there to help."

"No." I gave her a kiss on the cheek. "You go home, Bessie Mae."

"But my home is. . ." She gazed at Bob, who slipped his arm over her shoulder.

"I would feel so much better if you headed to your new place, Bessie Mae," Mom said. "The fire is headed toward us, not you. But if things get bad at our place, we'll come to you. It will be a safe place for us."

"Yes, please come to stay with us if you need to. I'll get the guest rooms ready." My aunt was suddenly a woman with a purpose, and nothing motivated her more than taking care of others. Bessie Mae and Bob headed off to prep their house, just in case. I was happy to see her leave, knowing she would be safer in her new home.

My stomach did that weird flip-flop thing that often came with nervous news like this. In my heart I whispered the words, *Please, God, don't let that fire come near our property.* I couldn't help but think about my wedding, just a week off. Surely God wouldn't allow the whole plan to go up in smoke, would He?

Mason rushed our way, face tight with worry. "I heard. I'll come with you. You might need extra hands."

"Probably." It would take all of us working together.

Dallas and Tasha headed our way.

She looked at me, wide-eyed. "Did you hear?"

"Yeah, we're headed home to prep, just in case. No Fish Tales for us today, I guess." I would miss that fried catfish, but this was too important.

"Don't blame you. I wanted to come to your place with Dallas, but he wouldn't have it. Said I need to go to the restaurant to be with my parents."

"I agree."

"It doesn't look like we're at any risk here in town, but you never know. I'm guessing my dad will be cooking up a storm for all of the firefighters."

No doubt he would. That's the kind of town Mabank was. When folks were in trouble, the community rallied together, and rallying almost always involved food.

It didn't take long for word to spread among the congregants about the fire, and quickly we were all scattering, headed to our respective homes to take care of our properties. I could see the anxiety on every face.

Instead of riding home with my parents, I went in Mason's truck...the covered bed now filled with over forty quilts for our wedding. Hopefully they wouldn't smell like smoke by day's end.

I tried to make easy conversation to put the fire out of my mind as Mason drove faster than usual toward my house.

"Sorry if I put you on the spot about our wedding song."

"No, that's on me." He looked my way and shook his head. "I'm so sorry I've been distracted. There are just a few things I'm trying to iron out."

"Anything you can tell me?" I asked.

"Not yet. Patience is a virtue."

"I'm just glad you have a plan." I released a slow breath. "Did I tell you that Mom wants us to move into Bessie Mae's room?"

Mason's eyes widened as he gripped the steering wheel. "Um, no thank you. I don't think it's going to come to that."

"Think...or know?"

"Know."

"I told her it wasn't a good plan." A little sigh followed. "I mean, I'll miss my family, but we need our own space."

"Yes, we do." He gave me a knowing look. "And you shall have it."

"Above the garage at your shop?" I asked. "Because I really wouldn't mind, Mason. I don't need fancy."

"Someplace nicer than that, I promise. And I'm definitely not fancy, but comfortable and safe is good."

"Someplace with land?"

"Maybe. But I'm not saying anything just yet." He gave me a look that said, *Let's talk about this later.*

"You know, I heard the Jacksons were renting their house and moving into that little retirement villa that just went up in Athens. They have acreage. Not a lot but enough for a young couple, don't you think? Might work out for us. Pretty close to my parents too."

"RaeLyn."

"Okay, okay." So it wasn't the Jackson place. That was a relief, actually. Mom was right in saying it was run-down.

My gaze shifted to the skies, and I noticed what looked like smoke off in the distance.

Or maybe it was just my imagination. Surely the fire hadn't moved this far south so quickly.

As we pulled onto the road leading to our property, I definitely caught a better glimpse of the smoke to the north of us. My heart raced.

"Mason, look." I pointed in the direction that looked the darkest.

"Crazy how it looks so much closer than it is."

Or maybe it really *was* closer than we feared. With winds this high the flames were likely moving at warp speed.

As we pulled into the driveway I could see that the smoke was definitely getting thicker to the north, and it appeared to be moving this way. I felt sick to my stomach all of a sudden. No telling if it was the anxiety or the fact that I'd skipped breakfast this morning.

We got out of the truck and raced toward the house. Dad, Dallas, and Logan were already grabbing the hoses to water everything down. I watched as my father reached up to grab the brim of his cowboy hat so that the crazy wind wouldn't whip it away.

Riley ran back and forth in the driveway, panting. Animals always seemed to know when something was amiss.

I patted her on the head and tried to reassure her everything would be okay, but dogs had a sixth sense about these kinds of things. No doubt she trusted her instincts more than she trusted my words.

Still, I had to remain calm. This wasn't our first scare, after all. We had witnessed a lot of fires over the years, most in nearby towns or counties.

But my mom—usually calm, cool, and collected—seemed in a bit of a panic today as she stared at the skies, frozen in place. That wouldn't help.

Meghan seemed to be the calm one today, though this was her first time with us during such an event. She carried all our purses into the house and returned with a cooler of water bottles.

"What should we do?" Mom paced the driveway, her hair whipped about by the ever-present wind that tugged at her jacket. "I don't want to waste any time."

Before I could say, "We should pray first," Mason did just that. While the other guys sprayed the area down, he prayed a hedge of protection around our property and for safety for our animals and all the firefighters. It was a short, staccato prayer, but I felt the power behind his words.

Jake's wife, Carrie, rushed our way from their little house next door with baby Annalisa in her arms. We all made an executive decision that she should leave with the baby and go to her mother's place in Athens, where they would be safe. Jake had a hard time convincing her, especially when he told her that he planned to stay and help, but she eventually agreed it was the right thing to do for the baby.

We made another quick decision to load all the wedding quilts in her truck. Carrie passed the baby to Mom, ran for her truck, and pulled into our driveway moments later. While she got the baby situated in her car seat, we ladies shoved quilts in as fast as we could. Less than five minutes later Carrie was on the road, headed to Athens.

Minutes later we were all at work with hoses, forming a saturated area from the house outward a hundred feet or so. Would this be enough, should the fire come our way?

I gripped the hose with every ounce of strength, the wind threatening to pull it from my hands. The cold water blasted through my fingers, and I was soon standing in puddles of wet grass, the water sloshing beneath my boots.

My gaze shot to the sky, and my stomach felt heavy as lead as I saw the smoke in the distance. Purtis Creek State Park was just a few miles away. And if the fire really was moving as fast as Gage said. . .

No, I wouldn't let myself think about that. Surely the firefighters would get it under control before it traveled this way.

Firefighters. I paused to usher up a frantic prayer for my brother and his friends.

"Riley, stay back, girl," Mom scolded my cattle dog as she got underfoot while I tried to wrangle one of the hoses.

Poor Riley seemed more anxious by the moment. She paced back and forth, panting heavily.

I reached for my phone to check the weather update. No storm clouds in sight, but unfortunately the strong winds were predicted through evening. Ugh. They could push that fire our direction even faster. My silent prayers intensified, and before long I was praying out loud.

The howling wind caused the garage's side door to fly open suddenly. It hit the wall with a bang that startled all of us. My phone started pinging, and I glanced down to see a group text that included Tasha and several others in our Sunday school class, letting us know they were praying. I didn't have time to respond, but I was grateful for those prayers, especially now.

A moment of panic swept over me. Could I really trust God, even in a situation like this?

Off in the distance the animals began lowing and whinnying, a vocal response to the increase in wind. This really got Riley worked up. She ran in circles, barking at the air, which didn't do anything to settle my nerves.

"Calm down, girl," I said. "It's going to be okay."

I knew my dad was worried about the house, but he was also very worked up about the animals. He kept looking back and forth between the house and the back field, where most of the animals roamed.

"I've got to take care of them too," he said.

"Of course you do, Dad."

He released a strained breath. "I'm so torn between protecting my home and my livestock."

"We can do both," Jake said. "Let's get the animals loaded up on trailers. Delilah first. She hates the harness, but if we all work together we'll get her loaded quicker."

"Ladies, you okay to stay here? Logan, Dallas, Mason. . ." My dad looked at my sweet fiancé with the inclusion one would show a son. "Come with me?"

"Yup," they all replied in unison.

I glanced up to the crew of men, grateful for each one. Calm Logan. Practical Jake. Energetic Dallas. Helpful Mason.

They took off toward the pasture, and I kept hosing down the area as far as the line would reach.

One of our nearest neighbors came running from his place. "Y'all need help?"

"What about your property, Joe?" Mom asked.

"I've got a whole crew working over there. We've already got most everything taken care of. The wife and kids are on their way to Kaufman to her sister's, and my oldest boy just loaded up the animals and is taking them to his place in Eustace."

"Then yes, we'd love your help. I'm sure Chuck needs your assistance with the animals. That's going to be a huge undertaking." She pointed, and he took off running toward the barn.

Out of the corner of my eye I caught a glimpse of my sweet Tilly in the parking lot of Trinkets and Treasures. My heart did that weird thump-thump thing it always did when I was in a panic. After all I'd been through to win Papaw's truck back at auction less than a year ago, would I lose her now?

I squeezed my eyes shut for a moment. When I opened them, my gaze shifted back to the north. My pulse picked up as I noticed how much thicker the smoke was now. And was it my imagination, or was that a reddish-orange haze intermingled with it?

My thoughts shifted to my upcoming wedding. Every fear hit me at once as I pictured our beautiful property burned to the ground. My wedding site would be ruined. My wedding ceremony. . .destroyed.

"Don't think like that, RaeLyn," I scolded myself. "Where is your faith?"

I couldn't see the flames yet, but uncertainty gnawed at my gut. I could almost picture those flames, traveling across the acreage nearby, jumping roads and creeks. Had they already crossed 175? If so, we were in real trouble.

A gray-brown plume of smoke drifted across the sky, even thicker and darker than before, and now I could actually smell the smoke. A fluttering of ash rained down on us, a gift from the wind above. And I knew. . .knew it couldn't be more than a few miles away now.

And moving fast, from the looks of things.

As I pondered this reality, my breaths came in short spurts. Panic took hold of me suddenly, and I couldn't think clearly about what to do.

I forced myself to take in slow, steady breaths and paused long enough to offer up a prayer that God would save us all, and this beautiful land I'd grown to love so very much.

CHAPTER SEVEN

I'd always been a prayer, but today those frantic prayers felt more urgent than ever before. I did my best to calm myself and tried to remember that God wasn't caught off guard by any of this. He was Lord of the wind and the waves, after all. Surely He could handle a wildfire.

One of our cell phones rang. I couldn't be sure which one. Mom finally realized it was hers and she answered. Bessie Mae. She put the call on speaker so she could continue hosing down the front of the garage.

"I just thought about all of the items in the attic over at the little house!" Bessie Mae's words were rushed. "The baby blankets, the family Bible. Mom's hand-tatted table scarves. We can't let them burn."

"We can't leave our work to do that just yet, Bessie Mae." I suddenly felt a little breathless. "And I don't know where we'd put them anyway."

"I'll get them," Meghan said. "And I'll take them back to our place. It's on the opposite side of the pond, so hopefully it's the safest."

Before we could tell her not to, Meghan was racing toward the little house where Jake and Carrie lived to take care of the items in the attic. I prayed nothing would happen to that precious little house, where my grandfather had grown up.

"We'll do what we can, Bessie Mae," Mom said. "But I have to go now. We're hosing everything down."

"Where is Annalisa?"

"She's with Carrie, on her way to Athens. She took the wedding quilts with her."

"Oh, thank God. And the animals?"

"The guys are loading them on the trailer right now. I have to go, Bessie Mae."

"Bob won't let me come over there, so I'm just over here cooking up a storm."

"Bob is a good man," I hollered out. "Listen to him. And pray, Bessie Mae. That's the best gift you can give us right now. Pray."

"I have been. Won't stop."

Mom ended the call, and I kept spraying everything in sight, the water pressure feeling slightly diminished now. I prayed it would hold out.

Still, I found myself distracted by what I'd just heard in that phone call from Bessie Mae. My aunt's desperation was a clear reminder of her deep ties—to this land, and to her family legacy. Her connection to all things Hadley was evident. And the fact that she—we—might lose it all was truly heartbreaking.

I fought back tears and felt a sob rise up in my throat. I did my best to shove it down, but the idea of losing this home, this land, all our family belongings. . .was terrifying. Every memory from my idyllic childhood was wrapped up in this property, and I refused to let it go up in smoke.

I decided to turn my hose to the roof. Spraying down the shingles might be helpful as well as the siding. Keeping the house damp meant that flying embers wouldn't set it ablaze, at least not easily.

I adjusted the sprayer on the hose and pointed it upward to the siding and then the gutters. I ran for the kitchen step stool and returned with it moments later, along with a rubber band to pull back my tangled hair. That settled, I climbed up as high as I dared, which meant I could now guide a steady stream of water onto the roof.

Mom worked on the back porch area and the wooden railings. By the time Meghan returned, we were moving outward, away from the house.

In an ideal world we would dampen the ground all the way to the edges of the property, but from the looks of things, we didn't have much time left and the hoses simply wouldn't reach that far. The skies to the north of us grew darker with each passing moment, and the ash was leaving marks on my clothes now.

Tasha texted. "We've activated the prayer chain."

I was grateful to know we weren't alone in this fight.

"Oh my goodness, I just thought of something!" I gasped as the idea hit. "The sprinklers."

"You mean the big gun sprinklers we use in the garden?" Mom shifted her hose from one hand to the other.

"Yes! We have a handful of them in the garage. Maybe we could set them up in strategic places around the farthest perimeter of the house and attach the hoses to them, which would give us better coverage closer to the road."

I rushed to the garage and pulled out the sprinklers, and then Mom, Meghan, and I worked together to get them attached to the hoses. We placed ours at the front of the house, the north side. Mom placed hers on the west side of the house, in case the winds shifted. Before long, the *click-click-click* of the sprinklers provided a comforting sound. And I was pleasantly surprised at how far the spray of water shot out. Right to the edge of the road. This was a much better plan than simply hosing things down closer to the house.

I called Mason as soon as we finished setting up. When he picked up I quickly dove in, explaining that the big gun sprinklers had been set up around the edges of the property and were already at work, saturating the perimeter.

"They've got great reach," I explained.

"Your dad was just about to do that same thing. Great minds."

"Tell him he doesn't have to. It's already done."

"I'm glad. That fire's moving fast. I've had half a dozen texts from folks who are worried."

"Ugh." I paused but tried not to let panic take hold. Bessie Mae was praying, and her prayers were powerful. This I knew, from twenty-seven years of living with her. "How's it going with the animals?"

"We just got them loaded. Jake is driving them to his in-laws' place. He just pulled out."

"I'm so relieved, Mason." A sudden gust of wind tugged at the collar of my blouse, blowing the acrid scent of smoke into my nostrils. Ugh.

My gaze shifted back to Tilly, and I felt tears begin to sting my eyes. I'd loved that truck from the time I was a little girl. Was I going to lose her now?

He must've sensed my change in mood. "We'll keep praying. If God could part the Red Sea for Moses and the Israelites, surely He can perform a miracle here too."

"I know. I'm just so upset about Tilly. I know that's dumb, in light of everything, but I would hate to lose her."

"Conner's on his way to get her."

"What?" I could hardly believe my ears. "You called Conner?" Mason had really managed to contact his coworker in the middle of this chaos?

"He's headed this way with a tow truck to get Tilly. He's taking her back to the shop. The fire isn't going anywhere near town, so she'll be safe."

"Oh, Mason! Thank you!" I couldn't stop the tears that now streamed down my face. "I've been so worried about her."

"I needed to get her up to the shop anyway, since she's not running. But we'll get her off the property. That smoke is getting too close for comfort. I sure hope Conner hurries. I'm headed Tilly's way right now. Your dad and the other guys are headed your way."

"Thank you."

"I left the keys to my truck on the dash. I think it's time for you ladies to get to safer ground."

"But—"

"Promise you will."

"If it looks like we have no choice." And I meant it.

We ended the call, and I got another rush of the acrid smoke. It stung my nose and throat. Riley now ran in circles around us as we worked, barking toward the north. Her ears were pinned back, as if her awareness of the approaching danger was growing.

Conner arrived minutes later. I motioned for him to head up to the antique shop and hollered out, "Tilly's up there!"

He offered a nod of the head and plowed up the drive to the shop.

Moments later we heard sirens, and I looked up to discover the fire department had already sent a truck.

No, two trucks.

They weren't the big, fancy ones. These were the trucks driven by volunteers, with far less water on board. But at least it was something.

The firefighters stationed themselves near the end of our driveway and gestured for us to join them. I ran down the driveway in their direction, the distant glow of the deep red-orange haze on the horizon now impossible to ignore. It pulsed and flickered, a sure sign that we didn't have much time left before it would be upon us.

The young firefighter was just a kid, barely out of high school. I recognized him as being one of Jake's regular players on the Mabank High baseball team from a couple of seasons back. Timmy Hollinger.

"Folks, we've got flames less than a mile from here," Timmy said. "And they're headed straight for us. You've got to get out of here." He pointed to the vehicles in the driveway. "You need to take those vehicles and get as far away from here as you can. Head west toward town. You'll be safe that way."

I couldn't bear the idea of leaving anyone behind. Mom and I looked at each other, both of us unsure of what to do.

"You heard him," Meghan said. "We have to go. Mom, you take your car. RaeLyn, you and Riley can go in Mason's truck. I'll take our truck."

I had to give it to her. This gal was all business, and excellent in a crisis. Then again, she was a nurse. No doubt she was used to crises.

My gaze shifted back to Tilly. Conner and Mason were working fast to get her hooked up to the tow truck, but would they make it in time? And what about my dad and brothers? Why weren't they back yet?

My heart hammered so loudly I could practically feel the vibration in my ears. I couldn't get the image of rolling flames out of my head, racing across the fields I'd spent my whole life tending. Now, just one week before my wedding, it felt like everything was teetering on a knife's edge.

I thought of all the wedding paraphernalia in the house—the centerpiece items, my veil and shoes, my wedding gown. My wedding gown!

Before anyone could tell me not to, I ran into the house with every bit of speed I could muster and grabbed the dress, shoes, and veil. At the last minute I also grabbed the family Bible from the coffee table.

I came back out to my mother loading up her car with items she'd somehow managed to grab. By now, everything was covered in a thin layer of ash, tiny flecks landing like little gnats on everything in sight. I shoved my wedding dress in Mom's car, grateful for the bag covering it.

The pounding in my heart was so loud I could hear it in my ears now. Or maybe that was the roar of the wind and the flames, which now appeared on the lot across from us. I watched in horror as those flames moved at a rapid clip.

The smoke in the air left a distinct bitterness on my tongue, which increased the feelings of nausea.

Or maybe it was just the fear.

Conner safely towed Tilly off the property toward safety. Tears of relief flowed as I realized Papaw's truck was safe.

Now, to save the rest of the vehicles.

And us.

Meghan backed her truck out of the driveway.

Mom climbed into her car and slipped it into REVERSE while I took my spot behind the wheel in Mason's truck, lifting Riley into the passenger seat beside me.

I started praying aloud, that God would protect us as we finagled our way past the flames that now threatened to land on our property. I could feel the heat, even from across the street.

I also saw those sprinklers, still spraying a steady stream of water across the outer perimeter of our land.

As we pulled past the firefighters at the end of the driveway, I witnessed their tense expressions and could see their mouths moving as they hollered back and forth to each other as they pulled out the hoses. I couldn't make out what they were saying but had to trust they knew what they were doing.

Mom turned right onto the street, drove several yards, and then slowed her pace. I hollered, "Mom, keep going!" even though I knew she couldn't hear me.

I tapped the horn and she inched her way forward. I followed closely behind, still keeping a watchful eye in my rearview mirror at the firefighters behind us. I caught a glimpse of Dad and my brothers as they sailed past us in my father's truck.

Mason came running to join them, and before long they were all working side by side with the firefighters to guide the fire truck's hoses to further saturate the edges of our property.

Even from this distance I noticed Mason's sheer determination. This was a man I could trust. With my life.

By now the flames across the road had raced within yards of our place. I climbed out of the truck and stood in the road, watching, my prayers never stopping.

The flames crossed over the road, and for a brief moment, I saw the edges of our land spark and ignite. The firefighters set their hoses on the flames, and—for the first time in my twenty-seven years on the planet—I witnessed an undeniable miracle.

Somehow. Some way. They managed to stop those flames in their tracks.

CHAPTER EIGHT

The moment the firefighters got those flames squelched, I erupted in tears. Maybe it was the sense of sheer relief. Maybe exhaustion. . .or panic. I couldn't say. But I stood in the middle of the road and bawled like a baby.

A couple of minutes later Mason barreled my way. He pulled me into his arms, and Riley pressed into what little space was left between us, panting heavily.

"You okay?" Mason asked.

I just kept crying, my sobs louder than the noise still coming from the hoses, which the firefighters used to saturate the scorched land across the street. Gripping Riley's neck, I let the tears keep flowing.

Mom got out of her car and took several quick steps toward us. I wrapped my arms around her.

"I can't believe what I just saw." She shook her head. "It's. . ."

She never got the words out because Meghan pulled up next to us and barreled out of her truck as Logan ran our way. He pulled her into his arms.

"I think we just witnessed a miracle," Meghan said. "I. . .I. . ." Her eyes filled with tears, and she suddenly leaned over as if she might be sick.

"Probably the smoke," Mom said as she rested her hand on Meghan's back.

"No, I'm fine." Meghan righted herself. Only, she didn't look fine. I thought the poor girl was going to hit the ground.

"Let me get you back to our place," Logan said. "You need to rest and get away from this smoke."

She looked back and forth between my mother and me. "I'd rather go to the big house with everyone else."

And with those words, my mother swept Meghan into her arms. My sister-in-law had just endeared herself to my mom.

Dad headed our way with Dallas at his side.

"That was a close call, but I think those big gun sprinklers did the trick." My dad gave me an admiring look. "Good call, RaeLyn. Soaking the ground by the road, was I just what we needed."

I was shaking so hard I couldn't respond. Not yet, anyway. And my ears were still throbbing so hard I could barely make out whatever he was saying. My gaze shifted to the smoldering patches of burnt grass on our side of the road, and I coughed as the lingering smoke did a number on my throat. It would take a while for things to calm down—on every level.

We left the vehicles parked a distance away while the firefighters made absolutely sure the area was safe.

When they gave us the go-ahead we went indoors. I gasped when I saw the clock. Was it really 4:20? We had less than an hour of sunlight left.

I noticed the cooler of water bottles next to the house and started passing them out to the firefighters. I offered them other snacks, but they turned them down.

"We've got to check the perimeter of the fire across several miles," Timmy said. "Just in case. Sometimes these things spark up again."

"Will you check on Gage for me?" I asked.

"Yup. Will do. I'll have him call home when he can. Last I heard, he was still up by Purtis Creek."

My dad called Jake and told him to turn the trailer around and bring the animals back. A bit of a disagreement followed. No doubt Jake couldn't believe it was safe to do so. He reluctantly agreed to turn around and come back home.

About the time he arrived home, a line of cars pulled up. Our neighbors and church friends arrived, one after the other, to check on us and to bring food.

Always food.

Tasha was first in line with goodies from Fish Tales. Looked like I was going to get my fried catfish fix after all. Then came Melody and Pastor Burchfield, with all sorts of items in Tupperware.

Several of the men headed to the barn to help my dad and the guys with the animals. But the ladies set up camp in the kitchen, peeling back the covers of casserole dishes like they were checking under the hoods of overheated cars.

Before we knew what hit us, we had a full-blown potluck set up in the Hadley kitchen with at least a dozen of our closest friends.

Bessie Mae and Bob arrived next, entering the house with arms loaded down with goodies.

"I baked a couple of cobblers in that mediocre oven of ours," Bessie Mae said. "And made a huge pot of chili with corn bread. Enough to feed an army."

Which, apparently, we had. By now, an army of believers gathered in a circle in our kitchen to usher up thanks to God for sparing our property. And then, like any good Southerner, I ate. Boy, did I eat.

By the time the sun set off to the west, I decided to change into clean clothes. The smoke was giving me a headache. I headed to my room and caught a glimpse of my reflection in the mirror that hung over my dresser. Heavens to Betsy. Something needed to be done about that.

I took the world's quickest shower, then dressed and yanked my wet hair up in a clip. Afterward, nausea kicked in once again. I heard the voices radiating from the living room and kitchen, along with the clinking and clanking of dishes. That, along with the smell of all those delicious foods, was a little too much for my overactivated senses to take. I found myself in the bathroom, losing every bit of food I'd eaten. Chili, corn bread, and cake weren't nearly as appetizing coming back up.

Still, I felt better after getting sick. And I felt sure I'd also emptied my stomach of a lot of ash in the process.

I eventually made my way back out to the group.

Mason took one look at me and asked, "You okay?"

I nodded and said, "Better now."

It took a while, but by evening I had finally calmed down enough to have a quiet conversation with Mason—not just about my stomach upset, but about everything that had happened. He listened closely and then shared all he had been through.

"I wish you could've seen your dad in action with the animals earlier. He's a pro."

"Yeah, he really is," I said.

"He was shouting instructions at them like he was their commanding officer. And they all seemed to listen to him. He drove every last one of them to the trailer, and we all loaded them up."

"Hey, the Bible says the sheep know the shepherd's voice."

"True." Mason smiled. "Hadn't thought of that. By the way, I might've helped with a panicked cow."

"Freida?"

"Yep. How did you know?"

"I know Freida," I explained. "She's fussy. I'm so grateful for your help. I know Dad is too."

"I've seen animals spooked before, but never like that," Mason added. "There was a lot of stomping and snorting going on."

"And the noise from the animals was bad too," my dad said, all smiles as he joined us.

After the laughter died down, my father grew more serious.

"I think the animals picked up on the smell of the smoke even before we did. Freida was carrying on like she was dying. But Mason here did a fine job of calming her down."

"Just call me the cow whisperer."

"I will never call you that," I said. And I meant it.

Still, he was getting a lot of play out of that Freida story, going from person to person talking about how he managed to tame the savage beast. And Dad was happy to tell everyone that Delilah had come through it all like a champ. No doubt that foal would come out with a lot of stories to tell.

Bessie Mae made a pot of coffee and started dishing up servings of blackberry cobbler, my personal favorite. By now, I was completely myself again, so I allowed myself a tiny serving.

Afterward, I remembered that I'd left my wedding gown in Mom's trunk. Meghan and I went out together to gather it, plus my other things.

"Hey, thanks for everything you did today," I said as we walked that way.

"Oh, you're welcome." She popped open the trunk of Mom's car.

"You're really good in a crisis."

She turned my way with a shrug. "I've seen my share."

I grabbed the dress and slung it over my left arm.

Meghan reached for my veil and shoes.

I closed the trunk and turned back toward her. "I know that Mom really appreciated all that you did. I just want you to know how grateful I am. You were a steady force from start to finish."

At which point she erupted in tears and threw her arms around my neck, nearly causing me to lose my grip on the dress.

"I–I'm sorry." She sniffled. "I think it's just hitting me now. I'm an emotional wreck today. And that smoke really did a number on my stomach."

"Mine too," I admitted. "I couldn't keep that chili down."

"Me either." She groaned and rested her hand on her stomach. "And that ash!"

"I know." I released a sigh. "Hopefully we'll feel better in the morning, but if you think you need to be seen by a doctor—"

"No, I'm okay." She brushed off any concerns. "But I promise I'll go in if I start having airway issues."

"Good. I don't want anything to happen to you, Meghan. We need you." I paused and shifted the dress in my arms. "We love you."

"I love you too."

We went back into the house just as some of our guests were headed out.

By now, I was feeling it. The exhaustion. The pain in my arms and shoulders from manning the hoses. The aching in my hands from gripping the sprayer. The headache from the smoke. The pain in my neck from looking up at the roof for so long. The blisters on my feet from sloshing around in wet boots.

Pressure settled into my face, and I realized a sinus headache was threatening. After sending Mason off for the night, I went into the bathroom and looked around until I found an over-the-counter med to help. I'd just swallowed it when Bessie Mae and Bob left.

Which coincided with Gage's arrival.

There was really no comparing how any of us looked and felt to poor Gage.

As the family gathered around the kitchen table to hear all that he had to share, I couldn't help but notice the exhaustion in his eyes and the scent of smoke emanating off his body.

"I showered at the station," he explained. "Changed back into clean clothes. And I still smell like someone just plucked me off a barbecue pit."

"I'm just glad you're okay, son." Mom's eyes filled with tears as she rested her hand on his arm. "I've never prayed that hard in my life."

"Me either," he agreed. "I was stuck up at Purtis Creek State Park, but the minute I heard the news they'd stopped the fire at the edge of our property, well. . ." He closed his eyes, and for a moment I thought he might lose it.

He didn't. Gage managed to maintain his composure.

"It was nothing short of a miracle that they got it stopped before it crossed over onto the property. The winds were out of control today, so much so that we had a near-impossible task trying to get that fire out. It just kept outrunning us."

"I felt like I was watching a biblical miracle," Mom said. "Never seen anything like it."

"I think it helped a lot that we soaked the ground," Dad said.

"Oh, for sure." Gage nodded. "Some folks just didn't have time. It happened too fast for them."

"How did folks on the other side of 175 fare?" my dad asked. "Like the Millers and the Lutz family? How are they?"

"There were three houses lost on the north side of 175, but neither of the families you just mentioned. We had a harder time getting it contained there because everything was so dry. But the biggest problem was at the point of impact, where we think the fire started."

"Which was. . . ?" Dallas gave him a penetrating look.

"Just inside Purtis Creek State Park."

"At the campgrounds?" Dad asked.

"No. Investigators are looking at a particular spot right off the highway. Not far from where Buck Adler lives."

My heart skipped a beat as he mentioned Buck's name.

"Oh, that's right," my dad said. "I forgot Buck is right off of 316 opposite Purtis Creek."

"I always loved that piece of land," Mom chimed in. "Gorgeous."

"When we first got there, he was rushing to get his animals loaded up into a trailer," Gage explained. "The fire skirted his property but took out one of his barns. Thank God he got the animals out first."

"I'm sure he's relieved to have escaped the worst of it," Mom said.

"Very. But he was still really worked up. I guess he's really been through it, of late. But the chief assured him there's going to be an investigation."

"Does it look suspicious?" Mom asked. "Are they thinking someone set it intentionally?"

"Hard to tell at this point, especially with all of the lightning. But it took off fast once it crossed 316, thanks to those high winds." Gage rose and stretched, then looked toward the food in the kitchen. "That area is still too hot to make a determination yet. Investigators will figure it out soon enough."

"Sit, Gage," Mom said. "I'll get you some food. Bessie Mae made chili and corn bread."

"Of course she did." He laughed. "Anytime there's a crisis, she cooks."

"Coping mechanism," I said. "I, on the other hand, am no help in a crisis. But Meghan. . ." I smiled at my sister-in-law. "Well, she proved herself a real champ today. She's as steady as a rock."

Meghan chose that moment to look a little green around the gills. She pushed her chair back from the table and said, "This rock needs to get home and get some sleep. I'm feeling a little woozy."

She and Logan headed out, but not before my mother gave her a big hug and thanked her profusely. Then Mom went to work fixing a plate for Gage.

"Something else happened at Purtis Creek while we were there," Gage said. "There were two boys—preteen. Twins. They somehow got separated from the rest of their family. It took some time to find them."

"Wow, that's scary."

"The whole family was there for a family reunion." He took the plate of food from Mom's outstretched hand. "I think there were at least four or five RVs and fifth wheels. I'm not sure the adults were keeping a close eye on the kids. The boys had gone off to do their thing, and when the fire came rolling through, the rest of the family got out but they couldn't find the boys."

"Gage, that's awful." I couldn't even imagine how terrified those parents must have been when they couldn't find their kids.

"Turns out they had crossed over the highway to tell Buck Adler to call the fire department. They could see it was headed straight for him."

"Sounds like they got to him just in time. I'm sure he was grateful for them."

"Yes, but the whole thing was frightening. They said they dodged the fire at every turn and barely made it out. They somehow outran those flames."

"Wow. Thank God they're okay," I said.

"Trust me, I have." He took a bite of the meat, and his eyes brightened at the taste. "I did a lot of praying today, that's for sure."

"Are they going to make it?" Mom asked.

Gage nodded as he took another bite, which he chased down with a drink of tea. "Both inhaled a lot of smoke, and one of the boys broke his arm while trying to get to the road. But miraculously, neither was burned. Not one burn mark on them, even though they came through the thick of it."

"That's an absolute miracle." I rested my hand on my heart, relieved to hear this news. "Almost biblical, in fact."

"I know. It really is. They're going to be okay. They were life-flighted to Dallas, on the off chance that their lungs were compromised. It happens a lot, where you think they're okay, but they later succumb to the smoke. So they can't be too careful."

"Hopefully they'll be fine."

"We had news crews come all the way from Dallas to interview us," he said.

"Wow." We rarely had big news stories break in these parts. The reporter in me was suddenly intrigued. Maybe I could reach out to them as well.

Someone else crossed my mind at that moment. Gage's best friend. "Hey, what about Aaron? You two always work together, right? But you haven't mentioned him at all today."

"You didn't hear?" Gage glanced my way; then his gaze shifted downward to his plate of food. "The fire department let Aaron go almost a week ago."

"What?" I couldn't make sense of this. "Why would they do that?"

"How long do you have?"

"Well, now that I know we're safe, I have time." I glanced at the kitchen clock and realized it was almost ten thirty. I had to take care of some wedding prep in the morning. And I probably needed to set up a time to meet with Iva and Eva about the reception food. That had fallen through the cracks in the chaos of the day.

"Aaron didn't show up for his shift a couple of times. And he had an attitude with one of our superiors."

"Aaron always had a temper," I reminded him. "Remember that time he got angry at Mr. Jenkins, the science teacher?"

"Yeah, Jenkins caught him in the act, cheating. He tried to pin that on me."

"I never knew that." Mom's brow wrinkled.

Gage pressed his chili bowl aside and reached for his tea glass. "He wasn't the greatest at following protocol at work. There were a number of reasons he was let go."

"I can't imagine you working at the fire department without Aaron."

These words came from Dad, but I had to agree. Those two were as thick as thieves. Still, the worry in my brother's eyes clued me in to the fact that he wasn't as confident about Aaron's innocence as I might have thought.

"Sounds like they did the right thing." Mom reached to take the chili bowl off the table. "That boy always worried me. I've seen these behaviors in him since he was a kid."

"We all did." Gage sighed as he set down his tea glass. "I'll be honest, I really went out on a limb for him. He got the job at my recommendation. The chief wasn't impressed with him from the get-go, and I always worked double time to make him look better. But I can't go on covering for him forever. You know?"

"That's no friend," Mom said. "Not a good one, anyway."

Gage paused, and a thoughtful look came over him. "I guess. I mean, he's still my friend, even if we don't work together. But he's been in a bad state of mind since they let him go. I think he's drinking, to be honest. Like, more than usual."

Mom muttered something under her breath.

"The boys described a man matching Aaron's description in the park near the fire." Gage released a slow breath and seemed to be processing this information before saying anything else.

"Oh, Gage." I dropped into the chair next to his. "Surely you don't think. . . ?"

He rested his elbows on the table. "I can't imagine he would do something like that. If anyone knows the devastating effects of fire, Aaron does. He's incredibly knowledgeable about fire dynamics. And in spite of his temper, he cares a lot about protecting people. Remember that time he flew into action when a snake almost got you, RaeLyn?"

I did, now that he mentioned it. We'd been out berry picking as kids, and a snake slithered right up to me. Aaron jabbed it with a stick and told me to run.

I'd never run so fast in my life. Dropped all my dewberries in the process.

"He's impulsive. Defensive. But I think he'd do anything he could to help others. So I have to believe he had nothing to do with this."

"I hope you're right, son." Dad rested his hand on Gage's shoulder.

I hoped so too. But judging from the look on my brother's face, he wasn't so sure.

CHAPTER NINE

I'd been tired many a time in my twenty-seven years. The past several weeks had offered plenty of opportunities as I'd juggled my work at Trinkets and Treasures, my articles for *Mabank Happenings*, and my wedding plans.

But even with all of that, I'd never known exhaustion—mental, physical, and emotional, like I felt on Sunday night. I crawled into bed, torn between wanting to sleep and fearing that I shouldn't.

All night long I tossed and turned as I battled nightmares about the raging flames. During the awake moments, I wrestled with fear, wondering if the fire would spark back up again. Many times I got up out of my bed and peered out the window to make sure there were no flames. The Hadley property lay in quiet respite, dark and still. Peaceful.

The house still smelled faintly of smoke—and the clothes I'd tossed in the hamper had a lingering odor too, which caused more stomach upset in the night. So I got up out of bed and tossed them into the washing machine in the utility room.

Afterward, I tried again to sleep. When I finally dozed, the dreams kicked in. Terrifying, realistic dreams where flames crossed onto our family property and kept going. The nightmares also included Tilly, stranded and engulfed in flames, in front of the antique shop. On and on the Technicolor dreams went, playing out every terrifying scenario.

In one of the dreams I was in my wedding dress, running across the field on fire. I took refuge in Buck Adler's home. In another, I roused two little boys and carried them across a field ablaze to safety with Aaron running hot on our heels, a snake in his hands.

When I awoke, my body was trembling so hard I thought I might be physically ill. It took several minutes of lying still in the bed, praying it through, before I convinced myself I was really safe.

Unfortunately, my body simply refused to cooperate. Or maybe it was my mind. I just couldn't seem to function normally.

Oh, I tried. I crawled out of bed, groaning all the way, then threw on a robe and tried to join the others. But with so little sleep, I could barely manage even the simplest of tasks. Like brushing my teeth. Or my hair.

So I skipped all of that and simply dragged myself out to the kitchen, where I found my mother unloading the dishwasher.

She must have had a hard night too. Her poor swollen eyes had dark rings under them. And she wasn't standing up straight. Instead, she was hunched over like poor Buck Adler, as if experiencing too much pain to straighten her spine.

I walked over and gave her a big hug. "Today will be better," I said.

To which she responded, "Couldn't be much worse," then went back to work on the dishes.

Should I remind her that we had somehow escaped the worst of it? That our house was safe, our cattle alive, and the property basically untouched?

No. Judging from the look of exhaustion on her face, I'd be better off just offering encouragement.

And coffee. Always coffee.

So I made a pot. No doubt we'd need a lot of it this morning.

Mom put her hand on her back and winced.

"Did you hurt yourself?" I asked.

"I think I pulled something when I moved that cooler yesterday. I'm not sure. It'll probably pass on its own."

"Take some ibuprofen, Mom. The gel caps. They work better."

"Okay."

Only, she didn't. She kept unloading the dishwasher.

Before long, Dad came in with Gage and Dallas trailing behind him.

"How are the animals?" I asked.

"They were anxious to get back out to the pastures." Dad pulled off his baseball cap and swiped at his thinning hair. "Especially Freida. I've never seen such a happy cow. She took off running as soon as we let her out."

Because Mom looked somewhat wrecked, I decided to cook breakfast for everyone. I whipped up scrambled eggs, bacon, and diced potatoes, then warmed some flour tortillas. We loved a good breakfast burrito around here. And with such an empty stomach, I really needed to eat something that wouldn't make me sick again.

Instead of sitting at the table, we all headed to the living room to watch the news as a Dallas reporter zoomed in on the twin boys who'd been recovered from the fire.

Inside a hospital room the boys shared side-by-side beds. They looked nothing like the young boys in my nightmare. These two were older, and a bit disheveled.

"They're being kept for observation," their mother said, looking at the camera. "But other than a bit of smoke and one broken arm, they got off easy. No burns at all."

"I still think that's remarkable, considering they had to go through the flames," Gage said, interrupting the story. "If you could have seen the height of those flames, you would understand how much danger they were in."

"They sure look great now." Mom took a bite of her burrito and leaned back in her chair, wincing.

Gage rose, plate in hand. "They were pretty shook when we loaded them into the helicopters." He headed into the kitchen for another helping.

"I still can't believe you were that close to the fire, Gage," Mom said.

"We were all close to the fire," Dad reminded her.

She set her plate on the end table. "Yes. We were. I never want to be that close again."

The news story switched back to a different reporter, this one at Purtis Creek State Park. In the background, I saw Buck Adler's property. I was kind of startled at how good it looked in comparison to the scorched area across the highway from it.

"Man, you were right. Buck's place was barely hit at all," Dad said. "That's a wonder."

I was so relieved that his property had been spared, but something about all of this made me feel uneasy. I couldn't put my finger on it, but something felt off. Either we were witnessing another divine intervention—likely—or something else was at play. Was my imagination running wild? Why couldn't I shake the notion that Buck might somehow be involved in this?

Gage rushed to the TV and pointed out the area where he and the others had been stationed. "There!" He pointed to a fire truck.

"I see you, son." Mom gave him an admiring look. "You're on the Dallas news. Wow!" She practically beamed with pride.

We all shared our thoughts on that as the news story ended. Still, I couldn't stop thinking about Buck Adler's place, how he was mostly spared. Everything around him went up in flames, but he only lost his barn.

"The other day Buck Adler stopped in to drop off that sign," I said. "He was really angry about the Frasier Oil Company. Apparently, there's some kind of legal mess going on with his property."

Mom looked my way. "Oh?"

Dad nodded. "Yeah, Frasier's up to their usual tricks. Things got so bad Buck had no choice but to take legal action. But he said something alarming, that Frasier might end up acquiring his property if he loses the case."

Mom paled. "They could do that?"

"Maybe if he's behind on his taxes or something?" Dad shrugged and took another bite.

"Is there a way we can look that up?" I asked. "Are those public records?"

"Maybe." Dad shrugged.

I rose to carry my plate to the kitchen, but my stiff joints did not want to cooperate. "Buck mentioned something in passing about wanting to burn the whole thing down."

"People say things like that all the time and don't really mean it," Dad said. "He was just spouting off."

"Yeah, but in this case he said it just hours before someone literally burned the whole thing down." I turned to face my father. "You don't find that suspicious? Like, maybe he's trying to send some sort of message?"

"That's a stretch." Dad leaned back in his chair.

Another memory hit me just then. "When we went to get the Frasier Oil sign out of his truck, there was a gas can back there."

"Everyone has a gas can in their truck, through," Gage said.

"It's just interesting that the fire started inside of the state park opposite his property on the day after he told us he wanted to burn the whole thing down, the same day he had a gas can in the back of his vehicle. And the fire somehow missed him altogether?"

"It took out his barn," Gage reminded me.

"Which is nothing, in the grand scheme of things. But others lost their properties, their homes, everything."

"I think your imagination is running away with you, RaeLyn," Dad said. "Buck is an old man."

"Exactly. He's got nothing to lose. He's already lived most of his life."

"Good grief." Gage gave me a "You've got to be kidding" look.

"Not saying I agree with you," Dad chimed in. "But I do think Buck must be in dire financial straits. Losing a mineral rights lease can be pretty devastating to the pocketbook. I've known plenty of people who lost everything then got behind on their property taxes. Came close to losing the land they'd spent a lifetime building."

"I'll never understand why those big oil companies pull the rug out from under folks," I said.

"Several reasons," Dad explained. "The company might choose to drop a lease because of a decline in production. Maybe the well's not producing enough gas or oil. You know?"

"Yeah."

"Sometimes there's a change in the market. That's what happened in our case. A drop in prices meant they could no longer pay the same rate, which is why our monthly checks dropped so drastically."

I rested my hand on his arm. "Sorry, Dad."

"It's okay." He paused. "And sometimes the oil companies will choose not to renew due to environmental concerns. Maybe some sort of regulation is standing in the way of drilling on that site. It could be anything."

"Whatever it is, Buck could be trying to send a message to Frasier Oil—if he can't have the land, no one can."

"I think you need more sleep, RaeLyn," Mom observed. "Or maybe you inhaled too much smoke."

Likely. Or maybe my imagination really had just kicked into overdrive.

Before anyone could respond, a car pulled up in our driveway. Bessie Mae. Minutes later, she and Bob joined us in the living room.

"Hello, y'all!" Bessie Mae's voice rang out from the back door. "I've come bearing gifts!"

I took several steps toward her to take the cake carrier out of her hand. "What's this?"

"Butter pecan cake," Bessie Mae said.

"After all that food you brought last night?" Mom rose and walked her way.

"I've never seen a woman bake as much as she does," Bob chimed in. "My oven has been used more in the past few days than in all the years prior."

"Which is probably why he never noticed how lousy it is." Bessie Mae sighed and set the cake carrier on the counter, then turned to face me. "It's Monday, RaeLyn."

"Yes, it is."

"You told me to come on Monday to help with your centerpieces."

Oh! She was right. "I did. Hold on and I'll go get what we need."

I raced to my room and came back with a large cardboard box, loaded with supplies, which I set on the breakfast table. "Ready to get to work?"

"Yes, ma'am." Bessie Mae took a seat next to me.

"I'll be in the living room working on my Bible study if anybody needs me," Bob said. He waved the workbook in the air. "Joshua. Lots of battles."

"Kind of like life," Mom added.

I reached for a bolt of burlap ribbon and the box of mason jars. "Mom? Ready to fire up the glue gun and help us with these?"

"Please! Don't use the words *fire up*, RaeLyn." Mom shivered. "I could live the rest of my life without hearing about fire."

"Oops." I shrugged; then we got busy making the mason jar centerpieces for the reception. I found the process of adding the burlap ribbon and fake baby's breath relaxing. Therapeutic, even. Mom had always been very crafty, and she had some ideas to make the jars even more beautiful with lace overlaying the burlap. By the time we got ready to add the candles, I was blown away by how breathtaking they were.

We managed to finish the centerpieces around lunchtime, and I boxed them up and carried them to my room. It felt good to know I had that project behind me. Now, to connect with Iva and Eva. I shot off a quick text and they agreed to come by at two o'clock, after they closed up the tea shop. After that I sent a text to Mason, asking him to join us at that same time. He didn't respond, but hopefully he would get back to me when he could.

We ate a quick lunch—sandwiches and chips—and then Dad went out to check on the animals once more. I knew he was particularly concerned about Delilah, and I didn't blame him.

Gage left for work, and Dallas went out to help Dad before heading to Fish Tales for the afternoon.

Mom turned her attention to tidying up while I pondered my article for *Mabank Happenings*. My editor had already given me the week off, what with the wedding and all, but I had an idea that wouldn't leave me alone. Maybe I could write the story of the miracle we'd witnessed on our property yesterday.

And the miracle of the boys who went through the fire but weren't burned.

Yes, maybe I could pen a truly inspirational piece that would give people hope.

Before I could give this idea any more thought, Mom's phone rang. I glanced down at the phone on the counter and saw Dot's name.

"Your BFF is home!" I passed the phone to her and then paused as my mother answered it.

"Tell her she missed a doozy of a homecoming yesterday," Bob said from his spot on the sofa.

Mom nodded and turned her attention to the call. "Hey, you! Glad you made it. We had quite the day yesterday. You're never going to believe this story!"

A long pause followed, and Mom seemed to be listening intently to the voice on the other end of the line.

"Oh?" Mom said at last. "Well, sure, honey. Come on over. We would love to see you."

Mom ended the call and pressed her phone into her pocket. "That was a little odd."

"Who was it?" Bessie Mae asked.

"Dot. She got home from her cruise late last night. With all the chaos I forgot to check in on her, but apparently she made it just fine and wants to come by to tell us all about it."

"I can't wait." Bessie Mae's eyes sparkled. "A cruise sounds so lovely."

Mom nodded. "Must be more going on. Dot said there's something important she needs to share with us."

"Maybe she knows who set the fire," I said. I wouldn't be a bit surprised. Dot always seemed to have the scoop on, well, everything—long before the rest of us.

"She must know something." Creases formed between Mom's eyes. "She was acting mighty strange. And I felt sure I heard voices in the background. Could've sworn I heard someone speaking Spanish."

"Maybe we'll finally get to meet these elusive sisters of hers," Bessie Mae said. "She talks about them all the time, but I sometimes wonder if they're real."

"Oh, they're real all right," Mom countered. "I'm Facebook friends with both of them. But they're not Spanish speaking."

"Probably just the TV or something," I said. Then I lit into a conversation about quilts, which kept us preoccupied until we heard a car pull up in the driveway.

Bob glanced out the front window and let out a whistle. "Wow! Dot got a new car." He rose and walked to the window, then peered through the open blinds.

"Really?" Bessie Mae joined him and pulled the blinds up to see better. "Whoa. Y'all, come look."

We all rushed to the front window, and I instantly realized what all of the hoopla was about. The car parked in our driveway was a red Ferrari.

"Dot drives a Chevy," I said.

"A 2009 Chevy," Mom added. "Which she'll probably keep driving until it gives up the ghost. That Ferrari is *definitely* not her car."

Then whose was it?

"Has to belong to one of the sisters," Bessie Mae suggested. "That's my guess."

That made sense. And how exciting to think that we might finally meet one of Dot's family members. No doubt we would have a lot of stories to swap.

My curiosity got the better of me as I watched a stranger—a tall, tanned fellow with a thick mustache and salt-and-pepper hair—step out of the driver's side. He walked around to the passenger side and opened the door, and Dot stepped out. At least, I thought it was Dot. This woman had golden skin and shimmering hair, gleaming under the afternoon sun.

"Mom?" I glanced her way, more curious than ever.

My mother squinted to give the man a closer look, then turned my way, curiosity etched on her face. "Who's that?"

"No idea."

The tall, dark stranger seemed to be very familiar with Dot, though.

They laughed as they made their way up the driveway, arm in arm.

A minute later a rap sounded at our back door. Then, before we could holler, "C'mon in," it swung open and Dot stepped inside.

Well, at least I thought it was Dot. With the bright tan, colorful ensemble, and far more makeup than usual, it was a little hard to tell. And even indoors her silver hair looked brighter, like she'd added highlights or something. Apparently, her trip to the Caribbean had taken ten years off her life. And afforded her a complete makeover.

She took a couple of steps toward us, those beautiful blue eyes of hers twinkling, then turned back to take the hand of the man who stood in the doorway behind her.

Mr. Tall, Dark, and Handsome had movie-star looks, with a chiseled jaw and compelling smile. The golden skin was fabulous against his perfectly coiffed hair. Still, it felt odd having a total stranger saunter in with his hand in Dot's. Was this some brother she hadn't mentioned?

They stepped inside and closed the kitchen door, but it quickly opened again as my father entered on their heels.

Dad looked at the stranger, confusion registering on his face; then he snapped to attention. "Oh! You the fella I hired to work on the fence? That gate is really giving me fits, and I can't seem to get it fixed on my own."

"No, no, no." The stranger shook his head.

"Heavens, no." Dot laughed and rested her hand on her heart. "But that's the funniest misunderstanding ever!"

"Well then. . ." Never one to meet a stranger, Dad stuck out his hand and shook the fellow's with his usual display of force. "If you're not the worker I hired, who in the world do we have here?"

"That's my big surprise, y'all." Dot's cheeks flushed the prettiest shade of pink as she leaned over to give the handsome fellow a peck on the cheek. "I want you all to meet Enrique. My husband!"

CHAPTER TEN

"Your. . .husband?" Mom's eyes widened, and she wiped her hands on the dish towel she was holding.

At that very moment, a streak of white-hot lightning lit up the sky outside our front window. I let out a gasp as it seemed way too close for comfort.

Or maybe the gasp had more to do with Dot's news. Had I heard right? The suave fellow standing next to Mom's best friend. . .was her husband?

In all my years of knowing Dot—and they were many—she'd never let on that she was contemplating a husband. Yet here he stood, all six foot something of him, broad shouldered, with thick, dark wavy hair, silver at the temples, and a neatly trimmed mustache that framed out a mischievous smile. This fellow looked like he belonged on a Hollywood set, not in our humble Mabank kitchen.

"Gracias por recibirme." Enrique took a half step back as my father released his grip on his hand. "Thank you for having me. I've been anxious to meet all of you ever since Dot told me about you. The stories I have heard! *¡Extraordinario!*"

"Your. . .husband?" Mom repeated, her gaze never leaving Dot's face.

She twisted the dish towel. I finally reached over and gently tugged it away from her, so as not to give away her anxiety.

Dot patted Mom's hand, but her gaze never left Enrique's handsome face. "I know, Flora. I know. There's a lot to tell." She rested her hand on Enrique's back and then leaned into him, a lovely, innocent smile on her face.

"Clearly." My mother released a slow, calculated breath, and I could almost read her thoughts.

"Wait. Are you saying you two got hitched at sea?" Bessie Mae looked back and forth between Dot and Enrique. "Because if that's the case, we need to throw you a doozy of a party!"

Mom didn't look like she was in a party frame of mind. Right now she just looked shocked and somewhat horrified. Not that I blamed her. This was all rather startling.

Maybe I was still dreaming. Maybe this was another scene in that ongoing Technicolor drama that had me tossing and turning all night. Maybe I really was delirious.

"We got married on *Allure of the Seas* on Saturday night, our final night at sea." Dot slipped her arm through his and planted a kiss on his cheek. "By that point, neither of us could deny that the Lord had brought us together in that marvelous way of His. We were meant to be."

"But...but..." Mom, clearly still stunned, stammered out a half sentence then dropped into a chair at the kitchen table. "I need a minute." She opened her mouth a couple of times as if to speak, only to close it again. Her eyes darted back and forth between her best friend and this total stranger, the man now pressing kisses onto Dot's cheek.

"You've been married since Saturday and didn't think to pick up the phone to call me? Really?"

Okay, now Mom wasn't even trying to hide her anger. The pitch of her voice elevated more with each word she spoke. I had a feeling she was about to blow, so I handed her back the dishcloth.

"We were having such a marvelous time with my sisters," Dot explained.

"Ah, the sisters!" Enrique's face lit up. "How I love the sisters! Dottie and I drove them to Mulakofeefee."

"Malakoff?" my dad said.

"Dottie?" Mom's voice tightened. "He calls you Dottie?"

"Yes. Si." Enrique lit into something in Spanish and Dot responded to him. In Spanish.

"You speak Spanish now?" Mom's eyes widened as she looked her best friend's way. "Am I witnessing some sort of Christmas miracle here?"

"Definitely witnessing a miracle, though my Spanglish—that's what Enrique calls it—is very limited." Her cheeks flamed pink. "He taught me a few things."

"I'm sure he did." My mother quirked a brow and leaned against the counter as if to anchor herself from this news. Who could blame her? This was all a bit shocking, after all.

"Now what were you saying? In English, please."

Dot gave her a sympathetic look. "I'm sorry I didn't call or tell you before we got back home, but I figured this was news that needed to be delivered in person. I didn't think a phone call would do." Dot sat in the chair next to Mom and gestured for Enrique to sit to her left. "We've been flying by the seat of our pants."

"I would say so." Mom's gaze traveled back up to Enrique.

I could tell my poor mother was grappling to keep her composure in the face of this startling news we were all forced to swallow.

I glanced her way, wide-eyed, as if to say, *You're not the only one finding all of this hard to believe!* Dot had been known to pull a prank or two over the years. If this was a joke, it was a doozy.

Nope. Judging from the look of adoration in her eyes as she gazed at Enrique, Dot was really, truly in love. With a total stranger. Which now had my mother in an apparent tizzy.

Bessie Mae decided we all needed coffee, so she started a fresh pot.

This was Bessie Mae's hustle. She always managed to hang on around the edges of conversations, listening in while busying herself with food and drink. Talk about a great way to get the latest gossip.

I glanced at my aunt, who bent down to retrieve a dish from a lower cupboard.

Bob, on the other hand? He'd been content to hang out all day, quietly reading his Bible study lesson or snoozing in my dad's recliner. What Bessie Mae lacked in stillness, he more than made up for.

Right now, however, Bessie Mae put Bob to work in the kitchen, helping her. He didn't seem to mind a bit. I had a feeling he would fly to the moon if she asked him to. Love had that kind of spell on people, didn't it?

Enrique carried on and on about his feelings for his precious Dottie, his rich, Spanish accent filling the room with so much flavor I could practically taste the cumin.

Bessie Mae, God bless her, gave Dot a big hug and offered warm congratulations. Before long, Bob and Dad joined in the celebration, giving Enrique several slaps on the back.

Mom still didn't look convinced. Poor woman. Her world really was shaking, wasn't it?

Bessie Mae, still in hostess mode, snapped to attention. "I happened to bring over a butter pecan pound cake with caramel topping. What say I serve it up like a wedding cake? We really will have a celebration with coffee and cake!"

"That would be lovely," Dot said. "We had a small cake on the ship, but nothing comes close to your baking, Bessie Mae." She shot a glance Enrique's way. "Though my husband's skills in the kitchen are something to behold."

"Yes, I'm sure he has some skills." These words came from Mom, whose eyes had narrowed to slits. Oh boy.

"RaeLyn, want to help me serve our guests?" My aunt's words were really more of an order and less a request.

I nodded and joined her on the far side of the room. As I worked, I snuck another look at Dot's new husband. I took in the neatly trimmed mustache and that warm, genuine smile. Enrique wore pressed jeans and a starched shirt with rolled-up sleeves. His expressive brown eyes seemed to take in everything.

Enrique continued to charm everyone in the room—well, everyone but my mother—as Bessie Mae and I sliced up that delicious and beautiful cake, which I offered to the bride and groom first, along with fresh cups of hot, steaming coffee.

Bessie Mae served the rest of us, juggling plates as she passed them across the table.

Enrique took a bite of the cake and a look of delirium came over him. "*¡Delicioso!* I must have this recipe."

"Honey, I never use a recipe," Bessie Mae explained as she flashed a warm smile. "It's just a few ingredients filed away in my brain. They've been there for years. And I change 'em up every time I make it. This time I threw in some maple syrup for added flavor."

"I've never seen anyone work in the kitchen the way this woman does,"

Bob chimed in. "It's something to behold. I'm mesmerized."

"Why, thank you, Bob. That's the sweetest thing you've ever said to me." Bessie Mae gave him a kiss on the cheek.

"This is five-star cuisine." Enrique took another bite and then lit into Spanish. "*¡Madre mía, qué delicia! Este plato está espectacular, un regalo para el paladar.*"

"Come again?" Bob said.

"This is delicious! This dish is spectacular, a gift for the taste buds."

"Well, why didn't you just say so?" Bessie Mae laughed and asked if she could cut him another slice, which he willingly accepted.

By now the room was buzzing with conversation. Mom was the only silent one in the bunch. Bessie Mae, Dad, Dot, Enrique, and I kept the overly animated conversation flowing.

I glanced at my phone, wondering why I hadn't heard from Mason. Usually he texted when he was on his way, but I'd heard nothing. He was missing all the fun.

"So how did you two meet?" Mom poked her fork around her plate, not taking a bite. "Tell me everything."

"Enrique was a chef on board the *Allure of the Seas*," Dot explained. "So, when he says it's five-star cuisine, he knows what he's talking about. This man really knows his food."

"You're a chef?" Mom asked, her eyes narrowing as if she didn't quite believe him.

"I put in for—*¿cómo se dice?*—retirement two months ago," he explained, a chunk of butter pecan cake dangling from the tines of his fork. "I knew it would be *mi último* cruise. Perfection! But I never dreamed I would meet my bride on that last trip. How could I have known God would grace me with such a going-away prize?" He gave Dot a look warm enough to melt us all like butter left in the sun.

"And you got married, just like that?" Mom jabbed her fork into her cake and pushed it aside. "You didn't think to come home first and then do it?"

"The captain of the ship is a close friend," Enrique explained. "He was happy to do the honors, and it meant the world to me. *¡Qué noche de bodas tan hermosa tuvimos!* What a beautiful wedding night we had!"

I was pretty sure I heard Mom mutter, "Spare me the details," but he kept going, all in Spanish. She set her fork down with a clink and used her napkin to wipe a ring of moisture from the table.

"We got married in the little chapel on the top deck." Dot sighed and seemed to lose herself to her thoughts. "It was divine. My sisters were my bridesmaids. You should have seen their dresses. We got them in the gift shop. We all cried."

"Over the dresses?" Mom asked.

"No, silly, over how beautiful the evening was."

I had to give it to her. Dot still looked happy. Delirious, even. I'd never seen this version of Dot before. The all-business-all-the-time Dot, sure. The one running the Cedar Creek Chamber of Commerce like a well-oiled machine. The widow who busied herself to make up for the fact that her grown kids were too busy with their careers to spend much time with her.

But this woman with the doe-eyed grin on her face? I hardly recognized her.

Still, if anyone deserved a happily ever after, Dot did. Surely Mom would see that too, in time. She just had to get past the hurt over how this had gone down.

Kind of like she'd gotten over the hurt of Logan's elopement to Meghan.

And Bessie Mae moving out and taking the dishes.

And my upcoming move to. . .wherever I was going.

I glanced at my watch, wondering why Mason hadn't arrived yet. He was supposed to be here at two so that we could finalize our food plans with Iva and Eva.

As if on cue, a knock sounded at the front door. I rose and headed that way, half expecting to see Mason on the other side. Instead, I smiled as Iva and Eva Gabriel came into view.

"Sorry we're a few minutes late, honey." Iva gave me a big hug, nearly dropping the notebook in her arms. "We ran into a little complication at the tearoom. A leaky sink almost caused a disaster."

"But I happen to be handy with a wrench," Eva added. "So. . .crisis averted!"

I ushered them inside, but they stopped short as they saw the crowd gathered around the kitchen table.

"Have we come at a bad time?" Iva asked as she surveyed the crowd.

"No, no. But we might need to look for another place to meet. I suspect they'll be here awhile. Come on in and say hello." I ushered them into the kitchen to join the others. The ladies took one look at Enrique and practically swooned right there on the spot.

"Oh my. Who have we here?" Iva fanned her face with the notebook.

Enrique rose and extended his hand. "Enrique Delgado. I'm—"

"He's my husband!" Dot rose and threw her arms around Enrique's neck and gave him a kiss on the lips, right there in front of all of us.

CHAPTER ELEVEN

"H–husband?" Iva squealed, nearly dropping her notebook.

"Wait. . .what?" Eva's face paled as she gripped the back of a chair for support. "Dot, you're. . .married?"

"You're gonna need a slice of butter pecan cake to help you swallow down this chunk of news, honey." Bessie Mae pressed a plate holding a generous chunk of butter pecan cake into Eva's hands. "Would you like some Blue Bell to go with that?"

Enrique tilted his head, confusion knitting his brow. "What's a Blue Bell?"

At that exact moment a flash of lightning lit the sky outside the kitchen window. A collective gasp shot through the room. Every head swiveled toward Enrique in synchronized shock.

"You've. Never. Had. Blue. Bell. Ice. Cream?" Bessie Mae asked. "My stars! Honey, that's practically a sin in these here parts. I'm about to baptize you in homemade vanilla!"

"Where are you from, anyway?" Bob asked. "Not from around here, judging from the sound of it."

"Reynosa, Mexico." Enrique clasped his hands together in dramatic fashion and seemed to lose himself to his thoughts for a moment. "Born and raised."

"The Delgado family owned a small citrus orchard, which he helped run as a younger man." The edges of Dot's lips tipped up in a comfortable smile. "That's where his love of cooking began."

"Ah, such bittersweet memories of my childhood." He swiped at his eyes with the back of his hand. "When my parents passed I tried to keep it going, but a drought left us. . .how you say? *Devastado*."

"Drought. There's a word I understand." My dad rose and headed to the sink with his plate. "But weren't we talking about Blue Bell?" He yanked open the freezer door, rummaged past a bag of frozen vegetables, and came out with a tub of Golden Vanilla under one arm and Cookies and Cream under the other. Even in the heart of winter we Hadleys had to have our Blue Bell. We'd show this stranger a thing or two about how folks celebrated in Mabank, Texas.

I rose to help Dad, and Iva and Eva followed on my heels, always ready to serve up food to guests.

As I grabbed the bowls, Iva mouthed the words, "He's dreamy."

I couldn't help but agree. The man had a suave, sophisticated air about him, to be sure. And that rich accent made me feel like I'd ventured onto a movie set.

"He looks like Ricardo Montalbán," Eva whispered.

"No, Ricardo Montalbán was clean shaven," Iva argued. "I think he looks like Cesar Romero."

"For sure, he dresses like Cesar." Eva fanned her face with her hand. "So sophisticated. Dot's gone to sea and come back with a Latin heartthrob."

I had to admit, for a fellow in his age group he was still mighty handsome.

My gaze shifted to Mom, who was giving Dot the third degree. "So, you're Dottie *Delgado* now? Am I understanding this correctly?"

"Yes." Dot smiled. "Delgado means thin or slender."

Well, that was fitting, considering the woman's lean physique.

Bessie Mae flew into action, scooping up a generous serving of each flavor, which she passed to our guests. Then, with Bob's help, she passed out smaller portions for the rest of us so that there would be enough. I didn't mind. With a wedding dress to fit into in five days, I needed to take it easy on the sweets. *Delgado* was my wedding day goal.

Before long, we were all drunk on Blue Bell and further intoxicated with the Spanglish ramblings of this Casanova who'd mysteriously swept into our lives so unexpectedly. He continued to entertain us with stories of his childhood in Reynosa, which were peppered with Spanish phrases none of us could understand.

Well, none of us but Iva and Eva, who both happened to be fluent in Spanglish.

Eva looked back and forth between Enrique and Dot, a dreamy-eyed expression on her face. "Dot, where on earth does one have to go to find a fella like this?"

"A cruise ship, apparently." Dot giggled. "He was right there, just waiting for me, after all these years of single life."

Iva batted her lashes like a starstruck teenybopper. "Do they sell any more like him in the gift shop?"

"No, and I found him in the dining room, not the gift shop." Dot flashed Enrique a mischievous look. "Though he has turned out to be quite the gift, one I'm so incredibly thankful for. Would you believe, after all of these years, that the Lord has finally seen fit to bring me my Prince Charming?"

"Tell me everything." Iva sat in the empty chair across from Dot and Enrique. "Don't leave out even the tiniest detail. I plan to live vicariously through you for the next several minutes. Or longer. Take your time."

So much for our meeting about the wedding food.

Enrique repeated the story we'd already heard, adding even more elaborate and fun details about how their eyes had met across the dining room that first night. About how flattered he was that she had asked to speak to the chef to compliment the delicious ceviche.

"Ceviche is hard to get right," Dot explained. "Enrique's was sheer perfection."

He kissed her hand once again, joy radiating from his eyes. "Flattery like that will get you everywhere."

"Clearly," Mom muttered.

Enrique's gaze never left Dot's face. "When I laid eyes on this woman, *lo sabía en mi corazón*."

"You knew in your heart?" Iva sighed and rested her elbows on the table as she leaned his way. "How lovely! That's how it should be, love at first sight. This is all so perfect."

"Wait, does everyone in the room speak Spanish. . .but me?" My dad leaned back in his chair and rubbed his full belly.

"Si," Eva, Iva, Dot, and Enrique replied in unison.

"No," Mom, Bessie Mae, Bob, and I echoed.

Dad shrugged and pushed his chair back to stand. "Looks like I'm gonna have to take lessons if this keeps up."

Everyone dove back into the conversation while my father carried his bowl to the sink. I found myself lost in my thoughts once again as I pondered the romantic way Dot and Enrique had met. My mind slipped back to the first day I'd met Mason. We were children in school, and I saw him from across the playground. Had I known that very day? It was crazy to think about now, all these years later.

Mason.

I glanced at my phone. No response to my text. Ugh. Had it gone unread?

"Wait, what day of the cruise was that?" The creases between Mom's brows let me know that she still wasn't quite buying this story, at least not in total.

"Tuesday," Enrique said. "We always served our ceviche appetizer on Tuesdays."

"Wow, you two sure didn't waste any time to tie the knot." Iva rested her palms on the table. "Met on a Tuesday, married on Saturday? That's speedy business."

Enrique batted his eyes in Dot's general direction and spoke with passion: "*¡Cuando encuentras a la persona con quien quieres pasar la eternidad, quieres que esa eternidad empiece de inmediato!*"

"I think we're going to need a translator," Dad said as he leaned against the fridge, arms crossed. "I'm feeling a little lost in my own kitchen."

"He said, 'When you find the one you want to spend forever with, you want forever to start right away,'" Eva explained. "Is that not the most romantic thing you've ever heard?"

All the women but my mother offered up blissful sighs in unison.

"Oh." My dad gave him an admiring look. "Gotcha."

Mom didn't seem convinced, judging from the tight expression on her face. "I've heard of short engagements, but marrying after only knowing someone a few days? That's rather unprecedented."

Interpretation: Dot, you've lost your mind.

"What can I say?" Enrique rose and took Dot's hand and kissed the back of it. "Dot swept me off my feet faster than a salsa beat." He pulled her up, and they did a spin right there in the kitchen. Dot's cheeks turned the prettiest shade of pink.

We all offered applause as he dipped her and then gave her a sound kiss, one that messed up her tinted hair and made her blush.

Well, not all. Mom rolled her eyes and fingered her coffee cup, eyes diverted to the back door. No doubt she was plotting her escape. Or trying to figure out how to shove her once best friend out of that door.

"He's great on the dance floor and fast with a quip," Dot said as he lifted her back to a standing position.

"He's fast, all right." Mom brushed her palms on her slacks. "More coffee, anyone? Tea?"

"There's so much to love about Enrique." Dot batted her eyelashes at her husband.

Husband.

This was all too weird.

"I just can't get over this," Bessie Mae said. "One minute you're leaving for a trip with your sisters, the next you're coming home with a husband. I'm half afraid to take you grocery shopping. You might go in for baking soda and come out with a passel of children."

"I have children," Dot reminded her. "Grown and moved away. Rarely come to see me. They're workaholics like their mama. So it's about time I fill my life—and my home—with someone who actually takes the time to notice me."

She had a point. If anyone deserved companionship, it was Dot. Amazing, wonderful Dot.

"We're thinking of getting a dog," she said. "A chihuahua."

"Dot, you *hate* dogs," Mom said.

"I do not hate dogs." Dot cleared her throat. "I'm not a fan of big dogs. They scare me. But chihuahuas are tiny and—"

"Vicious," Mom said. "I was bit by a nine-pound chihuahua as a child, and it scarred me for years."

"Don't be silly, Flora." With the wave of a hand Dot appeared to dismiss any concerns. "Enrique loves chihuahuas."

"I could not wait to be back on dry land again so I could have a dog of my own once more." Enrique took that opportunity to begin to clear the table. He shared a funny story about his last night in the kitchen on the ship as he carried dirty plates and coffee mugs to the sink.

I could tell from the look on Mom's face that she was mortified to have a guest cleaning her kitchen. She rose and tagged along behind him, more plates in hand. Not that Enrique noticed. He knew what to do. He turned on the hot water and began to rinse the plates off, then stacked them in the sink. Then he reached for a clean dishcloth, dampened it, and wiped a few crumbs from the counter.

"He's a keeper, Dot," Iva said. "Any man who takes it upon himself to clean without being asked is a man worth having."

"My stars, yes." Eva turned her attention his way. "Do you, by chance, have a brother, Enrique? I'm asking for a friend."

Enrique nodded. "I do. Yes. He's a priest at Catedral de Nuestra Señora de Guadalupe in Reynosa, Mexico. An amazing man of God. He once fasted for forty days to be more like Jesus."

"Oh." Eva's nose wrinkled. "Never mind. I could never marry a man who turned away food."

So the priest part didn't deter her?

I glanced at my watch, wondering why Mason hadn't arrived yet. This was better than those telenovelas Iva and Eva were always talking about.

Iva and Eva! They had come for a reason. We needed to get to it. I cleared my throat, ready to get down to business. But how? Should I nudge these people out of the room or find someplace else to meet?

"Iva and Eva own a local tea shop," I explained to Enrique as he sat back down at the table. "They've come to talk to me about the reception menu. They're catering the wedding."

"Catering?" This got Enrique's attention. "A word I know well. But who is getting married?"

I pointed to myself.

"RaeLyn and her fiancé are getting married this coming Saturday afternoon," Mom explained. "He should be here any moment. Right, RaeLyn?"

I glanced at the clock on the wall to check the time. "Right." In theory.

"They're getting married outdoors in a field," my father explained. "In December." He muttered something under his breath about what a crazy idea that was, but I did my best to ignore him.

"Sounds wonderful!" Enrique clasped his hands together and gave me a broad smile. "I love outdoor weddings. I've catered many of them for our passengers who wanted to get married at the various ports. So fun!"

I could've given the man a big hug right then and there. But I didn't.

"Eva and I are going to be cooking up a storm," Iva explained. "You should see the menu."

"Oh, how wonderful! *He llegado justo a tiempo.*" He paused and offered me a warm smile. "I've arrived just in time for the happy celebration. How fun!"

No doubt Mom would fill my ears later over how presumptuous he was to assume he would be invited to my wedding. But of course he would be. How could I leave out Dot's husband?

Dot's husband.

Those words still sounded foreign to my ears.

Foreign. Ha.

Enrique dove into a conversation with Iva in Spanish, and before long they somehow eased their way into English once again. Iva laid out the plan for all the foods they would be serving on my big day. Sounded like we were having our meeting right here and now, guests or not.

I glanced at my phone once again to see if Mason had responded. Nothing.

"It's a Texas-themed wedding, through and through," Eva explained. "You'll love the appetizers: mini chicken and waffles, pecan-crusted cheese balls."

"Corn bread bites with jalapeño honey butter too," Iva added. "It's going to be so much fun."

"And for the main course?" Enrique leaned his elbows onto the table, fully invested in the conversation.

"Still finger foods," I explained. "We want the night to be casual, since the reception is in a tent outdoors."

"A heated tent," my father said. "Don't ask me how much those heaters cost me. A bundle."

"We're having brisket sliders, steak fingers, and mac and cheese puff pastry bites for the main course," Eva chimed in. "Oh, and green bean bundles wrapped in bacon."

"Delicious. And for dessert?" Enrique's eyes twinkled as if he'd already settled on the dessert menu himself.

"Bessie Mae's doing our wedding cake," I added. "I wouldn't have it any other way. I can't wait to show off the topper. And we'll have snowball cookies and some candies, just small things. Oh, and a hot cocoa bar with all sorts of mix-ins like peppermint, chocolate chips, marshmallows, and so on."

"You must have something else, something no one will ever forget." Enrique's face lit up and he snapped his fingers. "Yes, that's it! I will do my famous churros. My gift to you."

"Churros?" Bessie Mae looked intrigued. "What's that?"

"Churros are crispy, cinnamon-sugar treats with caramel or chocolate dipping sauce, Bessie Mae," I explained.

"What about a churro bar, right next to the hot cocoa bar?" Eva pulled out her notebook and opened it. "I think there's room, don't you?" She showed us the diagram she'd drawn of the reception tent, and before long we were all planning where the churro station could go.

Why wasn't Mason here to put his stamp of approval on all of this?

I shot off a quick text to him, but it went unread.

"I'm so excited!" Enrique rose and paced the room. "I will do a homemade caramel dipping sauce, some of my best chocolate sauce, and a variety of—*¿cómo se dice?*—accoutrements. My gift to you, RaeLyn. No charge." He flashed a broad smile, which totally won me over. Well, that and the "no charge" part.

I thanked him profusely and fought the temptation to give him a big hug.

I also fought the temptation to toss my phone at the wall. Why was Mason avoiding me? He was missing all this great news. And what if he didn't like the churro idea? Then what? I didn't want to hurt Enrique's feelings, but I should get Mason's input. Right?

Mom muttered something unintelligible under her breath. She rose and gestured for me to join her in the kitchen. I followed on her heels until we reached the sink, where she fussed with a couple of the dirty plates.

"Well, isn't he just the most perfect specimen of a man?" Mom muttered under her breath as she worked.

"Seems pretty great," I acknowledged.

"A little too great." She turned to face me, her whispered words strained. "So, this stranger is now helping cater your wedding, RaeLyn?"

I offered a little shrug. "I guess. I mean, I love a good churro and I'm never one to turn away an offer of free food."

"From someone we've never met."

"Who just happens to be married to your best friend of thirty years, Mom."

"Who could be an ax murderer. Or an escaped convict. Or a. . ."

A peal of laughter guided our focus back to the table, where Enrique had swept Dot into his arms to dance another little salsa with her.

"Or a perfectly wonderful man who's about to make all of your best friend's dreams come true, Mom," I said. "An answer to her prayers."

To which Mom grunted. Loudly.

CHAPTER TWELVE

Mason never did show up for the meeting with Iva and Eva, but—with Enrique's help—we managed to put together a plan that I felt sure he would agree with. Hopefully.

I filled Mason in on Tuesday morning when he stopped by with Tilly, who was all fixed up and running perfectly. I had just finished dressing for my bridesmaids' brunch and was putting the finishing touches on my hair and makeup when he came rolling up the driveway in my gorgeous red truck, freshly washed and running like a champ.

I didn't even wait for him to come to the door. By the time he had Tilly parked I was halfway to the driveway.

Mason took one look at me all decked out in my jeans and frilly ivory blouse and whistled.

"Whoa." His gaze traveled up from my clothes to my wavy 'do. "Love your hair like that."

I brushed it off my shoulders. "Thanks. Decided to add a few curls. They probably won't last long in the cold, but it's fun to try for special events."

"They suit you. And that outfit is. . .wow." His eyes widened. "I'm marrying a hottie."

I felt my cheeks grow warm, and all the more when my dad walked up. He rested his hand on the hood of the truck and smiled.

"You got Tilly up and running again, I see."

"Yep. Just the carburetor, as I suspected. An easy fix, but I had to order the part from Dallas and ran into a couple of hiccups with the delivery guy."

"Thank you." I threw my arms around his neck and gave him a hug, so relieved and grateful. "And sorry about the hiccups."

"Good to have a car guy in the family." My dad gave him an admiring look. "Where are you guys off to today?"

"My bridal brunch," I explained.

"Not me." Mason put his hands up. "Pretty sure I'm not invited to that one."

No, he was not.

"Was there something on that spreadsheet of yours that I was supposed to take care of today?" Dad shot a glance my way.

"Yep. I need someone to make sure the rental company is all set with what we need for the reception—the tent, the tables, the chairs, chair covers. . .everything on the list I gave you." I hesitated before adding, "They'll be needing the final payment today. Did you get the numbers I texted you earlier?"

"I did." He pretended to be having a heart attack, then quickly recovered. "I'm calling them now. Have a great time at your. . .thing." He reached for his phone and walked in the opposite direction.

Mason and I had some time to talk as I drove him back to his car shop on my way to Tasha's, but I found myself completely distracted. I glanced out the window and caught a glimpse of the field to the north, which was nothing but a charred black mess. This was my first time out since the fire, and it was more than I could take. My stomach churned as I observed the devastation.

"I know," Mason said after a moment of quiet reflection. "It's bad."

"It is." I paused to think it through. It broke my heart to know that people had lost their homes. "I still can't get over watching those flames come so close and then die down. I'm wondering why God spared our property, you know?"

"After my dad died I wondered just the opposite: why He took my dad and spared the truck driver who hit him."

"Yeah." We both grew silent, knowing full well we wouldn't get the answers to any of these questions on this side of heaven. But there was coming a day when all would be made right. We would cling to that—not just now but for the rest of our lives together.

Just one more reason to love Mason Fredericks. His faith in Jesus was the real deal.

"Speaking of my dad, I spoke to my aunt Lucy this morning. She's getting really excited about the wedding."

"I'm so glad she's coming. And her husband too, right?"

"Yes." Mason nodded. "I've been doing my best to stay in touch with her more now that both of my parents are gone. I think she's enjoying our conversations too."

"That's sweet, Mason."

"Good for both of us, I think."

He grew quiet, and I found myself incredibly grateful that he had someone from his side of the family to support him on our big day.

But I still had a few lingering questions about why he'd missed my messages yesterday. So I turned to face him, ready for details.

"You worried me yesterday."

"I did?" He glanced my way as I pulled up to a stoplight. "Oh, because I didn't see your text yesterday until I was done with work? Sorry about that. I was working on Tilly all day and left my phone in the office."

"You're not going to leave me at the altar, are you? Because I'm not sure I could stand being jilted in a field on a cold winter's day with all of my friends and loved ones sitting on quilts on hay bales that my brothers lugged out there to make me happy. Just seems extra tragic and I'm extra enough already."

Mason's eyebrows shot up. "You would prefer I leave you on a hot summer's day?"

"No, silly." I fought the temptation to roll my eyes. "I'd prefer you show up for our meetings."

"In my defense, I didn't see the text. And even if I had, getting Tilly up and running is pretty critical too."

"I know, but this is the second meeting you've missed. Remember the one with Pastor Burchfield a couple weeks back?"

"Yeah, I had to make a run to Kaufman that day, sorry. And the meeting yesterday wasn't on the spreadsheet you gave me last month."

"Right. True." I bit my lip. "Just making sure you're fully invested, that's all."

When the light turned I eased forward.

Mason gave me a pointed glance. "I am, RaeLyn. More than you know."

The cryptic tone of his voice made me sit up straighter. "Intriguing response."

"All will be revealed. Soon. Can you hang on in the meantime? I promise, you'll be as happy as a pup with two tails."

Interesting imagery. "I'm happy now, Mason. Giddy, actually. And I forgive you for not showing up yesterday, though you missed a doozy of a conversation with Dot's new husband."

He laughed. "Oh, trust me, I heard all about him from pretty much every customer who's stopped in this morning. Enrique's the hottest topic of conversation in town. Well, Enrique and the boys who were hospitalized after the fire."

"We saw them on the news yesterday morning. Have you heard anything about how the fire started?"

"No. Have you?"

"Nothing more than what Gage told us. I'm just wondering if the investigators have pinned down a culprit or if it was really just lightning."

"I'm guessing dry lightning," he said. "Just a freak thing."

"Yeah. Probably." Still, I couldn't stop the niggling suspicion that there might be more to this story.

"How are the boys?" Mason asked as I pulled into the parking lot of his shop. "Any update?"

"They're both doing remarkably well. It's really miraculous, when you hear their whole story. Thank God they're both going to be okay."

"I know their family has got to be so relieved."

"I'm sure." I pulled into a parking spot and put the truck in PARK. "I know that feeling of relief well, trust me. The minute they got that fire out at the edge of our property, I felt that same feeling wash over me. I don't want to admit how scared I was."

"You and me both," he responded. "But a couple of my customers weren't so lucky. One of them lost over forty acres and the other had a barn go up in flames."

"With animals in it?"

"No, he got them out just in time."

"That's a relief. Speaking of customers, how's it coming with Nadine's car?" I stared at the parking lot to see if I could locate it. Must be inside the bay.

Pretty good," he responded. "I'm plugging away at it. I'm completely repainting it in rose gold. I think she's trying to wash away all memory of her ex and thinks a new color palette will do the trick, something more feminine."

"I don't blame her."

He turned my way. "Did Gage tell you that Aaron's gone missing?"

"No! What do you mean, missing?"

"He didn't show up for his appointment this morning. I was supposed to give him an estimate to flip that old truck of his. And I heard he's missed a couple of other appointments as well."

"Wow. Maybe he's just getting away for a few days to clear his head?" I offered.

"Maybe. But he's not responding to my messages. I reached out to Gage, and he said Aaron's not responding to him either."

"That's so weird." Aaron might be the moody sort, but he'd never gone AWOL before.

On the other hand, what if something terrible had happened to him? He was Gage's best friend, after all.

Oblivious to my internal ponderings, Mason went back to talking about Nadine's car. He sounded pretty proud of himself for the work he'd done on it. Not that I blamed him. Mason Fredericks was a pro.

"Speaking of Nadine, she's going to be helping out at your bridesmaids' brunch today, isn't she?"

"Yes. Iva, Eva, and Melody are prepping the food, and Nadine and Dot are helping out by serving us. They said I'm going to be treated like a queen, and the bridesmaids will be treated as my royal subjects." I couldn't help but laugh at the image that presented. "I think Annie James is coming to take pictures."

"I saw some of her photography in the paper last week. She's really going places."

"Yes, we're blessed to have booked her for the wedding, for sure. And grateful Landon is playing the role of deejay."

"I'm sure he'll be great." Mason paused. "So, you ladies are going to hang out and eat crumpets and drink tea? That sort of thing?"

I laughed at the word *crumpets*. "I guess. Why all the questions?"

"Just curious. No big deal." He got out of the truck and came around to the driver's side.

I put my window down so we could keep talking. "Are you jealous you're not going to have tiny quiche and scones?"

"Um, no." He laughed and brushed a loose hair out of my eyes. "You ladies enjoy yourselves. I've got a bunch of errands to run. There's a lot to keep up with."

"Tell me about it." I laughed. "I'm in wedding-planning mode, remember?"

"Oh, I remember. And I'm very much looking forward to that wedding. In the field. In the snow. With the thermal blankets your father told me he's buying." Mason gave me a little kiss on the nose.

"Very funny."

"Pretty sure he wasn't kidding. Don't be surprised if you see a folded blanket on the end of each bale of hay."

"That's a lot of blankets. And a ton of money. He doesn't need to go that far just to make a point. Surely people will wear jackets."

"I guess we'll see." Mason glanced at his watch then gave me a proper kiss. "I'd better let you get to your shindig. I've got errands to run. Gotta see a man about a horse."

"I hope that's just Texas lingo for 'I've got plans.'"

"Hey, you love horses."

"I do."

But what an odd thing to say.

I waved goodbye, rolled up the window, then headed off to Tasha's place.

When I pulled up to her house at the lake, I slipped the truck into PARK and reached for my purse to touch up my lipstick. I pulled down the visor and looked at my reflection in the mirror, then swiped on the lipstick and smacked my lips together.

When I glanced over, I noticed Tasha standing on the porch, waving at me. It only took a few seconds to get out of the truck and head her way. As I did, the energy between us served as a magnet, drawing us together. Nothing new there.

In the world of best friends, I'd somehow inherited the best. Tasha Dempsey was saucy, had the most gorgeous red hair and bright green eyes, and my, oh my, could that girl dress! Her wardrobe lacked no spark or pizzazz. This was true on most occasions, but today she'd outdone herself with the jazzy teal top, sassy jeans, and sparkling jewelry. I could hardly wait to see this chick decked out on my big day in that sage-green bridesmaid dress. No doubt she would outshine the bride. Literally.

"RaeLyn, you look gor-geous!" she sang out as she came bounding down the steps of her quaint home. That fabulous red hair of hers practically glowed under the morning sunlight. Nearly as much as that shimmering blouse. "I love how you did your hair."

"Thanks. Mason liked it too."

"I can see why."

I ran my fingers through the lengthy strands. "I rarely curl it these days but decided to put some effort in."

"Is that how you're wearing it for the wedding?" she asked.

I shrugged. "There have been more than a few debates about that. I was going to wear it up, but Mason makes so many nice comments when I wear it like this, so maybe I'll consider wearing it down. Especially if it's cold out. It will keep my shoulders warm."

"I thought you were wearing a wrap?"

"Yeah. Probably." I still hadn't settled on that 100 percent.

We made our way into her beautiful vacation rental home, the one I'd helped renovate just a few short months ago, and were met by Annie James, who started snapping photos the moment we walked in the door.

"Give a girl a minute!" I laughed and then fussed with my hair before agreeing she could forge ahead with pictures.

"With your permission I'm going to put your photo in the paper in our new weddings section."

"We have a new weddings section?" I asked.

She nodded. "We do now. And you'll be first up at bat, so let's get some good shots."

As she gestured across the parlor, my attention shifted to the fabulous Christmas decor. Shimmering white Christmas trees decked out the far corner of the living room, clustered in varying sizes. All white, with some silver accents. And lights. Lots and lots and lots of white lights, twinkling their invitation to celebrate the season.

Looked like we had plenty of places to take photos, for sure.

My gaze traveled to the large windows at the back of the room, which let in generous beams of the beautiful morning sunlight as it reflected off the waters of Cedar Creek Lake just beyond.

I couldn't get over how beautiful everything was. And it smelled like Christmas in here—a combination of fresh pine and some sort of Christmas spice. Cinnamon, maybe?

Or maybe that delicious scent was coming from the kitchen.

I sighed as I took in the gorgeous room. Truth be told, I'd love to have a house like this someday, one by the water. But I would never tell Mason that. I just loved the bright, airy feel of this place with its high ceilings and homey decor. How fun would it be to look out over the lake every day and marvel at the ripples in the water?

Why Tasha was having trouble keeping vacation renters, I couldn't say. Maybe the winter months were just slow across the board. At any rate, I was happy she had opened her home for this brunch.

"It's beautiful!" My gaze traveled to the mantel, which she had draped in soft white tulle and tiny twinkling fairy lights. "You've really outdone yourself, Tasha."

"Thanks. I didn't have any renters this week and decided this would be the perfect bridesmaids' hangout. What would you think about getting dressed and ready over here on Saturday?"

"I love it. Well, as long as Mom's okay with it." At this point I didn't want to hurt my mother's feelings.

Over the next few minutes, Annie snapped several pictures of me in various places around the room. She eventually coaxed Tasha to pose with me by the main decked-out Christmas tree in the corner of the room.

As we wrapped up the pictures, she headed off to the kitchen to get some pictures of the other ladies. And the food.

Tasha looked my way, all smiles. "Well, I have news."

"You do?" My heart skipped a beat. Had my brother popped the question without letting any of us know, perhaps?

"Hope you're ready," Tasha said with a twinkle in her eye. " 'Cause this one's a doozy!"

CHAPTER THIRTEEN

"My parents are retiring."

Okay, so this was not at all what I thought Tasha was going to say.

"They're selling Fish Tales?" I asked. "Really?"

"Yep." She nodded, a hopeful smile now lighting her beautiful face. "To *me*."

"What?"

Tasha fussed with a centerpiece on the coffee table. "I knew this day would eventually come, but I always thought they would sell it to someone else in the business. But in the end, they wanted me to have it. It meant more to my dad to pass it down to someone in the family. And I can appreciate that."

"So, what do you think of the idea? You're going to keep it open?"

"Sure. I love Fish Tales. But if they're stepping away—and I think they'll do it slowly, over time—then I'm going to need help, and lots of it."

"Meaning?"

"I'm going to need Dallas more than ever. I'm thinking about making him my manager. You can't believe how good he is with all of this, RaeLyn. It's like he was made for it."

He was made for you, I wanted to say, but didn't. Instead I opted for,

"Wow. That's cool. Just don't tell my mother until after the wedding, okay? She's already flipping out that I'm leaving. If she thinks he'll be gone more often, it will do her in."

"Speaking of your mother. . ." Tasha looked around. "Where is she? And Carrie and Meghan? I figured all you Hadley gals would drive over together." She paused. "Unless she's still upset with Meghan. I know your mother doesn't exactly get along with her. If—when—Dallas proposes to me, she'll probably hate me too."

"No way!" I threw my arms around her neck. "How could anyone hate you? You're the best person I've ever known." And I was so very thrilled that the Lord had chosen to bless her with the family business. She certainly deserved it.

"I'm the brightest too." She gestured to her colorful ensemble and laughed.

"Yep. And the difference is, Mom has known and loved you for years. She barely knew Meghan when Logan proposed."

"Oh, I remember." Tasha laughed. "She was 'the one we don't speak of.'"

"Right. And running off and getting married at the justice of the peace was the nail in the coffin. I really wish they hadn't done that. It sure complicated things."

"I can absolutely assure you that if I get engaged—"

"When."

"*When* I get engaged, I'm going to have a huge church wedding, and both of our mothers are going to be in the thick of it, helping me plan and shop and everything. They will be the happiest duo on the planet, I promise."

I threw my arms around Tasha's neck. "Pretty sure that will seal your fate with my mother forever. But just so you're aware, things are better between her and Meghan now."

"Oh?"

"Yes. Meghan was so sweet the day of the fire. I think she won some brownie points with Mom, the way she took charge and kept us focused. Mom actually gave her a hug."

"Wow." Tasha looked genuinely intrigued by this.

"I think they'll eventually be close. Meghan's living there on the property, and Mom's going to need companionship." A lump rose in my throat. "Meghan is the logical choice."

"I hope you're right. It would be good for Meghan too. She doesn't have family nearby, right?"

"Right." I paused to think it through. "I really do think she and Mom will eventually be best friends, especially now that I won't be in the house. Mom's going to need someone to bond with. A female, I mean. She's got Carrie, but Carrie's pretty busy with Annalisa."

"How is Annalisa, by the way? She was sick, right?"

"They went to stay with her parents on the day of the fire, and I haven't seen her since. This will be the first time we've been together since then. I hope she's feeling better today. Meghan too."

"Meghan's not well?"

"I don't know if she got too much smoke or what, but she was feeling queasy and faint the day of the fire and stayed home from work yesterday. I had a similar reaction to the smoke myself. It made me sick that night."

"Ack."

"But I do feel bad for Meghan. Logan said she was in bed most of the day."

"Poor thing. Probably all of the adrenaline didn't help. Is she coming today?"

"Yes, she insisted. She and Carrie are stopping to pick up Summer on their way. They should be here soon."

"Perfect. And your mom?"

"Left the house early to help Bessie Mae with the cheesy grits and the biscuits and gravy. She won't have far to come." I gestured to the side window, which gave us a clear view of Bob's house.

"I love having her as a next-door neighbor." Tasha laughed. "You can't imagine how many times she's stopped by with cookies. Or cake. Or pie. Did I mention I love her pie?"

"Only a thousand times." I gestured to the empty living room. "But does that mean you're staying here now?"

"More often than not. I've had such a hard time keeping it rented." Her smile faded. "I know God has a plan. He'll show me soon enough what to do about all of that. I have a mortgage to pay. You know?"

"Right. Maybe Fish Tales will do so well that you can take care of the mortgage payment that way?"

"Maybe." She shrugged. "But I was less stressed talking about your mother. Mortgages make me nervous."

"I can't even imagine. Yet."

Perhaps soon.

We headed into the kitchen, where I found Melody working alongside Iva and Eva around the spacious island. As they worked, the ladies buzzed with anticipation, bustling about with their last-minutes touches. Their laughter was welcoming and put me at ease right away. How blessed I was to have each and every one of them in my life, not just on good days like this one but on days when everything around was threatened by fire.

A swirl of mouthwatering aromas hit me at once: freshly brewed coffee, the delicious scent of bacon, and cinnamon and sugar from a tray of cinnamon rolls.

I looked over the food on display and gasped. Iva and Eva had outdone themselves with trays of mini quiches stuffed with ham and cheese and the most delicious fruit-topped French toast casserole I'd ever seen. It was a colorful and tasty-looking display that surpassed all my expectations. As I took it all in, Annie snapped photos—of both the food and my reactions.

My mouth watered at the sight of it all, and I was suddenly glad I'd come hungry.

"It's amazing!" I said and then made the rounds, giving every food item a closer look. Melody brought a large bowl of mixed fruit out of the fridge and reached back inside for a container of yogurt. I picked up a huge strawberry and pretended to shove it in my mouth. Annie got a great picture of that. Hopefully she wouldn't choose that one to go in the local paper.

"We've got coffee, sweet tea, and orange juice on the sideboard." She pointed at the beautiful arrangement, flanked with flowers on either side.

"Y'all went all out!" I couldn't believe the effort they had gone to, or me.

"We did." A tender look came over Tasha's face. "You're my best friend. Did you think we would do a shoddy job?"

"No, but I sure didn't expect all of this."

Iva and Eva fussed over the food items, describing each one with great animation. They had left no detail unattended for this bridesmaids' brunch, and it showed. I gazed at the pastel flowers in vintage mason jars that lined the countertops and sighed. "You gals have a gift."

One that Annie was capturing on film, one snapshot after another. She turned the camera around to show me the angled photo of the mason jars. It took my breath away.

"You're the gift," Melody said before giving me a warm hug. "And you have no idea how many times I've praised God for sparing you and your family from that fire, RaeLyn."

"It's truly miraculous," Annie said. "We've all said so."

"Yes." My eyes welled with tears as I saw the concern etched in their eyes. I was genuinely loved by all of these ladies, and it made my heart so happy.

"Speaking of miracles, did any of you see that story on the news about the twin boys who were caught up in the fire at Purtis Creek?" Tasha asked.

I nodded. "Yes! Mason and I were just talking about them. I'm so relieved they're okay."

Melody nodded. "We all are. I know the whole community is really rallying around the family. It's great to see people band together like this."

"Sure is." Iva fussed with the flowers. "The fire department asked if they could put a fundraiser bucket for the family in our tea shop and we agreed, of course. Folks are already contributing."

"Did you realize that Grace Oberdeen is the aunt of the boys?" Melody asked.

"No!" I couldn't help but gasp at that connection.

Melody nodded. "She says they've got quite the testimony."

This raised several questions in my mind. "I wonder if they would be willing to let me do a write-up in the paper about them when they're better."

"Probably. Do you know how to reach Grace?"

"I'm sure Mom has her number. Or Dot." My thoughts shifted. "Oh, speaking of Dot. . ."

"We know, girl." Melody laughed and pointed at Iva and Eva. "What do you think we've been chatting about in here? *Everyone* knows."

"It's the talk of the town." Annie snapped another picture of the decor. "Dot went off to sea and came back with her own personal chef."

"Her own personal Casanova, you mean." Iva's cheeks flushed. "And honey, is he ever a looker."

"For a man in his sixties, yes he is." Eva fanned her face. "I'm telling you, he's more handsome than Ricardo Montalbán!"

"But. . .enough talk about all of that." Tasha interrupted the chatter as she faced me. "Today is all about *you*, my friend. Not the television. Not the fire. Not Enrique, though I've had an earful about him from pretty much everyone in town. Today is your day and nothing will spoil it."

I decided to put her mind at ease right away. "Tasha, I hope you know me well enough to know that I don't need everything to be about me. In fact, I'm more at ease when we're talking about other people. I could use a distraction from all of the wedding chaos, to be honest."

Melody looked up from her phone and glanced my way. "I just sent you Grace's phone number, RaeLyn. I'm sure she would love to talk to you."

"Great!"

Mom and Bessie Mae arrived moments later, carrying on about Bob's lousy electric oven.

"Nearly burned the cheesy grits," Bessie Mae exclaimed as she brought the casserole dish to the counter. Steam rose from the container, and the most luscious buttery aroma filled the room.

"Yum!"

"Thank goodness I caught 'em just in time. That oven of his is an abomination, I tell you. The temperature isn't regulated. I sure miss my oven. My real oven." She sighed and set the dish on a hot pad on the counter. Iva quickly snatched it up and placed it on a beautiful pewter trivet.

Annie snapped a picture, of course. Because who didn't like a great picture of buttery grits?

I glanced at the clock on the wall and saw the time: 10:52. "You gals help me keep an eye on the time. Mason's coming to meet me at our place at two fifteen so we can do a final walk-through of the property so we're clear on where everything is going."

My sweet aunt looked my way with a smile. "If I know you, RaeLyn, you've got the whole thing mapped out down to the last foot."

"Inch," I countered. "But what's a few inches between friends?"

"Depends on how wide your neighbor is when you're sharing a bale of hay." Bessie Mae started giggling, and before long we were all laughing.

And honestly? I needed a laugh. After the past few days, the relief that laughter brought was long overdue.

Carrie, Meghan, and Summer came buzzing in a couple of minutes before eleven, making apologies for their tardiness. Right away I picked up on the look of exhaustion in Carrie's eyes. And I was pretty sure I saw a sippy cup peeking out from her oversized purse, which she slung onto the back of a chair.

Annie tried to snap a picture, but Carrie put her hand up. "Over my dead body. You're going to wait until the baby is at least two or three before you get any pictures of me."

Should I remind her that she was about to be in my wedding photos in a few days?

"How's Annalisa?" I asked.

"Better," Carrie said, "but I'm awfully glad Jake is on Christmas break with the school district right now so he can be with her. I hated to leave her, but I can't tell you how badly this mommy needed to get away for a few minutes."

"Hopefully more than a few minutes," Tasha said. "Just relax and enjoy yourself, Carrie."

"I will. I hope." But she didn't look very relaxed. The poor woman looked like she needed a massage ASAP.

"What about Dot and Nadine?" Tasha asked. "Anyone heard from them?"

"Dot's running late," Mom said. "I did not ask her to elaborate when she called, but there were Spanish phrases flowing from the background."

"Ooh-la-la!" Eva giggled.

"I'm sure she has a very good excuse." Iva fanned her face and turned toward the fridge to get some ice.

"No idea about Nadine," Melody said. "But she skipped out on me yesterday. We were supposed to have lunch together, and she had to cancel at the last minute." Melody paused and offered a little shrug. "I've been trying to spend more time with her since her divorce. I feel so bad for her after what Clayton put her through."

I did too.

Just as quickly, Melody jumped into the role of hostess. "Until Dot and Nadine get here, I'll be happy to serve you ladies. Please have a seat at the table." She gestured to the dining room. "Would you like to start with some juice or coffee? What's your pleasure?"

"Coffee, please," I responded. "Bessie Mae brought over that butter pecan cake yesterday and I almost made myself sick eating it."

"Speaking of. . ." Meghan rose from the table. "I think I overdid it with the cake too. I've been feeling off all morning." She headed toward the bathroom looking a little squeamish.

"Oh dear." Bessie Mae looked mortified by this. "I hope it wasn't the cake. I can't imagine what I might have done wrong, unless it was that terrible oven at Bob's place."

"You mean *your* place, right?" I gave her a knowing look.

"Right. Right." She sighed. "We really need a new oven, though. And Bob's not one to replace anything unless he has no choice."

"I say you deliberately burn everything that comes out of that oven until he buys you a new one." This idea came from Tasha, who didn't even look one bit guilty about suggesting it.

"Tasha!" Bessie Mae shook her head. "That's awful. I could never deliberately burn perfectly good food."

"Sounds like you're never getting that new oven, then." Tasha shrugged and took several steps toward the dining room.

I had to admit, she had a point. Sometimes extreme situations called for extreme measures.

CHAPTER FOURTEEN

Meghan returned a few minutes later, convinced she felt a little better, and joined us in the dining room around the beautifully decorated table. I couldn't get over all the little details—flowers in the center, along with candles and slender silver Christmas trees about a foot tall.

Each place setting was beautifully decked out with lovely dishes and hand-painted bridal gown cookies, all in white. No doubt Iva and Eva were wearing themselves out on my behalf, and we weren't even to the wedding yet.

Annie couldn't get enough of it either. She oohed and aahed as she snapped photo after photo.

"You're getting copies of all of these," she said as she showed off her work. "It'll all be part of your wedding package."

I could hardly call it a package when the woman was barely charging me. Still, I didn't argue.

Dot came rushing in and went right to work, serving up food with Melody. Eva tried to quiz her about her tardiness, but Dot brushed it off.

"No, ma'am. Today is all about the bride and her maids." She turned to face me. "Tell us about the wedding, hon. What's it going to be like?"

Okay, I would take the bait. Dot had missed a lot over the past week, after all. I started by talking through the layout of the property, and then I walked her through the ceremony, top to bottom. "We've got a beautiful arbor to stand under and lots of Christmas trees to frame out either side. Simple. . .just green with white flocking and clear lights."

"Sounds beautiful." Melody sighed.

"Are you offended that we're getting married at home and not the church?" I asked. "I've wondered that all along."

"Why would I be offended?" Melody looked genuinely perplexed by this question as she passed a tray of biscuits my way.

"It's usually every little girl's dream to have a big, fancy church wedding."

"It's easier on us that you're doing it at home," she countered. "There's a ton of work that goes into getting the church ready for a wedding and reception, so I'm okay with not having to work so hard." She laughed. "But I would imagine it's a much larger workload for you."

"Yeah, but totally worth it." I shot a glance in Mom's direction, and thankfully she nodded.

"It's going to be beautiful," my mother said. "And even though it might be chilly out, I'm honored that RaeLyn cares enough about her family home to get married there."

Wow. I half expected her to add, "Now, if only she would keep living on the property after she marries. . ." But she did not. Thank goodness.

"Do you girls all have your dresses?" Dot looked back and forth between the bridesmaids.

"Oh, yes!" Tasha clasped her hands together. "And they're beautiful. Want to see?"

"Well, of course." Dot reached for the container of tea bags and offered me one. I chose Lady Earl.

We kept the conversation going while Tasha headed up to the master bedroom. Less than five minutes later she came back down wearing her soft sage-green gown and holding the honey-brown shrug in her hands.

"Wow!" Dot started clapping. "Oh, this is fabulous! Perfect colors!"

"I thought so." I'd always loved green.

Tasha posed in exaggerated fashion as Annie snapped several photos. She slipped the shrug over her shoulders and made a Marilyn Monroe face. Crazy girl.

"Love the shrugs." Dot reached over and ran her hand over the fur. "Gorgeous."

"What did we decide?" This question came from Summer. "If it's below fifty-five we wear the shrugs? Above fifty-five we wing it without?"

"That's up to you ladies," I said. "I'm fine either way. I want you to be comfortable. It really doesn't matter one bit to me. Honest. And I love that honey-brown color. It goes so beautifully with the sage."

"Oh, wear them, ladies," Dot said. "They're everything!"

"They match the guys' suits perfectly," Meghan said. "Logan and I compared notes the other day and thought it all looked great together, so I'm in favor of wearing them, no matter the weather."

"The guys should be fine if it's chilly. They're all wearing long sleeves," Mom said.

"Mason's the only one in a jacket," I reminded her. "The guys are wearing tweed pants and vests in that same honey brown. White shirts. Sage-green ties. Cowboy boots."

"Sounds dreamy," Melody said. "And perfect for a ranch wedding in Texas."

"Classy but definitely giving off that ranch vibe," I assured her. "And the tweed was actually Mason's idea. It's a cold-weather fabric."

"Are you wearing anything over your shoulders?" Dot asked me.

"Actually. . ." I looked my mother's direction. "Mom found the most gorgeous white fur stole online. It's got a gorgeous silver clip on the front. If it's really cold out I'll wear that for the ceremony and go without it during the reception. We'll have heaters in the tent."

Iva and Eva were happy to share details about the food.

Which somehow led back to a conversation about Enrique.

"There's a rumor going around town that he's talking about opening a restaurant," Summer said.

We all looked Dot's way.

She put her hands up. "I can neither confirm nor deny. But if he was setting out on a venture like that, we would all be incredibly blessed. You have no idea what a good cook he is."

Eva and Iva looked nervous about this.

"If he does, I can assure you it won't be a tearoom," Dot explained. She turned my way. "But speaking of food, just make sure you remember to eat something at the reception. You'll need your energy—and I'm not talking about dancing." She quirked a brow.

To my left, Mom cleared her throat.

I felt my cheeks grow warm.

"Just don't do what I did on my honeymoon night." Dot lowered her voice. "Silk sheets and a silk nightie are *not* a good combination. Slippery!"

The whole room erupted in laughter.

"Dot!" Mom looked downright horrified. Well, for about ten seconds. Then she started laughing so hard she could barely catch her breath. It felt good to hear my mother laugh again.

Eventually the conversation turned back to Enrique and his churros.

"We think a full-on churro bar is going to be so fun," Eva said.

"Churro bar?" Tasha looked my way, confusion registering in her eyes.

I nodded. "Yeah, Enrique makes a mean churro, from what he told us. So Iva and Eva came up with this idea to have a churro bar right next to the hot cocoa station."

Eva went off on a tangent, talking about what it could look like. "Guests can pick their own toppings and dipping sauces. Everything from cinnamon sugar, powdered sugar, or sprinkles to melted chocolate, dulce de leche, caramel, or even berry compote. I'm sure Enrique will think of everything."

"Yes, and best of all, he said it would be his gift to me," I explained. "So I won't have to add it to the food budget."

"Wonderful! Tell us more about your reception layout." Meghan shifted her gaze my way.

I dove in, sharing details as best I could.

"I love that you're getting married at Christmas. Sounds dreamy." Meghan sighed.

"We would have thrown a Christmas wedding for you too." My mother gave Meghan a pensive look. "If you hadn't run off and gotten hitched without the family there."

Welp, this shindig was going just great, wasn't it?

I decided to change the subject.

"We ordered lots of mistletoe from the florist. The whole place is going to be overloaded with the stuff."

"Oh?" Meghan's lips curled up in a smile.

"Yes, we're adding it to the arbor Dad made, which we'll stand under when Pastor Burchfield announces we're husband and wife. And we're using it under the chandeliers in the tent. People will be kissing all night long." I couldn't help but laugh at the image that created.

"Better be careful who you agree to dance with," Bessie Mae said. "The whole night could go awry if you're standing with the wrong person under the mistletoe!"

"I'll be on the prowl for every piece of mistletoe I can find," Dot said, her cheeks flaming pink.

Mom rolled her eyes. "My goodness, Dot. This is a side of you I do not know."

"Well, get to know it," Dot countered. "Because I'm deliriously happy."

"And so deserving of happiness," I responded with a smile.

Meghan looked my way, her nose wrinkled. I had a feeling she was worried that so much of the conversation was about Dot and not me, but I didn't really mind.

"I still can't get over the fact that you're married." Tasha said. "You're the only person I ever knew who went off on a holiday and came back with a husband."

"Not the only person in town who's eloped, though," Mom said. Her gaze shifted to Meghan.

No matter how many times my poor sister-in-law asked Mom to forgive her for the impulsive way she and Logan had tied the knot, my mother simply wouldn't let it go. Maybe one day.

"I found my Romeo on a cruise ship and lost my heart in the process." Dot sighed. "I haven't felt like this since I was a kid."

"This is about RaeLyn's big day." Meghan diverted her attention to me, likely in an attempt to shut the older ladies down. "How are you holding up, RaeLyn? Really, truly?"

"The only thing standing between me and a mild panic attack about weather is a lot of prayer and the support of my friends."

"It's going to be beautiful," Tasha chimed in. "And I checked the ten-day weather report. We might get a few showers in the next twenty-four hours, but things are supposed to be dry and unseasonably warm this coming weekend. I think you're in the clear, RaeLyn."

"Well, that's good to know." Though the darkening skies outside suggested otherwise. "As most of you know, I work off of a spreadsheet."

"Oh, we know." Tasha laughed. "Trust me."

"Well, it's easier for me to think about what's left to do when I can look at it. I convert the sheet to daily lists and check things off one at a time. So far, I think I'm on track. Flowers are ordered. Food is decided." I gave Iva and Eva a warm smile. "But I can't predict the weather, no matter how good my spreadsheet is."

Someone asked about the wedding cake, which Bessie Mae was happy to talk about. According to her it would be three tiers of old-school wonderment, complete with the wintry decor and a lovely topper I had chosen, one that was sure to bring a smile to all faces.

I could hardly wait to share that first bite with my groom.

A few minutes into this discussion Nadine arrived, looking breathless. She took one look at all of us gathered around the dining room table and groaned. "I'm so sorry I'm late," she said. "You ladies wouldn't believe the morning I've had. Please forgive me."

We did, of course, and all the more when she revealed the loveliest tray of scones.

"Lemon lavender." Nadine set the plate down, and we all gathered around to look at the gorgeous little triangles of perfection. Wow.

"I've never baked with lavender before," Nadine admitted. "But I decided to branch out. And there's just a hint, not much. I thought they'd be perfect for today's little party. So fancy and fun."

"Scones are perfect with tea, and I've got Earl Grey, chamomile, and a bunch of others." Tasha gestured to the buffet near the window.

"The last thing my waistline needs is more sweets," Meghan said. "I'm already worried about my dress fitting."

"I told you I'd help with that, honey," Mom said. "Just bring me that dress, and I'll let it out a little."

"You're the tiniest little thing ever," Eva said. "How could anything be tight on you?"

"The dress was too big so I had it taken in, and now it's too small." Meghan sighed.

"I say we don't worry about calories today," Tasha countered. "We've survived dress fittings, registry drama, and at least forty Pinterest boards. I think we've more than earned these lemon-lavender scones."

Nadine's phone rang, and she excused herself to answer it. She stepped outside, and we all watched through the dining room window.

"Does anyone else notice anything strange about Nadine lately?" Tasha asked. "She seems distracted. I think she has a beau."

"Oooh, you think?" I gave the beautiful woman another look as she paced back and forth on the back porch, phone to her ear. "If anyone deserves a second chance at love, Nadine does."

"After what that scoundrel Clayton did to her," Bessie Mae chimed in, "I totally agree."

"I hope she's found the perfect fella," Tasha said.

"But it hasn't been very long since her divorce was final." Mom didn't seem to care for this idea. "She doesn't need a rebound relationship. And we sure don't want her moving off."

"Hopefully she won't," Melody agreed. "We're getting to be such good friends."

"Now that Clayton and Meredith have broken up, she's probably more content to stay put," Dot chimed in.

"I would get as far away from Dodge as possible." These words came from Bessie Mae. "I'd go live with my sister."

"You have a sister?" Tasha looked stunned.

"No, but Nadine does, right? If I were in her shoes, I'd shoot for a whole new life." A smile tipped up the edges of her lips. "There's something to be said for a whole new life, you know."

Oh, I knew, all right. And I was about to experience it firsthand.

Nadine made her way back into the house.

"Sorry about that, ladies." She pressed her phone back into her purse. "I have a situation going on at the house."

"A situation?" I turned to face her.

"Yes." Her nose wrinkled. "Just a repair thing. Sort of. Nothing I need to worry you with."

This led to a conversation about Nadine's big, gorgeous home on the lake, the one with the fabulous Texas decor. I still remembered the first time I'd laid eyes on it. The grand foyer with its towering ceiling and the massive rustic wrought iron chandelier had completely blown me away. But what really left me breathless was the huge kitchen. And the breathtaking view. Situated in one of the most beautiful spots on Cedar Creek Lake, the house was a dream. Still, I found it hard to imagine such a fancy new place needing repairs already.

"Did I ever tell you that my papaw wanted to buy that patch of land?"

I asked. "He was going to open a fishing resort for tourists."

"I remember hearing all about it," Dot said. "They were going to put in cabins and such."

"Papaw was the best fisherman in the area."

"Yes." Mom nodded. "He won all sorts of competitions."

"He taught me how to fish when I was about three, I think." I lost myself to my thoughts for a couple of moments. Suddenly I was seated on a pier off Cedar Creek Lake, pole in hand, with Papaw to my left and a basket for our catch to our right. We went home with a mighty lot of fish that day.

Feelings of nostalgia washed over me.

Papaw.

His beautiful red truck, Tilly.

Now *my* truck. And running fine, thanks to Mason. Tilly was safe and sound and ready to play her role at my wedding in just a few short days.

"Your grandfather and Clayton were going to go into business together." Dot's words roused me back to attention. "They planned to set up cabins for tourists and offer guided fishing expeditions and sunset tours on the water. That sort of thing. And then. . ." Her words drifted off and she glanced Nadine's way. "Anyway, it fell through."

"I vaguely remember something about my ex-husband double-crossing your grandfather." Nadine sighed as she lifted the tray of scones and set it on the buffet table. "I suppose I'll spend the rest of my life apologizing for the awful things Clayton Henderson did to the folks in this town, even the ones who are long gone."

"You will not, honey," Dot said. "You owe no one an apology. If anything, we all need to apologize to you for not being more observant and seeing him as the scoundrel he was even sooner."

"He is a scoundrel." Nadine released a loud sigh. "But it probably won't surprise you to hear that he's been looking for any excuse in the book to call me. And text me. And email me."

"Good grief." I hoped she wouldn't allow herself to be drawn back into that trap.

Then again, it wasn't my story to write.

Write.

My mind shifted back to the story Melody had told me about Mrs.

Oberdeen being an aunt to the boys who'd been hurt in the fire. I couldn't stop thinking about the possibility of reaching out to her to get an interview with the boys.

I would work on that as soon as I got home.

CHAPTER FIFTEEN

"Did y'all hear about Aaron Bradford?"

This question came from Tasha. I turned to face her. "Being missing, you mean?"

"Yes!" She leaned forward and reached for her orange juice glass. "Gage called right before you got here, asking if Aaron had come into the restaurant. He knew that Fish Tales is one of Aaron's favorite hangouts."

"And he hasn't?" Mom asked.

Tasha shook her head. "Nope. No one has seen him for days."

"So weird," I acknowledged. "Mason said he was supposed to show up for an appointment at the car shop and didn't come. He also didn't respond to Mason's calls."

Summer leaned back in her chair. "Gage told me how worried he is. One minute Aaron was carrying on about being fired from his job and the next. . .he's gone."

"Wait." Dot put her hand up. "Aaron Bradford was let go. . .from the fire department? Am I understanding this correctly?"

"Yes." Mom dabbed at her lips with her napkin. "It happened when you were. . .well, you know."

"You can say the words, Flora." Dot gave her a pensive look. "I was getting married."

"Right."

"But why was he fired?" Dot asked. "What was the logic behind that? They need all the help they can get, especially during a drought."

I filled her in by summarizing what Gage had told us on the day of the fire.

"Sounds like that kid is a real mess." Dot cleared a couple of the plates from the table as she spoke.

"He always was." Mom took a sip of her tea and then set the cup down. "But Gage tried so hard to befriend him from the time they were young. I guess we were all hopeful he would eventually make something of himself."

"Did I ever tell you that I used to have a little crush on Aaron?" These words came from Tasha, who pinched off the corner of another lemon-lavender scone.

"I thought you were in love with my brother," I said.

Her gaze shifted to my mom before she responded, "I *am* in love with your brother."

"No, I meant my other brother. Logan." I did my best not to arch my brows. "For as long as I can remember, you had a crush on Logan."

Tasha cleared her throat and took a big bite of the scone, then diverted her gaze to the window over the buffet.

"What's this?" Meghan gave her an inquisitive look. "Did you, now?"

Tasha's nervous laugh seemed to ricochet around the room. "That was a while back. And he never even picked up on any of my clues."

"Though she was throwing them at softball speed," I countered.

"As I was saying. . ." Tasha cleared her throat once again. "I *used* to have a crush on Aaron. Way back when. He was on the baseball team, and I was a cheerleader. I would swoon when he was up to bat."

"He's always been really good looking. I remember that much." Though I only had eyes for Mason, from junior high until this very moment.

"Didn't take me long to figure out that Aaron was kind of a hothead, though." Tasha sighed. "That's why I finally stopped looking his way. I saw the way he talked to his coach. And some of his teachers. Scary."

"You can't judge a book by its cover," Bessie Mae said. "Might look lovely on the outside but have a terrible story on the inside."

"This book has a *really* great cover," Tasha said. "But I'm glad God shifted my attention to Dallas."

"The Lord might have used me a little to help shift your attention," I reminded her.

"Yes. Now I don't know what I'd do without him. He's been so helpful with the vacation rental and, well, everything." Her cheeks turned the prettiest shade of pink. "Especially with this house. You're right about that. I can't tell you how many times he's stepped up and fixed a broken this or that."

Mom looked nervous all of a sudden, but she had to realize that her little boys—and her only daughter—were growing up. We were spreading our wings, learning to fly.

A quick glance her way clued me in to the mist of tears in her eyes.

Mom needed a project.

Or a friend.

My gaze shifted to Dot, who shared another story about the cruise. Oh boy.

We finished up the brunch and I offered to help with the cleanup, but the ladies wouldn't hear of it. I found myself out on the back deck with Meghan, who looked a little lost and forlorn.

I stepped into the spot next to her, the two of us now gazing out over the waters of the lake, which sparkled under the noontime sun overhead.

"Meghan, can I ask a question?"

She looked my way. "Sure."

"Are you okay?"

Worry lines formed between her brows. "What do you mean?"

"Well, you disappeared on us earlier. I just want to make sure no one has hurt your feelings or anything like that."

"Oh..." A tiny smile turned up the edges of her lips. "No, my feelings weren't hurt."

"Mom has a way of saying things sometimes without thinking."

"I'm used to her comments." Meghan's nose wrinkled, showing off a smattering of freckles. "They bothered me at first, but I've made it a life goal to win her over. I'm trying so hard, and I won't give up until she's fully in my court."

"Girl, you went above and beyond on the day of the fire. I was so impressed at how you handled things. You were calm, cool, and collected."

"On the outside. On the inside I was shaking like a leaf. But I guess I'm pretty good in a crisis."

"I'd say. Better than the rest of us, and you'd never even faced a fire before."

"Oh, I've faced plenty of fires. Just not that kind."

"So you're not upset about anything?"

I could read the conflict in her eyes, and her lingering pause made it clear that she wanted to say more. But she didn't. Meghan just offered a little shrug and went right back to staring at the lake with a quiet, "I'm fine."

Only, I had a feeling she wasn't.

"I just want to go on record as saying I'm so happy you married my brother. Logan deserves the very best, and I truly believe he found it in you."

"RaeLyn, thank you." She reached over and threw her arms around my neck. "That means the world coming from you. I can't tell you how many times I've prayed for God to give me just the right situation, the right person. After all I've been through. . ." Meghan shook her head. "Well, you know my history. Being married before to a guy who traded in wives like old cars, I didn't come out of that having the best opinion of myself."

"God redeems every situation, if we let Him. And clearly, you've let Him. Now He's given you the desires of your heart."

"Yes. He has." A pretty little smile lit her face. "In a thousand ways. And—bonus!—I got a sister in the deal!" She threw her arms around my neck and gave me another tight hug. "And a mom too. Like I said, I plan to win her over."

Through the plate-glass window I caught a glimpse of Annie snapping our picture. Oh well. This was one we would look back on with fondness.

We walked back inside, and Meghan went straight to my mother to ask if she could ride home with her.

"Well, sure, honey." Mom patted her on the shoulder. "I would like that."

I offered one last time to help with cleanup, but our hosts wouldn't hear of it.

"You go spend time with that sweetheart of yours," Nadine said, arms submerged in a sink full of soapy dishes. "We've got this, RaeLyn."

I thanked them profusely and offered little gifts I'd put together for each of them. In just a few short days several of these precious ladies would stand alongside me on the most important day of my life. I wanted them to know just how much that meant to me.

I headed out, my gaze shifting up to the skies above. Was it my imagination, or were those dark clouds hovering over the area east of here? Would it rain?

I found myself driving home alone, which was fine. I had a lot to process, including the information about Aaron going missing. Also, I couldn't stop thinking about those two boys who'd been caught up in the fire, what a miracle they were.

I decided to reach out to Mrs. Oberdeen while driving. I put the phone on speaker and dialed her number. She answered right away.

"Mrs. Oberdeen, this is RaeLyn Hadley."

"Well, RaeLyn. Aren't you supposed to be planning a wedding or something?" A sweet little giggle followed.

"Yes, ma'am. I'm on my way home from my bridesmaids' brunch. A little birdie told me that the boys in the fire are related to you. How are they doing? We've been praying for them."

"Oh, Karter and Kenner are doing well," she said. "Thank you for asking, and for praying. We're so grateful for the outpouring of love we've received from folks, not just here, but all across the state."

"You're welcome. You might recall that I write a weekly article for *Mabank Happenings*."

"Well, of course. Your story about the Thanksgiving food drive was lovely."

"Thank you. I like to focus on stories that touch the heart, and that's why it occurred to me that I might interview the boys when they're feeling up to it. I wanted to come at the story from a different angle than the ones I've heard on the news."

"How is that?"

I turned on my signal as I approached the corner in Payne Springs. "Well, you know that scripture from Isaiah 43 where God says we can go through the waters and not drown, and go through the fire and not be burned?"

"Yes."

"Those boys are both walking miracles." I turned to the left and slowly picked up speed as the roadway cleared. "It's really remarkable that they were both that close to the flames and came through them unscathed. No burns at all."

"Yes, it's all we can talk about. They both ran straight through the fire to get to the highway. I have no idea how they managed to do it without those flames touching them. The Lord just led them through. But I do know they got into the lake at one point, so when they did take off running they were sopping wet."

"I'm sure that helped. But clearly they had more than a little help from on high." I flinched as I looked to my left and saw a field completely burnt and dry. It was a vivid reminder of how badly things could have ended for Karter and Kenner.

"Honey, I thoroughly believe it," Mrs. Oberdeen said. "Do you want me to reach out to my niece to see if it's okay to share her number with you?"

"Please. And go ahead and give her my number while you're at it."

"Will do."

When we ended the call, I pulled up to my house, and in that moment a flashback sent me reeling back to the events on Sunday. I could still see those firefighters working so hard to quench the flames as they crossed the road.

And then. . .nothing.

No flames.

No fire.

Nothing of any danger.

Everything came to a halt just as the flames threatened to take down my family home.

If the Lord could take care of that, surely He could handle all the details of my life.

I paused to thank Him once again for sparing us that day. Afterward, I went inside and changed into more practical clothes. With the temperature dropping, I needed to be warm.

Mom arrived a few minutes later and headed into the living room to put her feet up.

"I don't know why that wore me out, but it did."

"You and Bessie Mae worked hard, before and during the brunch. And I'm so grateful."

"It was beautiful. And don't you just love Tasha's place?"

"I do. I'm a little worried that she's having trouble renting it out. But she's enjoying using it when she doesn't have guests." I paused. "Which reminds me, she asked if I might like to have the bridesmaids get ready at her place on Saturday before the wedding. How would you feel about that?"

Mom's smile faded. "You mean you won't be here?"

"Well, we have an appointment with Lorelai at Curl Up & Dye that morning, and I had planned to come back here to get dressed." I couldn't help but smile as I mentioned Lorelai, the stylist who had cut my hair since I was a kid. "But it might be fun to get ready at Tasha's place. It's big, and it's got a great view. I could ask Annie to get some beautiful pictures of us by the lake. You and Bessie Mae could come too, of course."

"I see." Mom couldn't seem to hide her disappointment.

"Tell you what," I said. "Maybe we'll get ready there and then come here early, say an hour before the wedding, to get pictures on our property too. How would that be? I'm sure Annie would be happy to do that. And she's coming on the night of the rehearsal to get some photos of that too. We'll have plenty of the house and property, I promise."

"Sounds good."

Only, her face didn't have a "sounds good" look on it.

"I know this is all a lot, Mom. I understand."

"Mm-hmm." She reached for the remote and turned on the TV, then rested back in her recliner. "Gonna rest my eyes."

"Okay."

Though I didn't feel okay. I felt kind of sick to my stomach when I saw the sadness in my mother's eyes.

Mason arrived at two fifteen and I was so relieved to see him that I greeted him on the back patio with a big hug and a sigh.

"You okay?" He ran his finger along my cheek.

"Yeah, it's all just. . .a lot."

"I understand."

And from the look on his face, he did.

"How was the shindig over at Tasha's place?" he asked as I released my grip on him.

"Oh, you know." I reached down and took hold of his hand as we walked toward the house. "A bunch of ladies eating crumpets and tea and talking about wedding stuff. After the wedding prep and fire, it was nice just to have some downtime to be together without any stresses."

"Well, hopefully we can keep that stress-free vibe going," he said.

I hoped so too. "I think Mom is still upset with Dot for running off and getting married."

"That one will take time."

"Right. Oh, and I learned that Tasha once had a crush on Aaron Bradford."

"Well, sure." He offered a little shrug. "*Everyone* knew that."

Clearly not everyone.

"I'm glad she didn't pursue it," he said. "Aaron's got a temper. Always felt like he was a firework about to blow. I used to worry that he might rub off on Gage and Dallas, if I'm being honest."

"I guess I didn't know that side of him. But then again, my brothers were a few years behind me in school. And when I was at Mabank High I only had eyes for one fella." I batted my eyelashes at Mason.

"Good to know. In case I ever begin to doubt it, I'll reflect back on this moment."

I jabbed him with my elbow. Seriously? How could he doubt it?

"Okay, okay." Mason rubbed his side and laughed. "Ready to head out to the field?"

I slipped my arm through his. "I thought you'd never ask. Just let me grab my laptop," I said as I reached for the back door handle.

"Laptop?"

"Yep. I have diagrams of everything."

"Of course you do." He laughed.

"And we'll need my spreadsheet to compare notes."

We walked into the house through the back door and found Mom dozing in her recliner. She stirred and opened her eyes as we walked into the living room.

"Oh, hey. I was just resting."

"You deserve it," Mason said.

"How are things coming with your housing plan?" Mom was wide awake now, asking the hard questions.

"Oh, they're coming." Mason smiled. "Wrapping up some final details."

"Do tell," I said.

"When the time is right. I promise, I've been hard at work on it."

"Anything you can talk about?" Mom asked.

"Not yet." But from the twinkle in his eye, I could tell he was happy with the progress.

"But here's something I can talk about. I got an email confirmation today about our flight to Playa Del Carmen on Sunday at one o'clock and we're all set, so that's good."

"Hey, I might not know where I'm going to live, but at least I know where I'm going to honeymoon." A nervous laugh followed on my end.

I headed into my bedroom to grab the laptop but could hear my mother peppering Mason with questions about the honeymoon.

The resort we'd chosen was luxurious. All-inclusive. We would have unlimited beachfront access, which made my heart so happy. What really blew me away, if the pictures could be believed, was all the lush greenery that stood between the resort and the turquoise waters at the beach. It all looked so vibrant and fun.

I walked back into the living room just as Mason described our lodging. "We've got their most spacious suite with an ocean view and private balcony."

"Wow." Mom's eyes widened. "You can sit out there in the morning and drink your coffee and listen to the waves." She pinched her eyes shut, as if trying to live vicariously through us.

"There are several pools," I said. "But I don't know what the temps will be like in December."

"They have hot tubs too," Mason reminded me. "Those are heated. And I saw pictures of lots of hammocks strung between palm trees."

"Sounds dreamy." Mom sighed.

"We picked this one because it seemed more intimate than the others we looked at," I explained. "Not so much a party place as a family place."

"Sounds amazing. Maybe someday I'll see the Caribbean for myself." She pushed the recliner back to a seated position and tried to stand. When she wobbled, Mason headed her way and extended his arm.

"Thanks, hon," Mom said.

Only, it almost sounded like *son*, not *hon*, which made all of us smile. Before long, he would be her son.

Wow. Mom would have five sons.

No wonder she was tired.

CHAPTER SIXTEEN

"I'd better thaw out some meat for supper." Mom hobbled toward the kitchen, wincing with every step. She kept her right hand on her lower back, as if to steady herself. "It's moments like these I really miss Bessie Mae. She sure knew how to keep up with all the cooking."

"You could always pick up takeout," Mason said. "That's what I do when I don't feel like cooking."

Mom turned to face him and flinched in pain. "I tried that the other night," she said after a moment's pause. "I never heard the end of it. I thought the pizza was delicious, myself."

"It was, Mom," I said. "And don't overdo it. Just warm up some leftovers or something."

She shrugged and opened the freezer.

Mason and I headed outside to walk the property. When we were out of Mom's hearing, Mason looked my way. "Do you think she's okay?"

I couldn't help but sigh as I offered up my gut-honest answer: "I don't know."

"She seems kind of. . ."

"Sad? Depressed? Despondent?"

"I was going to say overwhelmed, but all of the above, I guess."

He was probably right. I did feel really bad for Mom right now, in a weird sort of way. "I think it's been hard on her. I don't think she realized just how dependent she was on Bessie Mae. We all were. I mean, the woman is a wonder. She was born to cook. It's second nature to her, to feed people. Also, I think Mom's battling some jealousy right now."

"What's she jealous of?"

"Well, Dot, for one thing. She went off on a Caribbean cruise and came back with a Latin heartthrob. Now we're headed off to Playa Del Carmen for a week of R&R."

"Among other things." He pulled me into his arms, and I felt my face grow warm.

"And Bessie Mae and Bob had a great time on their little four-day trip to Fredericksburg. Mom's stuck here with—"

"All the menfolk."

"Yeah." I laughed. "And I think it's getting to her. She's kind of an emotional basket case these days. Dad says she's going through the change."

"Hope it's a positive one." Mason shrugged as he took my hand and led the way to the field where we would soon tie the knot. "Because I'm a little worried about her."

"Me too." I shivered as a gust of wind blew over us. "Brr. Wish I'd worn a heavier coat."

"Here, take mine." He pulled off his jacket and slipped it over my shoulders. Poor guy was probably going to freeze to death, but I didn't want to wound his pride by offering it back. He always pretended to be tougher than the weather. Still, this simple gesture went a long way in solidifying how comfortable and safe I felt with Mason. Even in the middle of the chaos, he could ground me with a simple gesture like offering his jacket.

I slipped my arms into it then led the way to the large field where the ceremony would take place and took note of the darkened skies above us. Ugh. "Looks like it's going to rain."

"Sure does. We could use it."

"Dad will be happy. Everyone else too." Still, the idea that it would wait until today—Tuesday—to rain? Ugh. Talk about cutting it close.

"Hopefully it'll last just long enough to saturate the ground and ward off any more fires." He gestured to the dry, parched ground in front of us. "That's some thirsty land right there."

I wasn't too worried about how the ground looked, though. In just a few days it would be covered in fully decked-out hay bales with a beautiful wide aisle and a gorgeous arbor for us to stand under at the front. Along with those gorgeous white Christmas trees framing everything out. And Tilly, of course, in her place of prominence. No one would notice the grass.

Still, his comment about fires reminded me that I still hadn't shared one pertinent piece of information with him. I turned to face Mason and grabbed his hand. "Did I tell you that I might have an interview with the boys who got caught up in the fire?"

"No." He gave me an admiring look. "Wow. That's gonna be some article. They were really lucky to get out with no burns."

"It's truly a miracle. And that's the angle I want to cover, how God protected them. If the mother agrees to let me talk with them, that is. Did I tell you she's related to Grace Oberdeen at church?"

"Hadn't made that connection."

"The boys' mom is her niece. They live in Dallas but were here for a family reunion."

"With Mrs. Oberdeen? Was she there when the fire broke out?"

"No." I shook my head. "Apparently, it was the other side of the family having the reunion." I turned my attention back to the field. "Okay, sorry for that interruption. Just didn't want to forget to tell you."

"It's important," he said.

"And so is this." I gestured to the grounds in front of us. "I know we've gone over and over this, so you're probably bored with hearing about it."

"Not at all." I could tell from his expression that he genuinely meant it.

I fiddled with the snaps on the jacket as a brisk breeze sent a chill up my spine. "You know how anal I am. I just need to talk it through one last time, in the location."

"Agreed. We both need that."

"So I'm thinking this is the section of the field we'll use since the ground here is really level."

"Agreed."

"Now, since we're getting married at four thirty, we have to keep in mind the position of the sun." I squinted and looked up, noticing the dark clouds gathering overhead.

"You've really given this a lot of thought."

"I have." I pulled my gaze back down to him. "If the guests face west they'll never forgive us. They'll spend the whole time with the sun in their eyes. If we face west, you'll never forgive me, and neither will the wedding party."

"So, what's the solution?"

"We all face south, away from the house. It's a prettier view. Oh, and I want Tilly to remain at the back of the wedding field after Dad and I pull up for my big entrance. I was thinking we could rest a Christmas tree in the bed of the truck, all decked out, along with some other Christmas decor. Like you see in all of the pictures these days."

"North, south, east, or west?"

I pointed north—toward the house—and he nodded. "All this talk about facing east or west—"

"South."

"South—is making me wonder if I'm going to need a compass to survive this wedding."

"Hey!" I put my hands on my hips. "Never use the words *survive* and *wedding* in the same sentence. Rude!"

He laughed.

"But if you like, we'll hand out compasses as wedding gifts," I teased.

"No thanks. What next?"

I showed him where the arbor would go. "We'll be standing here with Pastor Burchfield. I plan to leave the horses in the field behind the arbor. I think they'll make a nice backdrop."

"Unless Delilah decides to drop her foal in the middle of the I dos. Then we'll have a whole different story to tell our kids one day."

"Good point. We'll leave her in the barn." I paused and made a sweeping gesture to my left. "Obviously, the bridesmaids will be here. . ." I gestured the other way. "Groomsmen will be there." I gestured to the field. "Guests all seated out there on those gorgeous bales of hay."

"What about the elderly folks, like Bessie Mae and Bob? Will they be comfortable sitting on hay bales? They strike me as more of a 'padded chair with lumbar support' crowd."

"I offered Bessie Mae a different option—a special chair near the front—but she wouldn't hear of it. Said she didn't want to stick out. So we'll get the ushers to help her, if she needs it. But I'm sure she'll be fine."

"So, shivering guests on bales of hay. With or without thermal blankets your father might buy."

"Pretty sure he was just kidding about those." I paused. "Now, we have sixty bales of hay in total. I'm thinking a total of fifteen rows with four bales each. . ." I gestured with my hands to the right and then the left. "And a center aisle dividing right from left. And a deliriously happy bride and groom at the front."

"Facing south. Because of the sunset."

I nodded, still in my thoughts. "Speaking of which, if we time this just right—and I think we will—the pictures after the ceremony should be gorgeous. We can send the guests to the tent ahead of us while we take pictures."

"Gage said you guys rented some large space heaters for the reception?"

"Yeah, just in case. That way no one will complain for long. But after they head that way the wedding party will take pictures at sunset."

"Facing west."

"Facing east, with the sun to our backs," I explained. "Annie will be facing west with the camera in hand."

"I didn't realize how directionally challenged I was until this very moment." Mason laughed.

I walked over to where the first row of bales would be placed and pointed to an imaginary spot. "I was thinking we have empty places to commemorate those we've lost."

His laughter faded. "That's nice, RaeLyn."

"I want one on my side for Papaw, and I figured you'd want to create places for both of your parents. That way they're here with us in spirit."

"I like that." He slipped an arm over my shoulder and pulled me close to place a kiss on my forehead. "I wish my parents could've lived to see this day. Mom always knew I would marry you one day."

"You never told me that."

"She did. And my dad gave me a really hard time when I moved away. I heard all about how I was going to break your heart. . .and his."

"He was right about that. But God was good. He brought you back."

Mason smiled. "Yes, He did."

"I was thinking about putting Papaw's cowboy hat in his spot," I said. "Be thinking of what you want for your parents."

"Mom left behind her favorite quilt. Maybe we put that on their bale of hay, along with my dad's boots?"

"I love it. I asked Dot for a large white rose in my bouquet to represent your mom."

"She was a Texas gal through and through. I think she would've loved that."

"What would you think of having Pastor Burchfield mentioning those who've gone before us? Maybe something about honoring their memory?"

"I love it."

We wrapped up our conversation about the ceremony, and then I led the way to the area where the large reception tent would be erected. Dad had paid a pretty penny for the tent, and I was so grateful, especially since it would be heated.

"Wedding party will sit here." I gestured to the space that would occupy the front of the tent. "Guests there." I made another sweeping gesture opposite. "We have tables coming that seat eight. Centerpieces are made."

"Glad to hear we're not sitting on hay bales."

"No, everyone will be perfectly comfortable in here, and warm."

"Where's the memory table going?" he asked.

"At the back of the room. It will be the first thing people see. Speaking of which, I found a perfect frame for that wedding picture of your parents."

"You really do think of everything."

"I'm a detail person. I made a really pretty sign that says 'Forever in our hearts, always in our lives.'"

"I like it."

"Over here we'll have the hot cocoa bar. And next to that we'll put Enrique's churro bar."

"A churro bar *and* a hot cocoa bar? You trying to marry me or send me into a sugar coma?"

I laughed. "But the most important thing of all—Bessie Mae's wedding cake." I gestured to an area to my right. "It's going to go right here, in a place of prominence."

"In the middle of the room?"

"Just before the dance floor."

"Sounds dangerous. Sure you don't want to reconsider that?"

"I want to show it off."

"Oh, you'll show it off, all right, when someone cha-cha-chas straight into it."

"Don't be such a worrywart, Mason."

Okay, that made him laugh. Clearly, I was the worrywart of the two of us.

We wrapped up our planning and I closed my laptop, satisfied that we'd covered everything on my list. Up above, the skies grew darker still. Looked like we were really in for a doozy of a storm.

As we walked back toward the house, I was surprised to see a familiar truck in the driveway. We made our way toward it and watched as Buck Adler hopped out. Well, *hopped* was a bit of a stretch. The man was moving very slowly these days.

He hobbled toward us. "Hey there."

"Hi, Buck. How are things faring over at your place? I heard your barn took a hit."

"Yup. But I'm okay. Though I haven't slept much since the fire. Heard about all the damage and really had me shook. Just out checking on all the neighbors."

"Fire crossed the road onto our property, but by the grace of God they got it out at just that moment."

"That's good." He kicked the ground with the toe of his boot. "How's your brother, the one who works for the fire department?"

"He's fine. It was a hard day for him—for all of us—but I think we're better now."

"Good. He helped out a lot at my place that day." Buck's expression shared his gratitude. "I sure appreciated him, and the others too. They came just in time."

"Glad to hear your place is okay."

"Me too." He looked around our property, as if searching for something. "And the fire didn't affect your wedding plans?"

"No."

"That's good." Buck looked genuinely relieved. "What are folks saying?"

"About?" Mason gave him an inquisitive look.

"About how the fire got started."

"Ah." Mason shrugged. "They're going to do an investigation, but for now the rumor is lightning."

"Hmm." He didn't look convinced. "You know, they found those two boys just north of my property," Buck said. "I know folks are calling them heroes for saving me, but something about their story doesn't sit right with me."

"You think those boys set the fire?" Mason looked surprised by this.

"Well, sure. Hanging out by themselves in the densest part of the park right before everything lit up? That big, dramatic story about how they ran right through the flames but weren't hurt? C'mon now." He went off on a tangent about the twins, eyes narrowed as he shared with great emotion.

When he paused for breath, I invited him to come inside, but Buck said he needed to move on. And he did, but not before giving us another earful about Karter and Kenner.

When he left, Mason turned my way. "Man. He was all too quick to blame those boys."

"Sure was."

Mason's gaze remained affixed to the back of Buck's old truck as he pulled away. "I can't put my finger on it, but something seems off with Buck."

I had to admit, it certainly did. But this only gave me more reason to want to interview the boys. Hopefully if they saw something, they would let me know.

When we got inside we found Mom in the kitchen, hard at work.

"Need help?" I asked.

She looked relieved at the offer. "I hate to ask because I know you've got so much on your plate, but I'm getting some of the food prepped for tomorrow night's meal. I'm so glad you suggested we do a potluck so I'm not stuck with all of the cooking on Christmas Eve."

"It was the only thing that made sense. And don't worry, Mom. No one is expecting perfection this year."

"Because Bessie Mae's not here?" she asked.

"No, because we're all so busy. And besides—" I paused as I heard a crack of thunder. A streak of lightning lit up the area outside of the kitchen window, causing us both to jump.

"Whoa." Mom peered out the window. "I pray that's not more dry lightning. I would hate to think. . ." Her words drifted off, but I knew well enough what she was thinking. If we had another lightning storm, we were at higher risk than ever of another fire. And right now, that idea sent my stomach churning.

I felt my blood pressure begin to rise as I glanced up at the skies, now opened up and pouring.

"First a drought. Then a fire. And now a storm?" I said. "What's next? A hurricane?"

CHAPTER SEVENTEEN

I barely slept on Tuesday night. By midnight, torrential rains poured so loudly that they beat against my bedroom window, which shook with a fury. Howling winds only served to upset me further.

A flurry of activity outside my bedroom door alerted me to the fact that my father and two younger brothers had flown into action. I heard the back door slam as they headed outdoors, no doubt to make sure the animals were enclosed in the barn.

Streaks of lightning lit my room from time to time, usually following loud cracks of thunder that made the window shake. Though I knew we were safe from fire, the lightning still had me on edge.

About half an hour later they returned, and the noise level rose from there as everyone gathered in the living room. I ventured out there to hear the latest but ended up back in my room when I couldn't stop yawning.

I needed sleep, but it refused to come.

At one point I thought I heard hail, but the wind was whipping outside my window with such speed it might've just been the raindrops coming down at full force.

I'd always loved a good rainstorm, and we did need the moisture. No doubt about that. But this was beyond anything I'd imagined. By three I was pacing the room, wondering if we should build an ark. And by four, the house shaking from repeat thunder, we faced another sort of problem—a power outage.

Terrific. Who could have guessed this would happen on Christmas Eve, and so close to my big day?

What more could a bride dream of on her wedding week? A fire. An epic flood. And now, no power. If we kept this up, we might as well throw in a tornado or hurricane.

Or a snowstorm.

I shivered just thinking about it.

Should I call Pastor Burchfield and let him know we were moving the ceremony to the church? Common sense would say so, but it broke my heart to think about giving up on my childhood dream of marrying on our property.

I finally dozed off around four thirty. Honestly? I think I gave up on worrying, realizing that things were so far out of my control it didn't matter anyway. And what was the point in fretting? This storm didn't take God by surprise. And hadn't I just told Grace Oberdeen that God would protect us, both in the flood and in the fire? I had to keep my trust in Him, no matter how loudly the winds howled outside my window.

And boy, did they roar. The storm quieted for a bit but then hit with a bang about the time I crawled out of bed around nine thirty. My head throbbed, my pulse raced, and I could hear my family members in the living room, talking. Loudly. Actually, yelling.

By the time I made it out there, Mom was fumbling around in the dark kitchen. It was weird to see the house this dreary at nine thirty in the morning, but with overhead skies a deep gray, it felt like nighttime in here.

The back door opened, and my dad came rushing in. He paused to stomp his feet on the mat then set his umbrella down.

"Well?" Mom asked.

He shook his head. "We've got water so deep I can't get out to the barn to feed the livestock. The pastures are waterlogged. Some of the lower-lying areas are completely underwater, like pools."

"Oh no." Mom groaned. "Awful."

"The soil is a muddy mess, and slippery, so I don't want to risk it. I'm pretty sure we left enough feed out last night to get them through till later in the day. I'll go out later, when things calm down."

Only, they didn't seem to be calming anytime soon.

I could tell Dad was worried about Delilah. He mentioned her several times, hopeful that moving her to the highest spot in the barn would keep her safe.

Mom managed to get our gas stove lit and cooked some oatmeal. She put the old-fashioned percolator on, and before long we had coffee as well. She even managed some bacon. I had to give it to her. Mom was pretty good at adapting, even on a few hours' sleep.

We had a call from Bessie Mae as we settled down to eat. Mom put it on speakerphone.

"How's it going over there?" my aunt asked.

Mom managed a tight, "We're surviving."

Bessie Mae fussed about Bob's electric stove and fumed over the fact that they had no power and no way to cook. I took a few bites of my warm, sweet oatmeal, grateful for the feelings of comfort it brought.

"I had to feed the man cereal from a box," my aunt said. "Can you believe it?"

"I'm sure he's used to it. He lived alone for years," Mom responded.

"Well, I'm not. If I had a gas stove, I'd—"

"Make oatmeal," Mom countered. "That's what I did."

Bessie Mae sighed. "I'm going to fight for my gas stove when the time is right. But first we have to get through this storm. You should've put 'rain boots' on that registry of yours, RaeLyn. You'd be fashionably prepared and practical, all at the same time."

"Hopefully by Saturday I won't need them," I said.

"Weatherman says things are going to be better for the next several days, so let's hope he's right," she said.

"Amen," I replied.

"Hey, at least we won't need decorations," Dad chimed in. "Mother Nature's going all out with special effects!"

He headed out to pull the smoker under the awning while Mom prepped the brisket Dad planned to smoke for tonight's Christmas Eve dinner.

When I finished my breakfast, I headed to my room. Surely there would be something I could accomplish on a dreary morning such as this. Mason called before I could think it through.

"How are things looking over there?" he asked.

"Do you want the panicked RaeLyn version or the realistic version based on what my dad told me?"

"Somewhere in between?"

"We've got high water everywhere, including the field. It's basically a water park out there. We can put in a slip-and-slide, and I'll slide down the aisle in my gown."

"That's the in-between version?"

"The panicked version is that there's a zero percent chance we're getting married outdoors on our property in a few days."

"I wouldn't settle on that just yet. Things are going to improve today."

After the week we'd had, I wasn't so sure.

"Hey, if a tornado shows up we can say we went for a truly Texas-sized wedding." He laughed.

Unfortunately, he couldn't lighten my mood. I wasn't feeling very chipper about any of this.

"Did I offend you?" Suddenly I could read the concern in Mason's voice.

"No." I released a loud sigh. Maybe a little too loud. "I'm just discouraged. And kind of mad."

"At the weather?"

"At myself, for not having a normal, sensible wedding like everyone else on the planet. I'm not deliberately trying to be difficult. It's probably time to concede."

"Oh, I don't know. Let's make this a memorable one that folks will be talking about for years to come. 'Hey, remember that wedding where the wind gusts blew the groomsmen into the correct spots? They didn't even need the wedding coordinator!'"

"Very funny."

"I'm trying. Let's hold off on changing anything just yet. I've always heard you shouldn't make any big decisions in the middle of a crisis."

"Yeah, I've heard that too." I paused as my mother called out my name. "Hey, I have to go. I think they need me in the kitchen. Something about a leak under the sink."

"No way."

"Yeah. How are your plumbing skills?"

"Terrible. But I know a guy."

"Conner?"

"Yeah, he can do pretty much anything."

"Then ask him to dry up the land and blow this storm away."

Mason laughed. "Now who's the funny one?"

"I'm trying."

"The good news is, I know a guy who can do that too. And I'm going to talk with Him as soon as we end this call."

I expelled a huff of air, unable to come up with a spiritual response in the moment.

After ending the call I went into the kitchen to check on Mom. I found her under the sink.

"Mom?"

She poked her head out. "Got it fixed!" She held up a wrench. "I'm not completely useless."

"No one said you were. But we don't need a plumber?"

"Not at this very moment. I'll keep an eye on it."

Great. Now my mother was a plumber.

I extended a hand to help her up just as Gage entered the room.

He gave her an inquisitive look. "Mom? What are you doing on the floor?"

"Calisthenics," she said, then tossed the wrench back into the toolbox. "Does anyone else find it odd that we've had both fire and flood in the same week? These are biblical things happening right in front of us."

I quoted the scripture from Isaiah about the flood and the fire. Mustering all the faith I could, I said, "God will get us through this. The rain will stop, the ground will dry up, and everything will go back to normal."

"Please, Lord," Mom said, her gaze shifting to the ceiling. "I'm not sure my nerves can handle much more."

I could only hope and pray all of the water would be gone by Saturday. Sooner, even.

"I wonder if the church is canceling the Christmas Eve service." Mom peered out the window.

"If I know Pastor Burchfield, he's waiting to see what happens first." Kind of like I was.

By eleven o'clock the rain had halted, the electricity had popped back on, and we received news that the church service would take place after all. And I could tell from the weather app on my phone that we were probably in the clear for the rest of the day. For the next several days, if the app could be believed.

I walked out onto the back porch and looked out beyond the white horizontal wood slat fencing to the fields where my wedding would take place in just a few short days. Right now, it looked like we could pull out our Jet Skis and have a great time circling the grounds. Hopefully the parched land would soak all of that water right up.

I decided to put my concerns behind me and headed back inside to shower and dress for church service. I needed a distraction, and I certainly got one when my phone rang and I saw Grace Oberdeen's name on the screen. I answered right away to her chipper voice.

"How's our bride-to-be?" she asked.

"Trying to stay dry," I replied.

"Well, hopefully this news will cheer you up. I talked to my niece and she's happy to let you visit with the boys."

"She is?" I practically squealed my excitement. "Thank you so much, Mrs. Oberdeen!"

"You're welcome. She loved the angle. After all of the publicity, it only felt right to turn the attention back on the Lord to thank Him for saving her boys."

"I'm so glad."

"Sheila's not really what I would call a religious person, but this whole situation—how God spared her boys—has her rethinking that. So the fact that you want to share the miracle story has her really intrigued. She thinks it's more than a coincidence."

"I do too. And I pray she opens her heart to the Lord once we've talked."

"Me too," Mrs. Oberdeen said. "I explained that you're about to leave on your honeymoon, so I suggested you take care of the call quickly."

"Today?"

"Yes, I think they're all settled in at their house."

"Are you thinking I should pay them a visit?"

"Oh no, honey. Not in this weather. Maybe just interview them by phone? Or what's that other thing called? FaceTime?"

"Yes."

"They live in Dallas. Do you want their number? She said it was okay to give it to you, since we're friends and all."

"Absolutely."

She gave me the number and we ended the call. After I fixed my hair and put on a little makeup, I decided to give Sheila a call. I texted her first to ask if we could do a FaceTime so that I could meet the boys properly. She agreed.

Before long I was hunkered down in my room, making the call through my laptop so that I could take notes as we visited. Sheila answered quickly and we made introductions. I started with a bit of an apology.

"I'm so sorry to interrupt your holidays," I said. "But I guess you heard that I'm about to leave town in a few days."

"I did. Congratulations, by the way."

"Thanks."

"I'm so excited to meet you," Sheila said. "It's been quite a whirlwind."

"I can imagine. The fire came dangerously close to our place too, so we had our adrenaline going as well."

"The whole thing was terrifying. This is a family reunion we're going to be talking about for years to come."

"Can you start at the beginning?" I asked. "How many people were there? Where were you parked? How many kiddos were in the bunch?"

"There were two RVs, two fifth wheels, and a small pop-up camper. There were twenty-two of us altogether, including my twin boys and four other kids, mostly younger. I think my boys were bored because they were happy to be off doing their own thing while us older folks visited. We don't get to see each other very often, so we had a lot of catching up to do."

"I understand." I paused to type up the information she'd just given me about the family. "What was your first sign a fire was coming? And did you have any fires going at the time?"

"We had a campfire, but it was totally under control. We had also used the grills, but they weren't lit at the time. We saw smoke from the highway side of the lake, a distance from where we were. But we decided we'd better pack up and head out. That's when I realized the boys had run off."

She put the boys on the call and for the first time I could see them—Karter and Kenner. They were a disheveled duo—and rowdy to boot. Kenner was the one with the cast on his left arm, I learned. Karter was the one taking jabs at his brother and talking smack.

"I had told them to stay by the campground, but clearly they did not." Sheila released a weary breath. "These two decided to go for a swim in the lake without permission." She rested her hand on her heart. "In the end, that's what saved them."

"They stayed in the lake?" I asked.

"Nope." Karter shook his head. "When we got out we saw the fire and started running!"

"Unfortunately, they ran the wrong way," Sheila explained. "I guess they got turned around in the chaos and ended up in the middle of the flames!"

"The fire was going *so* fast!" Kenner interjected. "I got lost!"

"It almost got me!" Karter blurted out. "It was so hot."

"Any idea which direction it came from?" I jotted a few more things down.

The youngster looked at his brother and then back at me. "Nope. I just saw smoke and ran as fast as the wind!"

"So you ran for the highway?" I asked.

Kenner looked at his brother and then back at me. "Yeah. I saw that house on the other side and ran to tell that old man the fire was headed his way."

"And then what happened?" I asked.

"Fire trucks," Kenner said. "And a cop."

"Deputy Warren," Sheila said. "Works for Henderson County."

"I've known Shawn Warren for years." I paused and smiled at the boys. "You two were heroes. I hope you know that."

The boys looked at each other and then back at me once more with a shrug.

"I'm so grateful you're okay," I added. "Lots of people prayed for you."

"Yeah, we know. Mom said." Karter shrugged, then poked at his brother on his good arm.

"Well, I wanted to share a scripture I'll be using in the article from Isaiah 43:2: 'When you pass through the waters, I will be with you; and when you pass through the rivers, they will not sweep over you. When you walk through the fire, you will not be burned; the flames will not set you ablaze.'"

"Whoa," Karter said. "That's cool."

"You boys are living, breathing testimonies of that verse," I explained. "God kept you safe as you ran through those flames."

"Cool." Karter looked duly impressed at all of this.

"Thank God they took that swim," their mother said. "Being wet saved them in the end."

"Yes, it's truly a miracle they weren't hurt," I acknowledged.

"I broke my arm," Kenner said.

"And I breathed in smoke," Karter added.

"But you're both perfectly fine," their mother reminded them. "And it really is a miracle." She paused. "You know, it's been a long time since we've been in church. Maybe we should take this as some sort of a sign that God is really watching out for us."

"Clearly, He is."

Sheila nodded, and I could tell she was getting emotional. "Thank you for that reminder, RaeLyn. And thanks for not invading our private space. All of those other reporters were..." She shuddered. "Awful. When we weren't even sure how the boys were, they were rushing us, demanding we speak to them."

"That's terrible," I said. "And for the record, I'm really grateful you were willing to talk to me after all of that."

"Just felt right. And besides, any friend of my aunt Grace's is a friend of mine."

"Grace is amazing. We all love her."

"We do too," Sheila responded.

I then dove into my questions, asking one after the other. The boys and their mother answered in animated fashion. I had to admit, some of the answers were a little nonsensical. The boys couldn't seem to keep their story straight, and their mother spent more time asking them not to punch each other than she did answering my questions. Clearly, this was a rowdy lot. But I was still grateful for their time and told them so when we wrapped up.

"Thanks again," Sheila said. "Sorry about all the noise. I look forward to your article."

I agreed to let her know the moment it was published. Though it occurred to me after the fact that I would be enjoying my stay at an all-inclusive resort when my article in *Mabank Happenings* went to print.

CHAPTER EIGHTEEN

I ended up spending the rest of the morning looking over all the quilts, making sure they would work for the hay bales. I laid them out—still folded—all over the living room, to see which ones looked best together. Not that it really made any difference, but I wanted the seating to look nice.

We were short by two, but I had it on good authority—Dot—that she had a couple to offer as well. Hopefully she would bring them to the service today.

By two fifteen I was dressed for the Christmas Eve service. We arrived at the church twenty minutes early, the sun now shining brightly overhead, thank goodness. It gave me hope for the days ahead.

I located Mason in the foyer, talking to Nadine. Probably good news about her car, judging from the smiles on both faces. I greeted them both with a hug.

"You okay?" Nadine gave me a penetrating look. "You look tired, honey."

A yawn threatened to wriggle out. "I was up most of the night, thanks to that storm."

"I just love sleeping through storms." She released a contented sigh. "In fact, I slept so hard I didn't even realize it was raining."

Must be nice.

Then again, she wasn't the key player in a wedding in a soggy field in a couple of days.

"This time next week we'll be in sunny Playa del Carmen." Mason slipped his arm around my waist. "No more sleepless nights once we get there."

Nadine coughed and shifted her gaze.

A nervous chuckle rose up as I realized his point. So I countered with, "Probably experiencing a hurricane."

"Bite your tongue." He let out a hearty laugh. "It's going to be great. And so is the wedding. I have a good feeling."

I was grateful for Mason's upbeat response, honestly. I needed that.

Minutes later, I found myself playing the role of unofficial greeter, hugging folks as they entered through the front doors of the church. I tried to regroup, to make myself focus on the joy of the season. This was Christmas, after all.

I turned my gaze to the beautiful wreaths on the front doors of the church. They were adorned with red velvet bows and small gold bells that jingled every time one of the doors opened. Which they did. . .a lot. Before long, the foyer was full of happy, chatty parishioners. I lost myself momentarily to the carols playing on the overhead speaker and the cacophony of voices surrounding me.

Grace Oberdeen approached, all smiles. "Well? How did it go with the boys? Were they cooperative?"

"Yes, it was great! They gave me a lot of material to work with. I'm excited to write the article. I appreciate you connecting me."

"Of course."

"They remind me so much of Gage and Dallas at that age."

"Oh, I remember your brothers as preteens." Grace laughed. "They got into some trouble from time to time, as I recall. Remember, I was their Sunday school teacher for a while."

"Oh, yes. That's right."

"I've been hearing all sorts of rumors around town about how that fire started." Grace lowered her voice and leaned in close. "Have you?"

"What are you hearing?"

A look of concern settled on her face. "Well, folks are in a tizzy over who's really to blame. Lots of finger-pointing, including a few pointing at my sweet nephews."

"Oh?" I wondered if Buck might be behind those rumors, but I didn't say so.

"I know they're at a rough age, but I can't imagine they would cause something like that and not own up to it. You know?" She glanced up at me, and I thought I noticed a hint of tears in those soft blue eyes.

"Folks just like to gossip."

"Yes." Grace released an exaggerated breath. "Those boys are heroes in my book. Their quick thinking probably saved Buck Adler's property . . .and his life."

"I'm so glad they had the good sense to let him know the fire was coming so he could call the fire department."

"Yes, those flames were way too close for comfort. I'm most grateful the Lord saw fit to spare them. That's all I plan to focus on."

"Good idea." I offered what I hoped would look like an encouraging smile. "And amen to that."

I happened to notice Gage standing near the back entrance to the sanctuary, exchanging hushed words with one of his fellow firefighters. I could tell from his rigid posture that something had upset him, but what?

I took a few steps in that direction, hoping to ease my way into their conversation. I arrived just in time to hear the fire chief mutter the words, "We've got eyes on him. Still not sure about his motivation, though."

Who? I wanted to ask. *Whose motivation?*

"It's not illegal to camp at a state park." Gage glanced my way. "Oh hey, sis."

"Hey," I responded. "Sorry. Just trying to get through to the sanctuary."

He stepped aside and made room for me to pass through. I decided to move slowly, still in sleuthing mode, my hand on the door.

"Keep me updated," the chief responded as I passed through, causing a jingle bell ripple across the room. "After all he put us through last week, I don't trust that guy. I think he's got some kind of vendetta."

Vendetta? And what guy?

I would have to wait until I got home to ask. The music started, and before long many of our congregants had settled in for Christmas Eve service.

I had to smile as I took in the sanctuary. Melody and the other ladies had really outdone themselves with the Christmas decor. Just like all the years prior, a line of bright red poinsettia plants adorned the base of the pulpit, creating a vibrant floral accent. Off to one side of the choir loft, the large Christmas tree was decked out with white lights and bright red bows. And bringing it all together, a gorgeous oversized nativity scene filled the area where baptisms usually took place.

The whole room had a cozy, sacred atmosphere, one that sent a shiver down my spine, in a good way. And it smelled of freshly cut evergreen, the perfect aroma for a Christmas Eve service.

Gage stepped into the spot behind me and I turned his way.

"Hey—question. Were you guys talking about..." I lowered my voice to a whisper. "Aaron?"

His eyes widened like a kid caught with his hand in the cookie jar. "What makes you think that?"

I shrugged. "No idea. But was he the one camping at Purtis Creek?"

Gage shifted his gaze to the door as Summer entered, and he waved at her. "Maybe. But it's not against the law, so..."

"But he's still missing, right?"

"Right. He's not there now, but apparently he bought a permit the day before the fire and was inadvertently photographed by one of the other families the morning of the fire. He was in the background of one of their photos."

"Are they sure it was him?" I asked.

Gage nodded. "Yeah. No doubt about that."

The air in the room suddenly felt colder, and I turned to discover the wind had pushed open the doors to the foyer. One of the greeters grabbed hold of them and pushed them shut again.

I glanced up to the front of the sanctuary as "Joy to the World" played from the overhead speakers. In that moment, I willed myself to stop thinking—about the fire, Buck Adler, Aaron, the boys...all of it. I would never again have the opportunity to experience Christmas in my home church as a single woman after this service. I needed to make the most of it.

I relaxed and began to hum. The melody brought about the strangest swirl of emotions: relief that we were so near our goal of getting married, sadness at leaving home to move to...who knew where...and extreme gratitude for the people I adored, many of whom were in this room right now.

I also ached for my papaw. When I was a little girl, he had held tight to my hand in church on Christmas Eve, even helping me with my candle during "Silent Night." These days, I held the hand of a different fella.

Well, usually. I looked around for Mason, but he was missing again. I did find Mom in her usual spot near the front.

"Have you seen Logan?" she asked as I took a seat behind her.

"No, but I think he's staying home today. Last I heard, Meghan was still under the weather."

Mom didn't look one bit pleased by this announcement. "I can't believe Logan is missing Christmas Eve service. That has never happened before."

"I think he's worried about her. She inhaled too much smoke."

"Speaking of the fire. . ." She leaned in close and whispered, "Do you think they're suspecting Aaron? I overheard a conversation on the way in that made me wonder."

"I just heard something similar," I acknowledged. "Let's compare notes."

So we did.

"Apparently, he was seen near the campsite, according to the family of those two boys." Mom glanced at Grace Oberdeen. "The fire chief's wife just told me."

"The boys didn't bring it up when I talked to them. Why wouldn't they mention it?"

"Because they're kids?" Mom said. "Kids don't always pay attention to the details. The parents happened to have a photo of him."

"Yeah, I heard that part."

"Point is, he didn't stick around after the fire. But how strange that he was there right before it started. You know?"

"Yeah." A shiver ran down my spine once again.

Moments later, Pastor Burchfield approached the podium and greeted us. Before long, we were singing the opening carol. Several minutes into the service, something caught my eye. I glanced over to see that Buck Adler had slipped into the pew opposite us.

Others noticed him too. Several, actually, including Grace Oberdeen, whose eyes narrowed to slits when she saw him.

Buck looked uncomfortable and out of place. Was there a reason for that?

My thoughts shifted back to what I'd learned about Aaron. The idea that he had somehow been responsible for that fire didn't sit well with me. What would he stand to gain by burning down the acreage near Mabank? Was he trying to prove the fire department's inadequacy? Maybe trying to spread the message that they needed all the help they could get?

None of this made sense.

Pastor Burchfield rose to give the announcements.

"I want to ask you folks to keep praying for Karter and Kenner, great-nephews of our own Grace Oberdeen." He offered Grace a little nod. "They're back home from the hospital and healing up, but it's going to take time to get past the trauma of what they went through just a few short days ago."

To my left, Buck cleared his throat and shifted in the pew.

We ended the service with "Silent Night," as always. My eyes flooded with tears, just as they did every year. In spite of the chaos, in spite of the wedding, I still wanted to remain focused on the one thing that meant the most—the birthday of our Savior. Nothing was more important than that.

When the final song ended, folks gathered to say their goodbyes, many grabbing their coats and purses, ready to head out for Christmas Eve celebrations. I wanted to say hello to Buck, but he took off like a rocket ship as soon as the final song ended. Strange.

Dot and Enrique looked cozy, arm in arm at the back of the room. Should we invite them over for Christmas Eve dinner? No, they disappeared on us, not even looking back.

Honeymooners.

Mom lingered to talk to Pastor Burchfield about something, but I was anxious to get home.

"I'm riding with Mason," I explained. "See you back at the house."

She nodded and I went in search of Mason, who was now standing in the foyer talking to Gage. I could tell from the expressions on their faces that they were worried about something. I overheard Gage talking about a tip the fire department had received on Aaron. This made the hair on my arms stand up.

Thankfully, as I shot a glance his way, Mason extended his hand.

"Ready to head home?"

"Yep. I've got some food prep to deal with for this evening. Hopefully the power is still on."

"Hope so. Let's go." He took my hand, and we walked out together into the cold December air.

"So, you and Gage looked pretty serious," I observed as we made our way to the parking lot.

"Yeah." He slipped his arm around my shoulder. "I guess you heard there's a rumor going around that Aaron started the fire. He was camping out at Purtis Creek on the day the fire started."

"Yeah. I heard."

We reached the truck, and Mason opened the passenger door for me. As I climbed in, I spotted a figure lurking along the side of the building. I couldn't quite make him out. A male, judging from his height and clothing choices.

The man's face was obscured, but I happened to catch a glimpse of his Dallas Cowboys baseball cap.

"Mason, is that Buck Adler?" I nudged him, but the guy took off all of a sudden.

"Looks like it." Mason shrugged. "I was sure glad to see him in church. It's been years, right?"

"Yeah, but something about him showing up tonight just feels. . .off."

"What do you mean?" Mason started the truck and turned on the heater.

I shivered as I watched Buck get into his old truck and head out. He didn't make it very far. Moments later, Buck pulled into the gas station adjacent to the church.

"Follow him?" I suggested.

"Are you serious, RaeLyn? You want me to follow an old man who just came to church for the first time in years?"

"Please."

Mason grudgingly pulled his truck out of the church parking lot and eased his way off the road close to the gas station. We watched as Buck filled his tank. Then he walked to the back of his truck and reached for something.

The gas can.

Which he filled and placed back in the bed of the truck.

"Did you see that?" I whispered.

"A man filling up his gas tank? And why are we whispering?"

"That's the same can that was full to the brim the day he stopped off at our house last Saturday."

"RaeLyn, you're overthinking this."

"Am I?" I squinted to get a better view as Buck dropped a slip of paper into the trash can. Afterward, he got into his truck and pulled away.

"Last I checked, carrying a spare can of gasoline wasn't a crime."

"I know, but. . ." My thoughts went into a tailspin. Was Buck Adler behind last Sunday's fire? If so, was the gas can an indicator that he might be ready to strike again? How many others would lose their homes? Their properties?

"Mason, pull in there. Please. I want to see something."

To his credit, Mason didn't even argue. Likely, he knew I'd keep pestering him until he relented. He pulled into the very spot where Buck had just been. I climbed out, the cold night air now slicing through the opening in my coat. I watched as Buck's truck disappeared from view up the road before leaning in to look in the trash can. Where I found a scrap of paper perched atop the rest of the trash, as if begging me to take it.

I reached down and snatched it up, then jumped back into the truck.

"RaeLyn Hadley!" Mason looked my way. "What have you done?"

"Just a little snooping." I held up the paper. "You never know. It might be important."

Or. . .

I stared at the paper in my hand.

It might just be a gas receipt for $52.98.

CHAPTER NINETEEN

Okay, so it was just a gas receipt.

Still, I couldn't let this go. Was Buck Adler the arsonist we'd been looking for? Inquiring minds wanted to know.

I fussed and fumed all the way home. I decided to give our family friend Deputy Shawn Warren a call to let him know my suspicions. I put the call on speaker so Mason could chime in. I may or may not have sounded a bit exaggerated as I shared all we had seen. I also shared what Buck had told my father and me just a few short days ago, about burning his place down. And about the gas can.

After hearing all of that, Shawn promised to take my concerns seriously and said he would investigate thoroughly.

Before we ended the call, I decided to broach a completely different subject.

"Hey, I wanted to let you know that I had a FaceTime interview with Karter and Kenner today."

"Oh?"

"Yeah, I'm featuring their story in my upcoming *Mabank Happenings* piece. I don't have to turn it in till Saturday, so I was wondering if you had time to answer a few questions. It would be great to get a second source to quote for the article, and since you were on the scene, you're the perfect choice."

"Between now and Saturday?" He chuckled. "Two things: Tomorrow is Christmas, and Saturday I'll be attending a friend's wedding."

Okay, good point.

To my left, Mason cleared his throat.

"I know, I know." I paused and glanced at Mason before responding. "What if I just sent you a couple of questions by email? Sound okay?"

"Sure. I'll try to get them back to you by Friday morning. Would that work?"

"Perfectly." I thanked him profusely and ended the call. Afterward I shoved my phone into my coat pocket and leaned back against the seat.

"Can I ask a favor?" Mason asked.

"Sure."

"Once we get back to your place, can we let this go for the rest of the evening? I don't want to get everyone worked up. And we have absolutely no proof that Buck did anything wrong whatsoever. I'm inclined to think we're reading too much into this."

And by *we're*, he clearly meant *you're*.

Still, I agreed to drop it. We had more important things to take care of. It was Christmas Eve, after all.

By the time we arrived at my house, I was ready to shift my thoughts to the evening ahead. Thank goodness, the power was still going strong. Bessie Mae and Mom usually pulled off an amazing meal on Christmas Eve, but today my father did the honors, finishing up the brisket and some chicken thighs he'd put in the outdoor smoker earlier in the day. Mom whipped up a couple of appetizers, simple items that didn't take much effort.

Carrie arrived with her delicious cheesy potatoes and Bessie Mae brought along a dish of baked beans, as well as a couple of pies. I helped out with the rolls—not homemade, but who cared? I'd left them out to thaw during service, and the room was now filled with a lovely yeasty aroma. I popped them into the oven when we got home.

Gage and Dallas came in late, carrying fresh firewood. They were arguing about something, but we caught them on the tail end of it, so we didn't bother getting involved. I'd learned early on that arguments between twins weren't mine to solve. Besides, their raucous banter was almost fun to watch. It kind of reminded me of what I'd witnessed earlier in the day with Karter and Kenner.

Twins. Honestly.

About the time Gage and Dallas calmed down, Meghan and Logan showed up with some chips and homemade queso to be served as an appetizer. Yum. Looked like we were all set.

And Mason, God bless him, showed up late. He had a good excuse, though.

"I stopped to get Blue Bell." He held up a bag from Brookshire Brothers.

He shoved it into the freezer, pressing it behind some of Bessie Mae's frozen peaches.

"You're forgiven," Bessie Mae proclaimed. "But I don't mind saying we were about to put a MISSING poster on your chair."

"I have my own chair?" He quirked a brow as we all pointed to the chair next to the one I'd always sat in. "That's progress."

"Well, of course," I said. "You're a member of the family. One of Mom's five sons."

This got a funny look from my four brothers, who hadn't quite figured out that they now had another brother in the mix.

"Thanks. And you know I'd never stand you up." Mason took a seat.

"But you did the other day, when Enrique was here," Bessie Mae reminded him.

"In my defense..." Mason put his hand up. "I didn't see the text. And that particular meeting wasn't on the spreadsheet."

"Ah, the spreadsheet." My father laughed. "The infamous spreadsheet."

"Hey, I work better with a plan," I said.

"Speaking of Enrique, I hear he's got big plans for one of the old buildings in town." This comment came from Logan, who plugged in the slow cooker with the queso inside. "A restaurant?"

"We've never had a five-star chef in Mabank before," Bessie Mae responded. "Not that I can recall."

"Sure we have." I looked her way. "You!"

"Well, they sure didn't pay me very well, did they?" She laughed and slapped her knee, which got us all tickled.

Mom seemed to be preoccupied with something in the cupboards. She made a bit of noise as she moved things around. We all glanced her way as she set a dish on the counter and looked our way, hands on her hips.

"I have an announcement to make."

"What's that, Flora?" Dad asked.

"I bought myself an early Christmas present." She reached down and grabbed a gorgeous plate with a bright floral design, which she showed off with great flair. Very eye catching.

"You got new dishes, Mom?" I walked over to have a closer look.

"Two sets, so we'd have enough. What do you think of the design?"

"Colorful," Bessie Mae said. "I love 'em. They're perfect!"

"We still had plenty of older plates and such after you took your mom's dishes, Bessie Mae," my mother said. "I could've made do with them. But I just felt like getting something new."

"From Walmart?" Dad asked.

Mom's nose wrinkled, and for a moment I thought she wasn't going to respond. "No, Chuck," she said after a moment. "I ordered them online a couple days ago. I wasn't sure if they would arrive in time for Christmas, but they did. That poor driver must've delivered them in the wee hours. I found them on the front porch early this morning before any of you crawled out of bed."

I gave them a closer look and declared they were perfect for the Hadley household. Then I happily set the table with those new dishes, and before long we were filling our plates with a delicious barbecue dinner. It wasn't traditional Christmas fare, but it definitely hit the spot.

Nights like these made my heart so happy. So comfortable. Nothing about this evening was formal or pretentious. After the week we'd had, it was kind of nice just to have the family together for a simple, quiet meal.

Well, quiet until Annalisa started screaming. Turned out, she was getting a new tooth.

Carrie got her calmed down and the conversation turned to Summer and Tasha, who had both decided to spend Christmas Eve with their families. We would see them tomorrow for Christmas afternoon festivities.

Unlike so many of the stressful days prior, this meal was spent in peaceful banter, telling stories about Christmases gone by. Dad decided to share the one about the time I woke everyone up at five in the morning to open presents.

"I was seven," I told Mason. "You can't really blame a seven-year-old for being excited."

"Hey, at least she didn't unwrap and rewrap her presents," Mom said.

"Nope." I glanced at the twins. "I'm not the one who did that."

"You opened your presents and rewrapped them?" Mason looked back and forth between Gage and Dallas.

"Yeah." Dallas elbowed Gage. "We only got caught because Gage's wrapping skills are so terrible."

"They're *still* terrible." Gage laughed. "Did you see the present under the tree for Summer? *So* bad."

"More chicken?" Dad held up the platter. "Get it while it's hot!"

We continued to swap stories as we ate. As I listened to one of Jake's tales, I was reminded of something that happened when I was little, so I shared it with everyone.

"Remember that time—I think I was eight—when Papaw decided to take us kids out for a hayride in the back of Tilly on Christmas Eve to look at Christmas lights?"

"Who could forget?" Logan busted into laughter. "You made it a Christmas to remember, RaeLyn."

Meghan looked my way, creases forming between her eyes. "What did you do?"

"Papaw loaded up bales of hay in the back of the truck, and we climbed on board. But when he took off, I lost my balance and fell out of the back of the truck."

"Ouch!" Meghan gasped. "Did you break any bones?"

"No, just wounded my pride and bruised my shoulder. Papaw came and swept me up and kissed my tears away. Then he let me ride up front with him while the boys stayed in back. The whole time he drove he told me funny stories."

"Do you think that's why you had the idea to add hay bales to your wedding?" Meghan asked. "Maybe because of this memory?"

That thought had never occurred to me, but hearing it spoken aloud made sense.

"Could be."

"Were there quilts on the hay bales?" Meghan asked.

"Now that I think about it..." I paused, trying to remember. "Yes. He had Mamaw's quilts on the hay bales so we could keep warm."

"Sounds like a foreshadowing of things to come." Meghan offered a warm smile. "I love it. And you're riding up to the wedding in the back of the truck on a bale of hay, right?"

"Right."

"You're a sentimental soul, RaeLyn."

I was. For sure.

"And then there was the time. . ." I looked back and forth between Gage and Dallas. "When these two were playing with some leftover fireworks and set a bale of hay on fire in the barn."

"What?" Mom looked downright stunned at this news.

"Yep. You don't remember, Mom? I got blamed for it, but I'm not the one who lit that sparkler." I gave the twins a pensive look. "Was I, Gage?"

My firefighter brother paled. "I have no memory of this event."

"Sure you don't." I looked at Dallas. "What about you? Do you have convenient memory loss too?"

"I remember it," Bessie Mae said. "The boys said that RaeLyn was playing with leftover sparklers behind the barn. They even hid a few back there to make it look like she had."

At least someone remembered the correct version of the story.

"Bessie Mae was the only one who believed me," I said. "She's always been in my corner."

"And always will be." My aunt gave me a little wink.

Bob looked up from his plate and offered a warm smile, then took her hand and gave it a squeeze.

Gage cleared his throat and shoved a piece of brisket in his mouth.

"What do you have to say for yourself, Gage?" Mom asked. "Guilty as charged?"

"I need to speak to an attorney."

"Anything you say can be used against you in a court of law," Logan interjected and then laughed. "But I'm guessing even an attorney can't save you now."

Dad looked up from his plate. "Kind of ironic that you're a firefighter now, when you came so close to burning down the barn as a kid."

"Penance," Gage said.

Which was the closest thing to a confession we were going to get out of him.

"I got grounded for that," I reminded him. "Two weeks. Couldn't go to Carlee Ellison's roller-skating party."

"Oooh, I remember now." Mom's eyes widened and she cast her gaze to Gage. "Anything you'd like to say now, son?"

"Yes." He nodded. "Pass the barbecue sauce, please."

For whatever reason, I found my thoughts shifting back to Karter and Kenner as this exchange took place. My twin brothers were notorious at their age. Making up stories. Blaming people falsely.

Sometimes kids did that.

Made up stories.

"Hmm."

"You okay?" Mason rested his hand on mine.

I snapped to attention. "Yes. Just thinking."

A few minutes later we wrapped up the meal, and Logan and Meghan cleared the table, instructing the rest of us to take it easy.

We headed into the living room, and Dallas stoked the fire in the fireplace, adding another log. The conversation quieted, and before long Logan and Meghan joined us.

"Everyone ready for our Christmas Eve tradition?" Mom asked.

My heart skipped a beat as the words were spoken.

No matter how old we got, I would always perform one very routine but lovely task: As the only daughter in the house, I would take the little baby Jesus and place Him in the manger in the creche scene.

Tonight as I set Him into place, I thought about how many, many times I'd done this. For as long as I could remember.

But maybe it would soon be time to pass the baton to the next generation. Next year I would ask Annalisa to do the honors. She wouldn't be old enough to understand, but over the years she would grow to love the story of the baby in the manger. I sure had.

After I placed the baby, we sang "Silent Night." A cappella. A holy sweetness hung over the room, a reminder that this week—chaotic as it had been—wasn't really about all the turmoil and confusion. It was about that tiny baby in the manger, and the gift He was to each and every one of us.

After singing, my dad read the story from the second chapter of Luke, homing in on verses 10 and 11:

"But the angel said to them, 'Do not be afraid. I bring you good news that will cause great joy for all the people. Today in the town of David a Savior has been born to you; he is the Messiah, the Lord.'"

The room remained silent as we all pondered those verses. Bob finally broke the silence when he shifted positions in the chair and his knee made a popping sound.

"So sorry," he said. "I'm worse than a box of cereal these days. Snap, crackle, pop!"

When the laughter died down, we decided the time had come to open our stockings. This was our second Christmas Eve tradition, one I hoped would never change.

Mom passed them out, and Meghan looked startled as she realized there was one with her name on it.

"You have a stocking for me?" She ran her finger along the embroidered name.

"Well, sure. You're a Hadley now," Mom said. "Hadleys all get stockings."

Meghan's eyes welled with tears. "That's the sweetest thing ever. I can't remember the last time I had a stocking. If ever."

I gripped my stocking, ready to look inside. Not much had changed over the years, but I still loved this tradition of opening stockings on Christmas Eve. Inside we would always find a lottery ticket from Dad, a roll of Life Savers from Bessie Mae, and plenty of fuzzy socks from Mom.

Mom always scolded Dad for the lottery tickets, since she didn't believe in gambling. Dad didn't either, but that had never stopped him from buying those scratch-offs.

As for the fuzzy socks, Mom had kind of turned it into a game, sort of a "Who's got the wildest design?" challenge.

This year Logan won. His socks were covered in calculators. Funny, considering his work at the bank.

I had created a new tradition a few years back, which continued tonight. Homemade Christmas ornaments for each person. I always had fun making them, but especially this year. The ornaments were all wedding themed. We put them on the tree right away.

Afterward, the loveliest thing happened. Bob took a seat at our piano and began to play familiar Christmas carols. Bessie Mae—once a starlet in high school musicals like *Annie Get Your Gun*—blessed us all by leading a sing-along.

Mason sang out in that gorgeous tenor voice of his, proclaiming the majesty and beauty of the season. In that moment, I found myself forgetting all about the stresses of the wedding, all about the fire, the flood. . .and just enjoyed the moment.

After the sing-along, Mom decided we needed to play cards. This was our usual routine on Christmas Eve night. She particularly loved Spoons and Crazy Eights. We decided to start with Crazy Eights. After the nutty week we'd had, it just made sense.

As we settled in to play, I noticed that Mason was suddenly looking distracted.

"Earth to Mason. You okay over there?" I gave him an inquisitive look, and feelings of concern swept over me. This looked like a man who was troubled. Or. . .something.

"Oh, yes. Just thinking."

"About. . . ?"

"Family. About how good it is to have one that I can spend holidays with. Ever since my dad died. . ." His voice trailed off. "Anyway, it feels mighty good to be surrounded by folks I love."

"You're surrounded, all right," my dad said. "So, if you're looking for an escape route from the Hadley clan, you'd better move quick. Just a couple of days left before you're officially one of us."

"He's already one of us," I chided and then turned to face him. "And don't you dare think about running off."

"Trust me, I wouldn't. I'm feeling incredibly blessed this Christmas, that's all."

"Me too." I reached over and gave him a little peck on the cheek.

We were just a few minutes into the card game when Mason got a call. After glancing at his phone, he rose and walked to the back door, then disappeared outside.

"Must be serious," Mom said. "To interrupt Christmas Eve."

"I guess so." It was a little odd, this mysterious way he was acting. Pangs of insecurity swept over me again. No doubt he was dealing with something work related.

Or not. When he came back in, I could read the relief in his eyes. But why?

Everything okay?" I asked.

"Yup." A smile tipped up the edges of his lips. "I'm good. Really good, in fact."

"Anything you want to share?" Mom asked.

"Soon enough." He offered me a playful wink. "We're almost to the finish line."

"Didn't realize we were running a race," my dad said.

"Oh, I've been running faster than anyone knows," Mason explained. "But I promise, the end is in sight."

"That sounds rather ominous." Bessie Mae shuffled the cards like a Vegas blackjack dealer. "You might want to rephrase that."

"I've been running like a chicken with its head cut off."

"Slightly less ominous," I said. "But not by much."

"I've been running like a hound dog chasing a biscuit."

"This is getting weird," I said. "Want to try again?"

"I've been busy."

"Clearly." Bessie Mae laughed and slapped the cards down on the table. "Only, now I'm really wondering what in the world you've been up to. Inquiring minds want to know."

His eyes sparkled with merriment. "All good, I promise. Hopefully the best Christmas present ever."

"Better than my new dishes?" Mom asked. "Because they're pretty spectacular."

"How spectacular?" Dad's eyes narrowed to slits. "How much did those dishes set me back, anyway?"

Mom reached to grab the deck of cards and started passing them out one by one. "Chuck, you told me I could buy new dishes."

"I know," he said. "Just wondering."

Mom gave him a sideways look. "Well, sweetheart, keep right on wonderin'. It's cheaper than therapy—and much more entertaining for me."

My stars. Mom was on a roll tonight.

This exchange about the dishes led to a discussion about money.

Which led to a discussion about my wedding.

Which led to a discussion about the thermal blankets Dad still thought we needed for the guests.

Which led to Bessie Mae asking if she could bring an inflatable donut to sit on, on her bale of hay.

Which prompted Gage and Dallas to laugh so hard that Gage nearly fell out of his chair.

Which reminded me of that time I fell out of the back of the truck.

Which caused me to realize that the Hadleys, crazy as we were, hadn't changed much over the years. I hoped we never would.

At some point I gave up trying to weasel anything else out of Mason. I could tell he was brimming with excitement, though, and that gave me hope that whatever he had up his sleeve would be worth all the waiting and wondering.

Now, if only I had a gift to give him that was comparable.

Oh, wait, I did. I was giving him. . .me.

CHAPTER TWENTY

We shut the party down on Christmas Eve around nine thirty, and Mason headed home. I fell into bed around ten fifteen and didn't wake up until eight thirty Christmas morning. The house was strangely hushed—no squeals from little Colt, no rattling of pots and pans from Mom, no jesting from my brothers. Just the blissful stillness of morning. And I didn't want to break it just yet. After all, I wasn't that anxious seven-year-old anymore, waking my parents before dawn on Christmas Day.

No, in fact, I could have stayed in bed another hour, just relaxing. Especially as I contemplated the fact that my days in my childhood home were drawing to a close. But I knew that Bessie Mae would be here by nine, ready to start cooking for our big Christmas meal, which would take place at noon. And though we usually opened presents in the morning, we had opted to wait until Tasha and Summer could join us, later in the day this time. I didn't mind a bit. It gave me more time to relax and get ready.

Eventually I pulled myself from the warm cocoon of the blankets. A slight chill hung in the air around me as my bare feet hit the floor. I sank my toes into the plush rug and willed myself awake. A little shiver was enough to convince me I needed to start with a warm shower.

I pushed myself from the bed and headed to the bathroom, my thoughts swirling between the bliss of the upcoming days and the chaos of all we'd been through this week. Hopefully the worst was behind us.

I showered and dressed in comfortable but cute clothes, then headed into the kitchen to check on the others. Sure enough, Bessie Mae had already arrived and was bustling about, sorting through grocery bags with laser focus.

She looked my way with a mischievous grin. "Well, g'morning, sunshine! Merry Christmas!"

"Same to you." I walked over and gave her a kiss on the cheek. "You're early."

She flashed a smile. "Figured we needed to get started. There's a lot to do, as always."

It felt so perfect, having her here on Christmas morning, but someone was noticeably absent.

"Where's Bob?" I looked around, half expecting to see him in the recliner in the living room with his Bible study book in his hand.

She placed a casserole dish on the counter. "Hopefully in bed, snoring like a chainsaw. He tossed and turned all night. The man moves more than a rocking chair on a front porch. Very hard to get used to, I must say. Sharing a bed with Freida would be less problematic."

That certainly raised some interesting imagery.

"Why is that? Did we wear him out last night with all of the singing?"

"He's probably not used to staying up late, but I don't think it was that. When you get to be our age, sleeping is a luxury, one we're not often afforded. Our bodies wake us up at the most random times. And then there are the aches and pains."

"Like the snap, crackle, pop comment?"

"He's got an issue with his knee. And apparently my breathing bothers him when I sleep on my back. Which I do every night of my life. I told the man he was lucky I was breathing at all, at this age."

That got a laugh out of me. So much for thinking Bessie Mae and Bob were in their blissful honeymoon phase. She would rather sleep with a cow, and he would rather sleep after she left for the day.

On the other hand, maybe this *was* bliss to them. Being together. Weathering the aches and pains with the one you loved snoring at your side.

"You'll find out soon enough, honey, that being married isn't much more than two people ignoring each other's random noises." Bessie Mae went back to work and began to hum "Jingle Bells."

All righty then.

Mom joined us a couple of minutes later, and then Meghan showed up shortly thereafter, holding several wrapped gifts in her arms. She set those gifts under the tree, gave Bessie Mae a warm hug, and then walked straight up to Mom and threw her arms around her neck. "My first Christmas morning as a Hadley." The most delightful smile tipped up the edges of her beautiful lips. "I'm so happy."

Mom gave her a tight squeeze. "I feel the same, honey."

Progress.

Meghan's eyes misted over. "I just can't thank you enough for that stocking last night. I've never had one with my name on it before."

"You haven't?" Mom looked completely baffled by this. "Well, that's just criminal."

And that pretty much sealed the deal. The one we didn't speak of was truly a Hadley now, stocking and all.

Mom put Meghan to work making coffee and then diverted her gaze to Bessie Mae, who was tying on an apron.

"Everything feels so right when you're home, Bessie Mae." Mom then looked my way. "And you too, RaeLyn. Do you realize this is the last year we'll have Christmas morning with you at home?"

"You can't shake me that easily," I said. "I'll be back."

"No." She shook her head. "I know how it goes. When I married your father, we started our own traditions. It was hard on my mother, but I never regretted having Christmas morning in my own house with my own kids. That's how it's meant to be."

"Well, when I have kids we can talk about it, but for now, maybe I can still come on Christmas morning, at least the first few years."

"And you know I'm not going anywhere," Bessie Mae chimed in. "I'm harder to shake than a busted saltshaker. I'll be back every holiday if you'll have me."

"If we'll have you?" Mom looked stunned by this proclamation. "Of course we'll have you, Bessie Mae!"

"Well, good. Bob's got no immediate family but us. And besides, things are different when you're our age. We're not spring chickens anymore, like RaeLyn and Mason."

Right now I didn't feel like a spring chicken. After all the action over the prior week, my poor body was stiff and a bit sore. But at least we now had a real plan for the wedding. With the ground drying up, we were good to go, setting things up tomorrow as originally planned.

Before we could get too emotional, Carrie breezed in the back door, bringing with her a rush of crisp winter air. "I left the baby with Jake." She turned to close the back door, but a slight gust of wind threatened to open it again. "Figured we needed some solid time to get things done. How can I help?"

Bessie Mae already had a plan in mind and dished out the orders. Before long, we were her sous chefs, which was always how things had been. In spite of all the changes, much remained the same.

We had decided to do a semitraditional Christmas dinner this year—ham with a few sides. And Bessie Mae's homemade rolls, which had risen overnight on the tray that now sat on the counter. Even unbaked, they made my mouth water. I could hardly wait.

Mom prepped the Christmas ham and popped it into the oven. The rest of us simply did as we were told, and before long the room looked and smelled like Christmas dinner. That same sense of comfort and familiarity settled over me that I'd experienced every holiday for as long as I could remember. Oh, how I loved that feeling. And these people. I adored every single one, even the interlopers, as Dad called the ones who'd wriggled their way into the fold.

Speaking of interlopers, Tasha arrived around eleven thirty, arms loaded with presents. She set them under the tree and joined us in the kitchen, brimming with stories about her family's Christmas morning.

Summer came about fifteen minutes later with her son and joined the clan. Colt was so excited to put his presents under the tree and did so with lots of chatter. I couldn't get over how adorable he looked in his little Christmas suit and bow tie. Perfection. And Summer was downright gorgeous. That beautiful dark hair. Those rich brown eyes. The woman simply radiated warmth.

Summer looked my way as she slipped on one of the many worn aprons Mom kept dangling on the hook beside the fridge. "Good news! I checked the weather, and the next few days are supposed to be beautiful, RaeLyn."

A wave of relief washed over me. I hated to get my hopes up, but hopefully she was right.

"Looks like the temperatures are going to be in the upper sixties on Saturday." She brushed her hands along the front of her apron. "With bright, sunny skies."

"Really?" I threw my arms around Summer's neck. "Thank you!"

"Don't thank me," she said, pointing to the heavens. "Thank Him."

Still, I didn't want to get my hopes up completely just yet.

Mason arrived mid-celebration and confirmed that he too had checked the weather report.

"It's really happening, RaeLyn," he said. "Your childhood dream of getting married in a field facing north is coming true."

"South."

"I know." He gave me a kiss. "Just making sure you're paying attention."

One person was still noticeably absent. Bob. But he came hobbling in just as we dressed the table for the meal. The poor fellow looked plum worn out, as Bessie Mae was prone to say.

"Hard night?" I asked.

He grunted and grabbed a radish from the vegetable tray.

We settled down at the table moments later and my dad led us in prayer. I tried not to get too emotional as a holy hush fell over the room, our own personal sanctuary. I felt a lump rise in my throat. Yes, I would still be here next year, Lord willing, but it wouldn't be the same, not living here.

As the prayer ended, I glanced over at Mason, who looked perfectly at home in the seat next to mine. Or maybe he was just preoccupied by all of that food on the table. Talk about a feast! The mouthwatering ham looked delicious, but those creamy mashed potatoes and green beans? They were calling my name.

Mason took a look at that gorgeous ham in the center of the table and rubbed his hands together. "Come to Daddy!"

This got a laugh out of everyone at the table, especially Bessie Mae.

Bob looked duly impressed by the display of food as well. He reached for his napkin and placed it in his lap, his gaze never leaving the table. "That ham's more dressed up than I am today, and I actually put in some effort."

"You look wonderful, sweetheart." Bessie Mae reached over to give his hand a squeeze. "Merry Christmas to my handsome husband."

He leaned over to give her a little kiss on the cheek.

And I knew. I knew that someday—when we were quite old—that

would be Mason and me, still in love, and still with eyes only for each other.

Only, right now he definitely wasn't looking at me. Mason grabbed the serving fork and jabbed it into the ham and said, "I'll do the honors!" Then he took on the role of meat server.

We all loaded up our plates with ham, rolls, sides, sides, and more sides. Then the eating fest began, with lots of oohing and aahing.

The sounds of bliss were interrupted by Bessie Mae as she took her first bite of the ham. "Whoo-ee! This glaze is hotter than a billy goat in a pepper patch!" She reached for her water glass and guzzled it down.

This led to raucous laughter from all of us.

What happened after that was too lovely for words. Eating. Visiting. Reminiscing.

Eating more.

Swapping stories. Remembering Papaw and so many of the tales of days gone by. How I loved those stories. How I loved my life.

A lump rose in my throat, and in that moment I wondered if I would actually be able to leave all of this. Yes, I wanted my own place, but a part of me had always longed to raise my children with strong family ties, right here on the Hadley acreage.

I pushed that lump down with a big spoonful of mashed potatoes and looked at Mason. He reached to grab my hand and gave it a squeeze. And in that moment, I decided I'd go anywhere he asked me to. Within a certain radius.

Thank goodness, Dallas interrupted my internal wrangling by tapping his glass with a spoon. When we looked his way, he said, "I've got something to share."

"What's that, son?" Dad asked.

"Y'all know I've been picking up a lot of hours at the restaurant, which is great news. But Tasha's folks have told her that they're retiring. They want her to take over."

"I'm glad to hear the restaurant will stay open," Mom said, her gaze turning to Tasha. "But I can't imagine it without your mom and dad running the show."

"I'm sure they'll be in and out, but they're really wanting to travel in their RV for a while."

"Can't blame them there." Mom sighed. "I hear that some folks retire at our age. They travel. They see the world." She shot an odd look at my dad, who shifted his gaze to the mashed potatoes.

"Anyway, Tasha was counting on income from the vacation rental, but she's had a hard time keeping it rented."

"I still can't figure out why." Tasha released a sigh.

"So she really needs Fish Tales to not just stay afloat but to actually take off and make more money," Dallas said. "And that's where I come in."

Dad gave him an inquisitive look. "What do you mean?"

Dallas offered a bright smile. "You're looking at the new manager of Fish Tales."

Mom dropped her fork. It clattered against her plate.

"But what about your work here?" Dad said.

"I'll do what I can to help out, but eventually it was going to come down to this, Dad," Gage said. "Everyone else in the family is juggling a full-time job and work here. Logan's got the bank job, and he still manages to do the finances for us. Jake coaches and works at the school, but still takes care of a lot of things around the ranch."

"Well, yes, but..." My mother's words trailed off.

"Gage fights fires and still helps care for the animals. I'm just adding my name to the ever-growing list of Hadleys looking to supplement their income. It's important at my age. And my stage of life." His gaze shot to Tasha, whose cheeks flushed pink.

My dad grew quiet and I knew what he was thinking. In times past, when the ranch brought in more money from mineral rights, he would have had the income to pay us kids to help out. But those days were behind us now.

"It's going to be okay," Gage interjected. "We'll figure it out."

"I can help more," Carrie said.

"But you're already so busy with the baby," Mom argued. "I don't want to wear everyone out."

"Eventually we all have to grow up and get real jobs," Dallas said.

Though he meant the words well, I don't think my father took them that way. To him, the Hadley acreage *was* the real job, the only one that really mattered. But surely he realized that times were different now.

Or maybe he didn't. Judging from the disappointment on his face, this news from Dallas was hitting hard.

After a moment Dad offered Dallas a gentle nod, then quietly said, "I understand, son."

And that's all that was spoken on the matter.

By the time we finished eating, I was so full I could barely move. But move I must. We still had presents to open, so we headed into the living room. Dessert could come later.

I sank into the oversized sofa and reached for a throw pillow to cover my too-full belly. Mason settled into the spot next to me and swiped my pillow, which he propped behind his neck. That lasted about ten seconds before he handed it back with a wink.

Mom kicked things off, handing out gifts right and left. We didn't have any methodology, but eventually everyone had a gift in front of them, even little Colt, whose eyes bugged as he looked at all of that wrapping paper.

In that moment, as I watched Colt open his gifts with wide-eyed wonder, my mind flashed back to so many of the Christmases I had shared in this very spot as a little child myself. Two older brothers, two younger brothers, all five of us opening gifts year after year.

I was six all over again, opening a Barbie doll.

Then I was twelve, opening a diary from my papaw.

Finally, at seventeen, a cell phone of my very own. Not an expensive one but my very first.

And I'd loved every moment of fun spent with all of my brothers.

My gaze traveled to the tree, filled with ornaments I'd loved since early childhood, many of which I'd made myself in Sunday school or VBS. I couldn't help but notice the tears in Summer's eyes as she watched Colt play with his new robot toy.

When I glanced her way, she swiped at her eyes with the back of her hand.

"I'm sorry, y'all," she said, her voice filled with emotion. "I haven't had a Christmas like this since my husband passed away. This is just too. . ." Her voice cracked. "Beautiful."

Gage pulled her close and slipped his arm over her shoulders, then gave her a kiss on the cheek.

This did it for Mom. She couldn't seem to stop the tears that flowed.

"You okay over there?" my dad asked.

She nodded and then insisted we keep going.

We did, but I could feel the shift in the room. Things were changing. . .and that wasn't a bad thing. Just different. And different was okay.

CHAPTER TWENTY-ONE

My gaze traveled up to the hand-painted sign on the living room wall from Ecclesiastes 3: THERE IS A TIME FOR EVERYTHING, AND A SEASON FOR EVERY ACTIVITY UNDER THE HEAVENS.

In that moment, the words felt providential. Holy.

As joy washed over me, flooding my soul, I knew I would cherish this particular Christmas forever. And I could tell from the looks on all the faces around me that they felt the same. I suddenly found myself overwhelmed with gratitude for the years I'd already shared with the people I loved, and even more grateful for the years ahead. I couldn't see them yet, but God could. And I could trust Him with them.

Suddenly all my concerns about the wedding washed away. No matter the weather. No matter the number of guests or the food eaten. My marriage to Mason wasn't about a day; it was about a lifetime. And watching my family in motion, I could almost imagine what our lifetime would be like.

I couldn't wait to see the look on Mason's face when he opened his gift. Before I could hand it to him, he passed one to me. I opened the tiny box to discover a vintage key inside. Attached, I found a note that read, "To our future."

"There's more," he said. "But it will come later."

I nodded and passed a package his way. When he opened his, I saw confusion register in his eyes. He held up the antique pocket watch and looked my way.

"It was your grandfather's," I explained. "Your aunt passed it to me, and I had it cleaned and repaired."

"Are you serious?" He stared at it, looking more perplexed than ever.

"She wanted you to have it, and I thought it would be a great chance to keep your family legacy going."

He leaned close and wrapped me in a hug so tight I could barely breathe. Clearly, he liked his gift. I had a couple of others, of course, but they weren't as personal.

Mom had special gifts for all the ladies in the room. She passed out bags to Bessie Mae, Carrie, Meghan, and me. I couldn't help but notice she'd left Tasha out, but my bestie didn't seem to mind.

"Now, I had these made special," Mom said as she looked from woman to woman. "Grace Oberdeen is the finest seamstress I know, and she did the honors. You can open them now."

And so we did. We pulled out matching Christmas aprons with our names embroidered on them.

"Oh my goodness!" Meghan's eyes widened. "You really did think of everything."

"Well, we're always wearing those old, worn aprons." Mom shrugged and shoved some loose paper back into a bag. "Figured we needed new ones." Her gaze traveled to Summer and Tasha. "Don't fret. I know how to reach Grace for more when the time comes."

And that settled it. Mom had fully made the transition. She would welcome not just Meghan but the other incoming family members as well. When the time came.

After we cleaned up the mess, Bob dozed off in one of the recliners, and Colt fell asleep on the sofa. Dad and my brothers went out to check on the animals, and we ladies kept up our conversation in the kitchen while we tidied up.

After a few minutes I realized Mom had disappeared on us. I searched her room but couldn't find her there. I finally located her in Bessie Mae's old room, lying on her back on the empty floor. For a moment I thought something tragic had happened. But I could see her belly moving up as she took in—and released—steady, successive breaths.

"Um, Mom?"

"Yes." She didn't bother looking my way.

"Are you okay?"

"Mm-hmm." She sighed, her eyes still closed.

Bessie Mae appeared in the doorway next to me and gasped when she saw Mom on the floor. "Did she fall? Do I need to call 911?"

"No." Mom's eyes popped open. "I'm just thinking."

"On the floor?" Bessie Mae asked. "Is that healthy?"

"I figured if it worked for King David it would work for me. The Bible says he laid prostrate before the Lord as an act of worship and obedience. So here I am."

Bessie Mae took several steps in her direction then turned back to face me. "Help me down, RaeLyn."

I looked her way, stunned. "Bessie Mae, are you sure?"

"Help me, honey. And no doubt I'll need even more help getting up, but this isn't the time to worry about that."

So I did just that. I helped my great-aunt ease her way down to the floor. Before long, she was flat on her back too, staring upward at the ceiling alongside Mom.

"If I start snoring, just roll me over," she said. "From what Bob tells me, I'm more dangerous on my back than a turtle." She grew silent and her eyes fluttered closed.

"What are you thinking about, Mom?" I peered down at her. "Are you worried about something?"

"No. Everyone else is going through changes. Transitions. I guess it's time I do the same, so I'm working on a plan. I'm just lying here, thinking about how I want to redo this room, to make it my own."

"Are you leaving Chuck behind in the other master?" Bessie Mae's eyes popped open.

"No. I guess I'll let him come along for the ride, if he plays nicely." Mom pointed to the far corner. "I'm thinking about putting in a recliner over there so I can sit and do my Bible study in the morning."

"I always loved this room in the mornings." Bessie Mae sighed.

"I think that's a fine idea," I chimed in. "Does Dad know?"

"Not yet. I'm still leading him along."

And at that moment I decided to do the only thing that made sense. I lay down on the floor in the tiny space between them. I took one of Mom's hands and one of Bessie Mae's, my heart flooding with joy. We lay there in the stillness, a quiet, peaceful trio of Hadleys, planning our futures.

Tasha popped her head in the door and looked our way. "What are we doing?"

"Trying out a new holiday workout," Mom said.

"Yes, it's all the rage," I added. "You lie very still and burn zero calories. It makes enough room for dessert."

"In that case, I'm in." Tasha took several steps in our direction and eased her way down on Bessie Mae's left. Before long, we were all staring at the popcorn ceiling.

Which Mom suddenly decided she wanted to change.

"Popcorn is so passé," she said. "I think a smooth ceiling would make more sense. This is the twenty-first century, you know. Out with the old and in with the new!"

"Amen," we all agreed.

"Is there a prayer meeting going on in here?"

A voice sounded from the hallway, and seconds later Carrie appeared in the open doorway. She took several quick steps toward us and said, "What in the world?"

"Don't panic," I said as she looked down with concern etched on her face. "We're just practicing synchronized sighing for the next family crisis."

"Well, hopefully there won't be a next crisis," she said. "We've had enough for one week, thank you very much."

"Agreed." I gestured for her to join us, and she lay down next to Tasha. "But for now we're trying to channel our inner decorators. Mom's decided she and Dad are moving into this room."

"Oh, that's amazing! It's about time!" Carrie gave her a thumbs-up. "What will you do with your current bedroom?"

"Dallas and Gage have never had their own rooms. They can fight over it."

"What about RaeLyn's room?" Carrie asked. "What's happening in there?"

"I'm turning it into my sewing room," Mom said.

Whoa. That was news to me. Then again, Mom had always wanted her own sewing room. Now she could finally have what she had always longed for.

We quietly talked through several decorating ideas, but one voice was noticeably absent.

Mom chose that moment to ask about Meghan, and I explained that she had dozed off on the sofa.

"Yeah, she's out like a light," Tasha confirmed. "Too much ham, I'm guessing."

"That's a shame," Mom said. "She's decorated their little place so cute. I'd love her input."

Dallas stuck his head in the door and looked from person to person. "Did I miss the memo? Is this some kind of postfeast nap session?"

"It's the horizontal holiday club," Tasha countered. "Women only."

"So unfair." He huffed off.

"Men." Tasha groaned and rolled my way. "Speaking of. . .you feeling better about the wedding, RaeLyn?"

"Yeah. I'm not having a nervous breakdown anymore."

"You were having a nervous breakdown?" This question came from my mother.

"Just a little one. I couldn't afford a big one. Too pricey. And too time consuming. I'll have more time after the wedding for a breakdown."

"Everything okay in here?"

I looked over to discover Jake standing in the doorway, holding baby Annalisa. My dad showed up on Jake's heels.

"What in the world's going on here?" Dad asked.

Mom didn't even give him a second look as she responded, "We're decorating, Chuck."

"Is that code for something else?"

"Nope. We're really decorating," she responded.

My dad quirked a brow. "In that position?"

"Mm-hmm," we all said in unison.

"Are you by any chance auditioning for the role of a throw rug?" he asked. "If so, you've got the part."

That got a laugh out of all of us.

My father took several steps toward us. "What's really going on here, Flora? Why are you doing this?"

Mom paused, then sat up and looked his way. "Are you okay with a few changes, Chuck?"

Concern etched his brow. "Well, I suppose that depends on what you mean by *changes*."

"Like, what if I get rid of our country-blue duck decor from the

1980s and go with something. . ."

"From the twenty-first century?" he asked.

"Different. Sometimes different is good. You know?"

"How much is this going to cost me?" Dad asked.

Mom gave him a pensive look. "Why is everything always about money?"

"Because it is," he said. "Life is expensive these days."

"I've been putting away a little money for a rainy day," Bessie Mae said. "I'd be happy to contribute to the redecoration fund. I'm the one who moved off and left the room empty, after all."

This offer from my aunt put my dad in a precarious position. It would wreck his pride to have Bessie Mae pay for his new bedroom furniture.

"No, it's okay," Dad said. "We'll get new stuff. I saw there's a new secondhand shop going in in Athens."

"Think again," Mom said. "I'm shopping in Dallas. I can't wait to pick out a new bedroom suite from one of those big, fancy furniture stores."

Dad grunted. But I knew he would go along with it.

Bob showed up next, eyes widening as he found us all on the floor.

"Oh! I saw this once at a revival meeting. Folks were laid out all over the floor like this. Slain in the Spirit, they called it."

"I'm not slain, Bob," Bessie Mae said. "I'm Baptist. But I *will* be slain if someone doesn't get me up."

"I think it's important to get a photo first," Dallas said. "Because nobody's gonna believe this."

And before we could argue the point, he grabbed his phone and snapped a picture.

"If that ends up on social media I'm never speaking to you again." Mom shot him a warning look.

He put his hands up and backed away.

"All right, ladies, back on our feet." Mom stretched but didn't rise just yet. "There's a mighty lot of pie in that kitchen, and I'm not going to let the men eat all of it."

Bessie Mae attempted to roll over onto her side and let out a groan.

"Do you need help?" Mason extended his hand.

My aunt nodded and reached to grip his hand. "You betcha. I'm not exactly a spring chicken. More like a well-seasoned hen."

He helped ease her to a standing position, then extended his hand to help my mother as well. She stood with a grunt and then looked around the room. "This is actually a really nice space. And I like that the windows are on the west. The early morning sun won't be a problem."

"Facing west is where it's at." Mason gave me a wink and then offered his hand to help me up. "Unless you're getting married in a field at sunset. Then it's a no-go." He grinned and then helped me up as well.

"Thanks." I gave him a little kiss.

"I hate to interrupt this sit-in, but I've got a little surprise up my sleeve," Mason said. "Would you care to trade in that plush carpet for a drive?"

"Right now?" Bessie Mae asked. "Before we've had pie?"

"No, we can have pie first," Mason replied. "But if no one minds, I plan to steal my bride after that. I haven't given RaeLyn her real Christmas present yet."

My heart rate began to skip to overtime as I saw the twinkle in his eye.

"And this one's a little too big to wrap up with ribbons and bows."

CHAPTER TWENTY-TWO

"Ready for a little drive?" Mason asked after we finished up our dessert.

"Absolutely." I rose and carried our pie plates to the sink. "Let me grab a coat."

All the tension melted as he pulled me into his arms and planted the sweetest kiss on my lips.

"Well, when you put it like that. . ." I kissed him back. Soundly. "Where are we headed?"

"There's something I've been wanting to show you. Something I think—hope—you'll like."

"Sure." My heart rate skipped as I pondered the reality of what might be happening.

"I've kept you waiting long enough," he said. "You've been very patient with me over the past few weeks."

"Meaning, I've been hanging in limbo, not knowing where I'm going to spend the next few years of my life?"

"Hopefully the rest of your life. If you're happy with it, I mean."

I had a feeling I would be.

We walked to his truck, and he opened the passenger door. I climbed inside, shivering—as much from excitement as from the cold. Mason talked about plans for the wedding as he drove up the highway toward town. I could tell from the little quiver in his voice that he was nervous. Excited, maybe? Still, I couldn't make any sense out of where we were headed. The Jackson place was in the complete opposite direction, so clearly not there.

My imagination kicked into overdrive. Had he picked out a new piece of property, perhaps? Maybe close to Tasha's?

We drove through Mabank, passing some of the businesses, and I smiled when I saw Dot and Enrique outside of what had once been a local Mexican restaurant, now boarded up. We pulled into the parking lot and Mason rolled down his window.

"Well, hello, you two," Dot said. "Where you headed?"

"I'm off to show the lady her Christmas present," Mason said.

Dot's eyes lit up. "Are you, now?"

He put his finger over his lips, and for the first time I realized Dot must've been in on this somehow. Whatever *this* was.

To her credit, she just looked my way, smiled, and said, "Merry Christmas, RaeLyn. And happy upcoming wedding day!"

"Feliz Navidad!" Enrique called out. "And *¡Feliz día de la boda!* We will celebrate with churros!"

We waved, and Mason put his window back up then pulled out onto the road once again.

I glanced out the window at Enrique and Dot as he pulled her into his arms and pressed a kiss onto her forehead.

"I've never seen this side of Dot before," I said. "It's kind of. . .lovely."

"Being in love definitely suits her," Mason agreed. "And I really like Enrique. That new restaurant of his is going to be a keeper. The man is an honest-to-goodness five-star chef."

I paused as the realization of what he'd just said set in. "So is that where he's opening his restaurant? Where Consuelo's used to be?"

"Yep. Right there."

"Wow. So in less than a week he's gotten married, agreed to cook for our wedding, and is planning to open a restaurant?"

"Hey, when the winds of change are coming, you move fast."

"Clearly." I glanced back but could no longer see the parking lot. "This is all very exciting."

"I looked him up online. Before he went to work for the cruise line, he had a really fancy restaurant in Mexico City. People came from all over to taste his food."

"I can't get over the fact that we have a world-class chef making churros at our wedding."

"We'll tell our children about it someday. How our friend Dot ran off and got married and came back with a wedding caterer."

"Our children? We have children already?" A nervous laugh followed, but it was clear we probably were a lot more blessed than I had realized to have Enrique on board, not just at the wedding but as a fixture in this town.

While we chatted, I paid attention to the direction Mason was driving, toward the lake. Interesting. I felt completely lost and clueless. As someone who loved to be in control, I was really unnerved by this feeling.

He turned off down a familiar road on the Gun Barrel City side of the lake, and I felt my breath catch in my throat as a familiar field came into view, one I'd fallen in love with last spring during bluebonnet season. This whole area was absolutely breathtaking in the spring and summer, with flowers in abundance.

Today, of course, it sat still and barren of color under a heavy December sky. But I could almost imagine what it would look like in a few short months.

My heart raced in anticipation as we drew nearer to the lake. No wonder he'd been so quiet about all of this. Mason knew how much I loved this stretch of Cedar Creek Lake. The properties on this side of town were the best to be had.

When we got to Nadine's beautiful lake house, he pulled into the driveway.

"What are we doing at Nadine's?" I asked. "Does she know we're coming?"

"She does. I told her we'd stop by around six thirty, so she's ready for us. Hope you don't mind a little pit stop."

"I never mind hanging out with Nadine." It would be nice to see her, in fact. No doubt the poor woman was spending Christmas alone this year. We should have invited her to our family celebration. I wished I'd thought of it sooner.

We got out of the car, and I stared at the huge home with its curved drive and vast yard. Even in the middle of winter the gorgeous tree-lined driveway was breathtaking. Mason slipped his arm around my shoulder, and we made our way up the flagstone walkway to the expansive front porch with its heavy wooden posts and gorgeous light fixture.

He rang the bell and seconds later the door opened. Nadine stood there, all smiles.

"C'mon in, y'all," she said. "I've been waiting for you."

I stepped inside the spectacular home and was blown away, as always, by the sheer magnitude of the space. And that Texas decor. It wowed me. Off in the distance, something smelled delicious. Had she been baking again? Nothing this woman did surprised me anymore. She could decorate. She could bake. She could arrange flowers. Truly, Nadine Henderson was a wonder.

"I'm sorry to pull you away from your wedding planning and all," she said. "But we have a little something-something for you, RaeLyn. An early wedding present. Follow me."

She led the way into the oversized kitchen. I ran my hand along the granite island, cold to the touch but gorgeous to look at. Nadine reached into one of the kitchen drawers and came out with a small pouch. She turned to me with a smile and extended it my way.

"Here you go, honey. Happy wedding!"

I took the pouch in hand, surprised by the weight of it. "What's in here?"

"Open it and see."

So I did. I untied the ribbon on top and jabbed my fingers inside, then pried out. . .

"Keys?" A whole set of them, in fact.

"Mm-hmm." A bright, wide smile lit her face as she shifted her gaze to Mason.

I looked at him, completely mystified.

"Welcome home, RaeLyn," he said as he gestured to the expansive kitchen with its breathtaking decor. "And. . .Feliz Navidad!"

I turned to Mason, my heart in my throat. "How did you. . . When did you. . . Why did you. . ."

He put his finger over my lips. "All the questions can come later. For now, welcome to your new home."

"My new home?" None of this made sense. This was Nadine's home, the one she had inherited in her divorce from Clayton.

In that moment I had that weird out-of-body sensation one sometimes gets before passing out. Was he really saying that—

"It's all yours, honey." Nadine's eyes filled with tears. "Really and truly. Please forgive us for keeping it a secret for so long, but there were some details to iron out with the purchase."

"The. . .purchase?" Surely Mason had not purchased this mansion on the lake. It was too much. Way too much.

"She gave me a deal I couldn't refuse," Mason said. "The word *discount* doesn't even begin to describe it."

"Consider it my wedding present." Nadine walked over and threw her arms around my neck. "This home was meant for a loving, godly couple. With Clayton out of the picture, my heart's just not in it. And I'm not interested in using it as a vacation rental investment anymore either. Too much to keep up with. I'd rather see it filled with people I love, people who have always treated me like family."

"But, Nadine. . ." I argued.

She raised her hand, as if to stop me from arguing with her. "I'm so happy it's going to the two of you. If anyone deserves a beautiful home to raise their family in, it's you two. I can just picture all of the baby showers and birthday parties you'll have out on that deck. And from what we all know, it's what your papaw would've wanted, RaeLyn."

My eyes filled with tears as she mentioned my grandfather. He'd once had his eye on this particular patch of land, after all. Back then, he wanted to put cabins on it, rentals for tourists to enjoy. How ironic that he might one day have great-grandchildren running and playing on this very piece of land. I got misty-eyed just thinking about it.

"I. . .I. . ." I hugged her so hard I thought I heard her ribs pop.

Nope, that was just Mason, opening a bottle of fake champagne. Which he poured into glasses and passed around.

"Now, I'm not saying you have to keep my furniture," Nadine said. "It wouldn't hurt my feelings one little bit if you swapped it out. But I sold the house fully furnished so that you could, at least for now, have a bed to sleep in and a sofa to sit on."

"Among other things." The whole house was decked out with that heavy, expensive wood furniture that felt like old Texas. It was my cup of tea, for sure.

My heart soared with joy. "Nadine, I can't think of a thing I would change. I love the colors, I love the furnishings, I love it all."

"Well, good. But if you do, don't ever worry about what I might think about it. This is your house now."

Those words caused my heart to swell with joy. Today I was a homeowner. Two days from now I would be a wife. And soon my husband and I would live in this home—this beautiful, marvelous home—with a passel of kids.

And a dog.

I couldn't do without my Riley. She would have to adjust to life on the lake instead of the farm, but I knew she would manage just fine.

Nadine took a couple of sips and then looked at her watch. "I'm gonna head on out," she said. "My sister is waiting on me. I kept my place in town, by the way. But you have to come see the sweet little place I've purchased in Kaufman. I plan to go back and forth between the two for now. But I'll be around."

"You'd better!" I said. And I meant it. Over the past year Nadine had become a friend, a mentor, and now a benefactor.

I gave her another long hug, and she parted ways with us.

I turned to face Mason, still unable to form proper sentences. "I. . . You. . . How in the world?"

"I've been noticeably absent over the past couple weeks, and I'm sorry. We ran into a hiccup with the inspection, and it took a while to iron out, but all's well that ends well."

"I'd say!"

We made our way from room to room, and my heart leaped for joy as I took it all in.

"Look, RaeLyn." He pointed to the gorgeous study. A heavy leather armchair sat near the huge bay window with a knitted throw draped over the back of it. I could picture myself here, sipping coffee in the early morning hours or watching the sun go down in the evening.

"Smells so good in here." Mason breathed in a deep breath. "It's that cedar they used for the bookshelves. Love it."

"Me too."

We stepped inside and I took it all in. The room wasn't pretentious. I wouldn't call it showy or grand. But it had a certain type of elegance in its simplicity. I imagined a lot of words could grow in this room—articles for *Mabank Happenings*, and perhaps more.

A book, maybe?

I gazed up at those beautiful cedar shelves that lined the walls. Nadine had left a few books behind, but I had plenty of my own to fill quite a few spaces. The rest of the shelves would be filled with framed photos and decor, things that made me feel at home. Because I could write best when I felt at home.

Like I did in my little room in the Hadley house.

Only, it wasn't home anymore. Not for long, anyway.

I turned my attention to the expansive mahogany desk that sat near the bay window. It was polished to a lovely sheen. I could imagine myself here, looking out over Cedar Creek Lake, tap-tap-tapping on the keys of my laptop.

In the daylight, the view from this window was spectacular. Even now, under the shadows of evening, I could see the pier stretching out over the water. Two Adirondack chairs sat on the deck on the end.

I would spend a lot of time in those chairs, my hand in Mason's. I could just picture it now. The lake would inspire me to write. The breeze off the water would carry my imagination to places I'd only dreamed of.

"Look, Mason. The window points west. We can watch a lot of sunsets here."

"Yes, we can. This is a great room."

"It's not just a room." I turned to face him. "It's the place where magic will take place."

"Okay, then. Who am I to disrupt magic?"

I released a slow breath, the weight of this gift now fully settling over me.

He had done all of this. . .for me. And I would spend the rest of my life showing him just how grateful I was.

CHAPTER TWENTY-THREE

Mason pulled me close and pressed a kiss onto my cheek. "I hope you don't mind, but I've invited your whole family over."

"They know?" I asked.

He shook his head. "Nope. I just told them to be at Nadine's house on the lake at seven thirty for a big surprise. They know nothing."

"I'm guessing Mom's already figured it out, and Bessie Mae's probably wrapping up leftover ham to bring with her."

"No need." He opened the refrigerator to reveal several trays of meats, cheeses, and desserts. "Nadine outdid herself. I told your mom not to bring a thing, just to come hungry."

"Wow!" How in the world had he pulled this off? Overcome with emotion, I punched him in the arm. Not very romantic, but it was the only thing that came to me in the moment.

"Ouch!" He rubbed at his arm playfully. "What did I do?"

"You managed to pull off the plot twist of the century. I don't know how you did it, but this is a sure sight better than the Jackson place."

He looked mortally wounded by this. "I cannot believe you actually thought I was buying the Jackson place. It's old, run-down, and overgrown."

"I would've been happy there, Mason." I threw my arms around his neck and gave him a big kiss on the cheek. "I'd be happy anywhere, as long as you're there."

"I really am sorry I've been so absent over the past couple weeks. We had the closing a few days back—the day of the bridesmaids' brunch, actually—and there were some complications with the inspection like I mentioned, something to do with the electrical panel. But that's all cleared up now and the paperwork is over and done with. We'll add your name to it after the wedding, but for now it just made sense to do everything in my name. I hope you don't mind."

"Don't mind a bit." Though my thoughts were reeling over all of this. I was the planner. The spreadsheet maker. The one who took the reins. How did he know I would be wonderfully, blissfully okay with all of this?

Because he knew me.

And if I ever had any doubts about becoming Mrs. Mason Fredericks, they were washed away in an instant.

"If you like, you can go ahead and start moving some of your things over right away," he said. "I was thinking we could stay here for our wedding night and leave the next morning for the airport."

"That sounds a lot better than staying in a hotel in Dallas," I agreed. Even the Gaylord couldn't begin to compete with this.

"I don't know if you realize it, but the land is bigger than just the lot the house sits on."

"Oh?"

"Yes." He held my hand and led the way outdoors to the back deck. We walked a distance, out to the point where the deck met the pier, and he pointed at the section of land to our left. "It actually goes about two acres to the east. I think that's the section your grandfather was hoping to put cabins on once upon a time."

"Really? How do you know?"

"I took a look at the original plans, which I found registered with the county—and it looks simple enough. If you ever want to do that, I mean."

"Put cabins on the property, you mean? For guests?"

"Yes. They could be rented individually. And there's a forested area between our house and where they would sit, so I don't think we would get much noise or foot traffic from the guests. We could even put up a little fence to separate the areas."

"Mason, you think of everything. And how did you know to look up all of that, anyway?"

"Dot. She's known from the get-go about all of this. We started talking before she ever left for her Caribbean cruise. I knew I would need her help, and she was invaluable."

"If you tell me that you knew about Enrique before the rest of us, I'm really going to flip."

"Nope. Didn't know about Enrique." He laughed. "But Nadine knew where to look for the plans for the original cabins. She pulled them, and I was able to see just how big the property really is. That's another place where we ran into a problem with the inspection, by the way, because the property lines were different on the current map from the original. They needed to be reconciled."

"But that's all ironed out now?"

"It is. And I'm happy to say we're now the proud owner of five and a half acres of prime Texas lakefront property with one of the most solidly built homes in Henderson County."

"I can't believe this is real. Pinch me."

He pretended to pinch me but ended up giving me a kiss instead. I shivered, in part from the cold and in part from nerves. This was all too much.

He slipped off his coat and draped it over my shoulders.

I gripped his hand, and we stared out over the dark waters of the lake, the overhead lights from the deck reflecting off the water. Suddenly I could see just how my life would be. Mason and I would live here. Entertain here. Host Bible studies and small groups. Have Christmas parties. Raise children.

Teach them to swim, to fish, to kayak.

Throw birthday parties for the little ones. Host slumber parties with their friends.

It was all too much. I couldn't hold the tears back any longer. They fell like rain—tears of joy, of shock, and of genuine gratitude for what God had done in my life, bringing me this amazing, godly man.

Mason pulled me into his arms and kissed me soundly. "Happy tears, I hope?"

"Very. I feel a connection to my family here, on this property. To my papaw, especially. To Tilly." I pressed back the lump that rose in my throat.

"This is more than I ever dreamed of, Mason."

"It just felt right."

"That's because it is." I brushed back the tears that brimmed my lashes. "You didn't just give me a house, Mason. You literally gave back a piece of my family."

"Speaking of, I know it's a fifteen-minute drive to your parents' place," he said. "But that's not too far, is it?"

"Not at all. And it's a beautiful drive."

He led the way back inside and we slowly walked each room, dreaming of all the things those rooms would one day hold. Then we headed into the kitchen so I could give those high-end appliances a closer look.

True to his word, my whole family showed up at seven thirty. It only took a minute to share the news that this home—this gorgeous, over-the-top home—was mine.

And in that moment, in the grand spacious foyer of my new house, my mom forgave Mason for moving me away from the Hadley acreage.

"I just can't believe you did this, Mason," she exclaimed. "We've always loved this home."

"I know." He gave her a knowing look. "I pay attention."

Clearly.

"It's truly a dream house." Mom gestured to the grand living room. "My stars, but we're going to have some amazing get-togethers in here, aren't we!"

I agreed, we would.

Bessie Mae nodded. "Yep. But I'm gonna need a map or one of those GPS thingies to find the kitchen in this place. Everything is so spread out."

I led her into the spacious kitchen, and Bob tagged along on our heels. When we got there, she ran her hand along the island and gasped. "Now this is a real kitchen. I say we renovate yours to look more like this, Bob."

"Ours," he countered. "It's our kitchen, not mine."

"I'll call it mine when it looks like this." She slipped her arm through his. "At the very least, can we have a new oven?"

"Sweetheart, you can have a new oven, a new refrigerator with ice in the door, a bigger pantry. . .whatever you like. *Mi casa es su casa.*"

"Now Bob speaks Spanish too!" Bessie Mae threw her arms around his neck. "We don't have to do all of that, Bob. Not right away, anyway.

But I would love a new oven."

"We'll shop for one just after the holidays. Now let's give this beautiful house a closer look, shall we?"

"We shall."

We walked into the master bedroom, and Mom practically swooned as she looked at the large four-poster bed with its tufted headboard upholstered in a soft cream fabric. She ran her fingertips along the deep button tufting and sighed.

"Now *this* is a bedroom suite," she said. "Pretty sure that bedding didn't come from Walmart."

Behind us, my dad cleared his throat.

"I'll take you shopping when I get back home from my honeymoon, Mom," I said. "You can make your new bedroom as beautiful as this."

"Hopefully not *quite* as beautiful as this," my dad countered. "Feels like a hotel in here. I'm more at home with a simpler style, thank you very much."

"We'll meet in the middle, Chuck," Mom said. "How would that be?"

"Reasonable. And for the record, I'm okay with the color scheme here. All of this..." He gestured to the plush bedding. "What color would you call this?"

"Sage green," I said. "And honey brown." And that's when it hit me. "Just like the wedding colors." Oh my goodness. And Mason hadn't even planned it that way. Nadine had picked out these colors ages ago.

We found Carrie, Jake, and Annalisa in a small bedroom opposite the master.

"I think this would make a great baby's room," Carrie exclaimed. "I can imagine it all decked out with a crib and dresser and changing table. And it's super close to the master. That's going to come in really handy, I promise. You'll want the baby close by but not necessarily in the same room."

She went off on a tangent, sharing plans for the child—or children—I would have one day. I didn't mind too much. There would be children. I felt sure of it. Still, she was overlooking one key detail.

"Right now, I'm still in wedding-planning mode, remember? And tomorrow morning we have to pull together that wedding area—get the bales of hay onto the field, set up the arbor, wait for the events company to come set up the tent and dance floor." I went into a lengthy list of all we had to do.

But somewhere mid-sentence Mason pulled me into his arms and kissed me. Soundly. When I tried to start talking again, he kissed me one more time.

"Each day has enough trouble of its own," he said. "Let's just focus on today."

But I couldn't. This house had my head spinning in a thousand directions at once.

Everyone split up, each person heading off to look at something new. Mom and Dad disappeared on us altogether, but we found them a short while later standing out on the deck, looking over the waters of the lake.

"I can't help but think of your papaw," my dad said as I stepped into the place next to him. "This was the very piece of land he always wanted to own. And now he's done it. . .through you. You've kept his legacy going, RaeLyn."

"Mason's kept his legacy going."

"Welp, Mason took your papaw's dream and gave it a Texas-sized upgrade." These words came from Mom. "I'm sure your grandfather never could have pictured anything as grand as this."

"It is grand," I said. "But it's also homey. I just love all of the Texas decor. Right up my alley."

Mason stepped into the spot next to my dad. "Do you remember when I said that I had to see a man about a horse?"

"Yes." I remembered, all right.

"Well, that man was your father. I asked him if he would help us set up a corral and barn."

"W–what?" I looked back and forth between my dad and Mason. "Dad, you knew Mason was buying this house, and you didn't mention it?"

Mom looked equally as stunned. "Chuck? You kept a secret this big?"

"I did." He squared his shoulders, looking more than a little proud of himself. "And for the record, I think my acting skills over the past few days could have earned me an Academy Award, don't you?"

No kidding.

"We've got plenty of property for a couple of horses," Mason said. "And I think we can put in a small barn as well. I've picked out a spot." He winked at me. "It's facing west."

"Are you serious?"

"Yep."

"I know Delilah is set to deliver any day now," my dad added. "So Mason and I have decided you can bring her and the foal here when they're ready. We figured you'd be missing ranch life over here, so a few animals would be helpful."

"Perfect! Thank you, Dad!" My mind reeled. If we had the space I could also have a couple of goats. Maybe some chickens. Riley would feel right at home.

Within seconds I had the whole thing planned out in my head.

Until I remembered I still had a wedding to plan. It came first.

A short while later we drove back home. Well, my childhood home. Saying good night to Mason was harder than ever, but by the time he left I was so exhausted I could barely stand, and we had a big day tomorrow.

Afterward, I headed into my bedroom to settle in for the night. It felt weird, knowing this would be my last time in this little bedroom. Tomorrow night would be spent at Tasha's place, after all. But this room? This precious, beautiful space? I'd spent twenty-seven years of my life here. In this small space I'd played with Barbies, learned my multiplication tables, written in my diary, confessed my love for Mason as a teen, mourned his move to College Station as an eighteen-year-old, and celebrated his return just a year ago.

I'd spent hours sleeping in this twin-sized bed, and nearly as many sitting at the desk, working on homework or articles. The walls were filled with memorabilia from my childhood. Could I really trade all of that in for the fancy master bedroom at Nadine's place?

Er, my new place.

Why, yes. Yes, I could. And I would, starting Saturday night. I would swap out my lazy daisy comforter for that high-end bedding, and I wouldn't even look back for a moment.

CHAPTER TWENTY-FOUR

Christmas Day—and night—felt like a fairy tale. When I woke up on Friday morning, I literally had to pinch myself to make sure I hadn't dreamed it all. But when I checked my messages and saw texts from Tasha, Nadine, Summer, and several other friends, I knew I had not.

Tasha was beside herself. She sent a string of messages:

"I'm so thrilled for you!"

"You totally deserve this!"

"Can we have a slumber party?"

To which I responded, "We're having one. Tonight. At your place."

I wanted to revel in the news about the house, but there was no time. We had to get everything set up before this evening's rehearsal. The events company would arrive at one o'clock with the tent, tables, chairs, lighting, and so on. In the meantime, we had some bales of hay to put out. But before any of that could take place, I had to get my ducks in a row. Er, my wedding dress, shoes, veil, and so on.

Everything I would need for tomorrow must be packed up and ready to take to Tasha's tonight.

That would take some doing. I hadn't created a spreadsheet for this, since Tasha only tossed out the idea a few days back. Still, it sounded like a lot of fun, a bridesmaids' bash the night before the wedding.

I showered and dressed quickly, then pulled together all the belongings I could think of. I made a master list to make sure I hadn't overlooked anything. If I did, surely someone would bring it to me. God didn't give me four brothers for nothing.

After getting everything prepared and ready, I headed out to the living room to find that Mom was hard at work tidying up.

Bessie Mae arrived a short while later with bags and bags of groceries, which she deposited on the kitchen counter. "RaeLyn, I'll try not to be underfoot while you're working," she said. "But I just *couldn't* bake your wedding cake in that ridiculous oven at Bob's house."

"*Your* house, Bessie Mae," I reminded her.

"My house. I just couldn't. But since you're mostly working outside today, would you mind if I baked your cake here?"

"Heavens, no." What a funny question. "Why in the world would I mind? I can't wait to see it!"

We talked back through the flavors—white with strawberry filling for the top two tiers and Italian cream cake for the bottom tier. I showed her the picture of the cake I'd found online, with its messy textured frosting, white silk roses, and lots of faux evergreen and frosted cranberries.

"I'll never understand why folks make the frosting so messy like that," she responded after giving it a closer look. "But it certainly makes my job easier."

"It's the trend," I said. And I knew it would be easier than trying to get perfectly smooth frosting. Bessie Mae's baking skills were stellar, but she wasn't a pro decorator.

Mason and all four of my brothers had taken the day off to help Dad set up the arbor and hay bales, so I turned my attention to that as soon as Bessie Mae and I wrapped up our planning session. Summer and Tasha would arrive at eleven to help me with decorating. And Meghan was working a shift at the hospital, but promised to join us when she got off at three.

Things were really coming together. And I would oversee it all like a stage director putting on a play, my trusty spreadsheet serving as the script.

When Mason arrived at the back door at ten, I greeted him with the biggest hug and kiss ever.

"Somebody's anxious." He laughed and pulled me in for another sweet peck on the lips.

"Just needed to make sure all of this is real." I pinched my eyes shut, as if willing it to be so. "I'm so afraid it's all a dream and I'm going to wake up." At that, my eyes popped open.

Mason gave a warm, easy laugh "I'm real. It's real. It's happening, RaeLyn." He shot a quick glance to the field just behind us. "Well, after we get set up. Do you have a plan?"

Was he kidding? I had every minute mapped out, all the way through to our rehearsal tonight.

He laughed and brushed a loose hair from my face. "Just joking. I know you better than that. And I've memorized my part of the spreadsheet." He reached into his pocket and came out with a folded piece of paper.

Oh, wow. He really had brought the spreadsheet. Talk about a validation.

We made our way out to the field. I carried my laptop, my guide for all things wedding related. Riley followed along on my heels, as if to say, *Don't leave me out of the plans, please!* I could never! Though I did need a plan for her tomorrow evening. Otherwise she might try to steal the show.

A low rumble sounded from the barn, and I looked up to see my father easing our old John Deere onto the field. The front-end loader cradled two bales of hay, which he deposited into place just in front of us.

"Mornin', y'all!" Dad called out. "We've got some work to do!"

We did, indeed.

It took some doing, but we finally got all of those bales lined up and in their proper places. My heart swelled with joy to see my plan coming to life before my eyes, especially that lovely center aisle, which I would walk down tomorrow.

Next came the arbor. The guys wrestled it into the spot front and center. Then, on either side of the arbor, they set up all of those flocked Christmas trees we'd been gathering over the past weeks. Nestled together in varying shapes and sizes, the flocked trees would be covered in twinkling white lights. From a distance, you could barely tell they were artificial. Sitting out here in the field like this, they blended in with the scenery.

Mom and Carrie went to work on the lights after we finished getting the trees in place. Dad had already worked out a plan to provide electricity for those. I had to leave that part up to him.

While the ladies strung lights, Mason and I met in the spot where we would exchange vows tomorrow afternoon. Hands clasped, we turned to survey the hay bales with tears in our eyes.

Okay, I was the one with tears in my eyes. Mason was apparently having some sort of allergic reaction to the hay, based on the sneezing fit that erupted.

"I'll take an antihistamine tomorrow, I promise." He laughed and swiped at his nose, then started sneezing all over again.

"Preferably a nondrowsy formula," I countered.

Otherwise, we might have a wedding ceremony folks would always remember but for the wrong reasons.

Mom joined us shortly after and offered her stamp of approval on the way things were coming together. Then she peered upward at the bright, cloudless sky above us. "Do we put out the quilts today or tomorrow?"

I wanted to see how it would all look but also realized the weather could easily take a turn, so leaving them out overnight wasn't an option. In the end we set everything up—with quilts—to establish the best look. I took pictures, and then we folded them back up and pinned numbers to them so that tomorrow's setup would be a breeze.

When Tasha and Summer arrived at eleven, we turned our attention to the arbor, a blank canvas ready to be decorated. I had opted for silk flowers in sage, ivory, and—of course—accents of honey brown. We worked on that gorgeous setup, covering it with all the flowers, silk fabric sheers, and gorgeous ribbons, then stood back and examined our handiwork. Breathtaking!

I snapped a picture with my phone and sent it to Nadine. She responded with one word: "Wow!"

I had to agree.

I followed that text up with a gushing thank-you for all she had done for Mason and me over the past few weeks. I owed the woman so very much.

Just about the time we finished the arbor, I remembered all the antique candelabras we needed to get from the storeroom of Trinkets and Treasures. Logan offered to walk over with me while Mom and the other ladies worked on the bows that would adorn them.

Logan led the way into the dark storeroom, and I bumped my foot on something. After letting out a loud "Ouch!" I paused to rub my aching foot.

I looked at what I'd hit. That Frasier Oil sign. I'd forgotten all about it.

Logan flipped on the light and then pointed at the sign. "Hey, where did that come from?"

"Buck Adler brought it over last weekend," I explained. "The day we moved Bessie Mae."

My brother gave the sign a closer look. "Seems to be in great condition. Is it here on consignment, or did you buy it from him outright?"

"Dad bought it from him. Paid three hundred dollars. I know that's a lot, but he seems to think he'll make his money back and then some."

"We've had good luck with some of these signs." Logan gave it a closer look. "I think it's worth a whole lot more than three hundred dollars."

If anyone would know that, Logan would. We leaned heavily on him with financial matters related to our antique shop.

"Apparently, Buck had some sort of falling-out with Frasier Oil and just wanted to be rid of it," I explained.

"He's not the only one. Half the folks in the county are fed up with Frasier." Logan ran his fingers over the raised lettering on the sign then looked my way. "Know what? We should list it online. I'll check the appraisal. And I might even get in touch with Frasier to see if they want it. Sometimes these companies buy back their own memorabilia."

I hadn't given it a close look but had no choice. The sign was blocking the candelabras I needed, so I hefted it out of the way, turning it sideways in the process. That's when I happened to notice a sticker on the back of the sign.

"What's that?" my brother asked.

I brushed the dirt off it and gave it a closer look. "Looks like it's a signature? Not sure."

"If this sign was autographed by the man who designed it, it's probably worth more than we think." He took a picture of the name scribbled on the back of the sign and then looked it up online.

Logan turned to me, wide-eyed. "Whoa."

"What?"

"RaeLyn, this piece could be worth a fortune. I say we call Frasier right now and let them know we have it. If what I'm reading is true, it could bring in enough money to cover your whole wedding."

"Wow." That would be great news for my dad, for sure.

We hauled the candelabras out to the field, and then Logan headed off to make the call to Frasier Oil. I wondered if I should call Buck to let him know the piece was worth significantly more. In the meantime, I filled my dad in.

"Don't count your chickens before they're hatched," I said. "Just in case Logan's wrong. But if he's right. . ."

My dad stared at me, bug-eyed. "Man, wouldn't that be something."

Logan returned from his call a few minutes later, just as we got the bows affixed to the candelabras. I could tell from his expression that he had good news.

"They came in with an initial offer of ten thousand dollars."

"W–what?" My dad looked stunned. "Are you serious? I only paid Buck three hundred dollars for that sign."

"They knew all about Buck Adler." Logan shoved his phone into his pocket. "Did you know there's a lawsuit between them?"

"Yes." My dad nodded. "Buck told us that they didn't renew his lease. I was confused about the details, but he said he was fighting it and he'd hired an attorney."

"He hired an attorney all right," Logan said. "But they had some choice things to say about that too. Apparently, there was some sort of dispute over whether or not Buck actually owns that piece of land. Someone else laid claim to it. And in the meantime, Buck fell behind on his property taxes."

"Oh, wow." My dad paused and grew silent. "Probably spent all that money on attorneys and didn't have anything left to pay the county or school district. That's too bad. Now I really feel awful about only paying him three hundred dollars for that sign. Poor guy."

"Not sure if he's a poor guy or not," I interjected. "I've had this niggling concern about him all along. The day we bought the sign from him he said he would rather burn his place to the ground than lose it to the likes of Frasier Oil."

Logan released a slow breath. "That's troubling."

"Exactly. And if he thinks he's about to lose his land—or that Frasier might end up with it—he might do something crazy."

"Like burn the whole place down." Logan repeated the line.

"Yeah."

"So, do we call the police?" my dad asked. "Because I'm more inclined to tell Buck about the ten thousand dollars. Maybe split it with him?"

Logan shook his head. "Before you split it with him, Dad, I think we need to make sure he's not the one behind the fire that could have destroyed our whole livelihood."

My father's nose wrinkled. "Well, when you put it like that. . ."

I snapped a picture of the arbor and bales of hay; then we headed inside to grab a quick bite to eat before the events company arrived. When we got in the house, I decided to place a quick call to Deputy Warren to get his take on the situation with Buck Adler.

After I explained everything, he agreed that the comment about burning the place down should be taken seriously.

"And remember, he had the gas can, which he refilled after Christmas Eve service," I reminded Shawn. "So, as far as we know, he could be ready to strike again."

"I mean. . ." Shawn paused. "I suppose that's possible. I'll talk to my sergeant and the fire chief. I'm sure we'll pay Buck a visit. But, RaeLyn?"

"Yeah?"

"Aren't you supposed to be getting married or something?"

I laughed. "Yes. We're setting up for the wedding now."

"Then go do that. And don't worry about any of this. Just leave it to us, okay?"

I promised to try.

We wrapped up lunch in a hurry—sandwiches and chips not taking long to wolf down—and headed out to meet the events team when they arrived at one o'clock. I couldn't help but cry when I saw that tent go up. And as the dance floor went in, as each table went into place, each chair was set up, each centerpiece placed, my joy rose exponentially.

Tomorrow night, I would be Mrs. Mason Fredericks.

I would live in that gorgeous house on the lake.

With my dog.

And my husband.

Not in that order.

And someday, perhaps, 2.5 kids.

Okay, three kids.

But right now? I would make sure the mistletoe was hung from that fabulous chandelier in the center spot, above the table where Bessie Mae's cake would sit in its place of honor.

Which is exactly what I was doing when Landon James arrived and needed help with the setup for the music. He'd brought a couple of tables from the church, one to be placed at the back of the field and another for the tent. Hopefully he had everything else he needed because I was clueless.

"Trust me," he said with a smile.

And I did. These were the kinds of things I couldn't put on my spreadsheet because I simply had to trust.

By the time Meghan arrived at three fifteen, we were almost done in the tent. She looked pretty tired as she made the rounds, but she seemed duly impressed by our work.

"Wow, RaeLyn." Her eyes misted over as she took in the space through fresh eyes. "This is beyond gorgeous."

"Thank you. I love it!"

And I truly did.

Meghan headed over to greet Logan, but something about their exchange seemed a bit off. I couldn't put my finger on it, though.

I approached Tasha to ask her opinion on the matter as Meghan and Logan took a seat at a table in the far corner opposite the dance floor.

"Do you think Meghan's okay?" I asked.

Tasha glanced her way, then back at me. "I've noticed she's been acting weird, but I think I've got it figured out. Want to hear my theory?"

"Of course. What are you thinking?"

"She and Logan got married at the justice of the peace."

"Yeah. Don't bring that up in front of my mom."

Tasha leaned a bit closer, lowering her voice. "And when she was married before, to Harlan Reed, they *also* got married at a justice of the peace."

"Oh, wow. Didn't realize that. So she's never actually had a real wedding ceremony." My heart twisted at that revelation. That had to be it.

"Right."

I gave my sister-in-law another glance through the lens of what I now understood. "You think she's regretting running off and eloping, wishing she'd done a big wedding instead?"

"Maybe on some subliminal level she's now seeing what she could have had," Tasha explained. "You know?"

I did. And it stung. But what could I do to make her feel better?

"Think on these things." Tasha said. "Maybe help her dream up an idea, one that makes sense for the situation. When you get back from your honeymoon"—she stressed the word in playful fashion—"maybe you can help her plan something fun. A reception. A party. You're so good at that."

"Great idea. And thanks for the kind words. I do love planning things."

"I noticed."

"But I'm not the only one who's good at it." I gave Tasha an admiring look. "You are too. And in case I haven't said it before, I am so grateful for you, not just because of the wedding, but in general. You're the closest thing to a sister I've ever had. I'm so glad God brought you into my life."

"Well, you're not getting rid of me." She nudged me and gestured to Dallas. "And who knows. . .maybe one day I really *will* be a sister. It could happen. Right?"

Judging from the look of pure joy on her face as she mentioned the idea, I had a very strong feeling it could.

CHAPTER TWENTY-FIVE

At three thirty I went tearing into the house to change into my outfit for the rehearsal. We were set to begin exactly at four thirty so that the run-through would look just like the real deal tomorrow. I was curious about the timing of the sunset, after all, and what that would look like.

I paused in the kitchen and gave a whistle when I saw the bottom tier of my wedding cake frosted and partially decorated. Bessie Mae, apron covered in powdered sugar and blobs of frosting, worked to tuck the faux evergreen and sparkling cranberries around the bottom.

"Is this what you were envisioning?" She turned the cake slightly so I could see her frosting job.

"Oh, it's perfect! Love that rough texture!" It was exactly what I was hoping for.

She stepped back to give the cake tier a solid once-over and wrinkled her nose, as if in objection to my thoughts. "It's growing on me. Though I can't tell you how many times I've been tempted to smooth it out."

"Please don't. This is the look I was going for. Rough and a little messy."

Kind of like I looked right now.

I gave her a kiss on the cheek. "It's going to be amazing, Bessie Mae.

I can't thank you enough."

I rushed to my room to get ready. As I dressed, my phone dinged. I looked down and saw a message from Shawn Warren. Just four words, but they took my breath away: "We have him now."

Whoa.

Was Buck in custody, or was I misunderstanding this?

Based on what? I wondered. *The little bit I shared, or something else? Was Buck really angry enough at Frasier to stir up trouble? To burn down homes?*

I shivered just thinking about it.

No, I shivered because it was cold in here. I grabbed my jacket and slipped it on.

I could learn more about Buck Adler later. Right now, I had a wedding rehearsal to attend.

As I changed into my favorite jeans, boots, and cozy sweater, I tried to put Buck out of my mind. Then I touched up my hair and makeup.

I paused to glance in the mirror and tried to see myself through Mason's eyes. Would he be content to marry the woman now staring at her own reflection, the one with the splattering of freckles on her nose and the messy lipstick?

Touching up the lipstick wasn't a problem, and the freckles were kind of my trademark, so I wouldn't even attempt to cover them up with foundation. Instead, I drew in a deep breath and ushered up a quiet prayer that God would be at the very center of everything we were about to do.

Afterward, I loaded my wedding attire—along with a bag filled with everything else I would need—into my truck. That way, we could go straight from the rehearsal to our scheduled dinner at Cedar Creek Prime, my favorite lakefront steakhouse in nearby Seven Points. From there, straight to Tasha's place. Whew!

Pastor Burchfield arrived at four fifteen with Melody at his side. I met them at the back door. By now, Bessie Mae had added the second tier to the cake and was pressing in the decor between the tiers.

"My stars, Bessie Mae!" Melody put her hand on her heart. "If I'd known you were this good at cake decorating, I would've recommended you to my brides. Folks use the church for weddings all the time, you know."

"I don't know that I'm up for that," my aunt said. "At least, not until I get my new gas oven."

"Gas is best for baking," Melody agreed.

"I'm not a pro baker," Bessie Mae acknowledged, "but it's been fun making RaeLyn's cake."

"You're coming out to the rehearsal, aren't you?" I asked.

She brushed some frosting off of her hand and her nose wrinkled. "Yep. I've got one more tier to go, and then I'll need some help moving this cake into the fridge overnight."

"I'll come back in and help you move it after the rehearsal," Melody said. "Don't you worry."

"Be outside by four thirty if you can," I said. "We're starting right on time."

She agreed to do so and then went back to work.

I led Melody and Pastor Burchfield out to the field, to the area we were now calling the Hadley Wedding Venue. Riley came along with us, and I patted her head. "I've got to figure out a plan for you, girl."

"She's not part of the wedding party?" Pastor Burchfield asked.

"Not as of yet," I said. "We'll see how she does during the rehearsal before I make a decision about putting her indoors tomorrow. She's usually a pretty good girl, aren't you, Riley?"

She chose that moment to jump up on me and nearly knock me backward. I brushed the dirt off my jeans and shrugged.

A gentle wind rustled across the open field as we walked that way. It carried the subtle scent of dry hay from all of those bales we'd set up. I couldn't help but gasp as the golden hue of the afternoon sun seemed to dance off the hay. And the flowers on the arbor sprang to life against the rays of sunlight as well.

Melody's eyes widened when she saw our handiwork in the field. "Oh, RaeLyn, it's gorgeous! I can see your whole vision now, and it's perfection."

"Thank you. It'll be even better when the quilts are on the bales of hay tomorrow. They're so pretty. Thank you so much for collecting all of those for me."

"Of course, hon. It's what I do."

I offered her a warm smile. "You do it well. Now, come look at the reception tent." I led the way to the spacious tent with all of its impressive decor. By now Mom and Carrie had finished adding the lovely fairy lights to every table, and even more on the food tables and tent poles. We couldn't turn them on until tomorrow, but I could already imagine how the whole place would spring to life.

I also loved all the fresh evergreen, which served to cement the wintry theme. Jake had done a fine job twisting those evergreen garlands around the tent's supports. And my oh my, did they ever give off a luscious scent.

We paused in the center of the room and Melody took it all in.

"I. . .I just can't even. It's fabulous! So much finer than I ever could have imagined."

"Thank you. What do you think of the centerpieces? Dad made the candleholders from tree branches. And check out the large tree ring the cake will sit on." I led her to the center table, which would feature the gorgeous cake.

"Everything is perfect. And I love all of the evergreen. And the twinkling lights are going to be perfect." She paused and looked my way. "Hey, I heard about your new house. Everyone in town is talking about it. We're just giddy for you. If anyone deserves such a beautiful home, it's you."

"Honestly, I still can't believe Mason did that." Tears rose to cover my lashes, and I brushed them away. "It's such a surreal thing."

"Speaking of surreal. . ." She pointed at the massive chandelier above us—the one with the mistletoe dangling from it. "What in the world? That thing looks like it belongs in a European castle."

"I know." I laughed. "Every wedding reception has to have the proper mood lighting, right?"

I finished up the tour, showing her the dessert table. And the hot cocoa bar. And the churro station. As of yet, all of these tables were still bare, but I could almost imagine how fabulous they would look tomorrow evening.

"I've heard all about the churros," Melody said as we paused in front of that area. "We had lunch with Dot and Enrique today. Did you hear that Enrique is opening a new restaurant where Consuelo's used to be?"

"Mason told me."

"Spanish cuisine," she explained. "Some Tex-Mex, but tapas and other interesting dishes too. He's very much into global cuisine, but I guess that's because he's connected to so many missions organizations around the globe."

"He is?"

"Yes, and he has direct connections to an orphanage in Reynosa, one we're already acquainted with. Enrique had all sorts of ideas for how we could go about raising funds to help with global missions. We just love him."

"And clearly Dot does too," I said.

"Sometimes when you know. . .you know." She flashed a smile at her husband. "That's how it was with John and me. I saw him walking toward me on our college campus and just had that fluttering sensation."

I knew that feeling, of course. I'd had it in high school, the first time Mason held my hand. I'd pressed those feelings aside when we parted ways during college, but God had brought us back together, and I couldn't be happier.

Mason approached us, looking mighty fine in his jeans, button-up shirt, jacket, and cowboy hat. I let out a little whistle.

"Thank you, ma'am." He took off his hat and offered a sweeping bow. "Happy to be here." He swept me into his arms. "Ready to get this show on the road?"

"Am I ever!"

He slipped his arm through mine and steered me away from the tables. A cool breeze rushed through the tent's side flap, as if to nudge us back outside.

At 4:25 we gathered at the arbor to get started. My gaze shifted to the late-afternoon sun, and I watched as it bathed the field in light, which reminded me to ask the obvious question: "Has anyone done a final check of the weather for tomorrow?"

Pretty much everyone in attendance lifted their phone.

Meghan seemed happy to chime in with a report that sounded like it could have come from the six o'clock news: "I'm happy to say we're expecting unseasonably warm weather, with a high of sixty-nine and a low of fifty-two, the fifty-two coming in the early morning hours and the sixty-nine later in the day."

"Bright, sunny skies," Tasha threw in. "I ordered them just for you."

"And sunset at exactly 5:29 p.m.," Mason said. "So, if we play our cards right—"

"And we will," I said.

"We'll get those sunset pictures you've been dreaming of since you were eight."

"Seven," I said. "But who's counting."

They all had a good laugh at that. But the truth was, I really had been dreaming about my wedding day since childhood. Call me girlie. Call me a princess. I didn't care. A girl's wedding day needed to be perfect. Or close.

Bessie Mae came barreling from the house to the field, all bundled up in a long, heavy coat, gloves, scarf, and cap. It seemed a bit much, considering the warmer-than-expected temps, but I didn't ask any questions. The poor woman was easily chilled, and I wanted her to be comfortable.

Pastor Burchfield opened with prayer and then gave us our marching orders. Annie was already hard at work, snapping photos.

I already knew the drill, at least in part. In the South, a bride rarely took part in her own rehearsal. I knew this Southern tradition from having attended many a wedding rehearsal over the years. So Melody stood in for me.

Landon took his spot at a small table in the back to man the sound system. At four thirty on the dot, the opening music kicked off. I could barely keep my emotions in check.

From my spot on a bale of hay at the front, I watched the whole thing play out.

Mason looked amazing, standing under the arbor with Pastor Burchfield, who was centered, Bible in hand. And now, time for the procession to begin, starting with family members. We kicked off with Bessie Mae, who was escorted up the aisle by Bob. He then eased her down onto a bale of hay on the front row, just to my left. She rested her hand in mine and gave it a squeeze.

Next came the groomsmen and bridesmaids parading up the aisle in pairs.

Summer and Gage made quite the production as they sashayed up the aisle in dramatic fashion. They parted ways at the front. She went to the left; he went to the right.

Meghan and Logan followed on their heels, a bit more subdued.

Next came Carrie and Jake, the most mature and responsible in the group, from the looks of things.

Finally, Tasha came up the aisle with Dallas on her arm. They beamed with such joy that you might have assumed it was their own wedding.

I found myself getting weepy when Mom came up the aisle pulling the small red Radio Flyer wagon with Colt and Annalisa inside. That sweet little boy held tight to that precious wide-eyed baby girl to make sure she didn't fall. My heart nearly burst at the sight of them. His protective little arm around her was more than I could take.

The children only stayed up front for a moment and then joined Mom on the bale of hay next to mine.

Finally, the moment we'd waited for. My father held tight to Melody's arm at the back of the aisle. He looked like a nervous wreck, and as they headed our way I couldn't help but notice the tears in his eyes.

He led her to the front and pretended to place her hand in Mason's at the pastor's request.

"Who gives this woman to be married to this man?" the pastor asked.

My dad must've gotten over his nerves because he looked Mason in the eyes and said, "If you break her heart, I'll repossess my girl faster than a stray cow in my pasture."

Not quite what I expected, but he managed to get a laugh out of all of us.

Just as quickly, he gave the right answer: "Her mother and I do," his voice cracking as the words came out. Dad then came and sat next to Mom for the rest of the run-through.

I found myself breathless as I watched the pretend wedding take place. This was just the practice round, of course. Tomorrow I would be wearing that amazing dress with its gorgeous tulle skirt. I would wear my hair down, curled, the way Mason liked it. And I would wear that gorgeous white stole to keep my shoulders warm.

The late-afternoon sun illuminated my groom's handsome face as he pantomimed—in exaggerated fashion—putting the ring on Melody's finger. Silly and fun, the whole thing felt a bit surreal. But tomorrow? Tomorrow I would be standing up there beside him, speaking words that would forever link us.

When the pretend I dos were spoken, a cheer went up from all in attendance. There was no kiss, of course.

Oops, erase that.

Pastor Burchfield gave his wife a romantic smooch right there—front and center.

I jumped up and grabbed Mason's hand and walked down the aisle with him, the other couples tagging along behind us.

When we reached the back of the aisle, I happened to glance back and saw—to my great delight—the perfect sunset, the one I'd dreamed of. It would make the ideal backdrop for our wedding photos. Now to replicate all of this tomorrow, for real.

With joy flooding my heart, I glanced up into Mason's gorgeous eyes and asked the obvious question: "How does it feel to be married?"

He offered a little shrug. "Great, but I kind of feel like I got duped. Ended up with the wrong gal."

"Let's fix that." I slipped my arms around his neck and gave him a kiss he wouldn't soon forget.

Pastor Burchfield chose that moment to holler out, "That's a wrap, folks! Nobody got trampled or accidentally hitched, so I'd call it a successful run-through."

Which caused all of us to erupt in laughter.

"See there?" I said. "You're still a single man."

"Hardly." He swept me into his arms for another passionate kiss then dipped me backward so low I almost toppled. He caught me and spun me in a circle, as if we were suddenly on the dance floor.

Which caused the crowd to cheer.

Well, until my dad stepped into the spot next to us, gave Mason a quirky look, and said, "I spent twenty-seven years raising this gal, son. If you break her, I expect a full refund."

CHAPTER TWENTY-SIX

Leave it to Dad to steal the spotlight. Everyone started laughing, myself included.

"I promise not to return her, broken or not." Mason held me tight as I stood aright.

Pastor Burchfield asked if we all felt confident enough with just one run-through, and I nodded. We needed to get a move on. With six thirty reservations at the steakhouse, we needed to get on the road. As we headed toward the vehicles, I realized I'd left something in the house—the gifts for our wedding party, which we planned to give out tonight.

I rushed in the back door and nearly lost my breath when I saw the gorgeous three-tiered wedding cake on the counter in front of me, completely decorated and ready to go. Underneath the glow of the overhead lighting I could make out the rough, textured design of the frosting. Those swirling ridges were perfect, catching the light just so.

A wave of nostalgia swept over me. I was a little girl, standing in this kitchen, sticking her finger in the frosting of her seventh birthday cake. Standing behind me, giving me the go-ahead? My papaw. In fact, I could still remember him whispering, *"Go for it, RaeLyn! You only live once!"*

This time, I wouldn't stick my finger in the frosting. I didn't dare.

Bessie Mae came in behind me and peeled off that long, heavy coat, her gloves, and her scarf. And that's when I realized that pretty much all of the clothes she was wearing underneath were covered in frosting, head to toe.

"Bessie Mae!" Giggles rose up. I wanted to hug her but realized I'd end up a hot mess.

She put her hands up, as if in protest. "Hug me later, kiddo!"

"I will." But man, oh man, was this cake a work of art.

That messy frosting. Those gorgeous sparkling cranberries, nestled in clusters between sprigs of evergreen. And those delicate white roses, tucked into place every few inches. Breathtaking!

Melody and Pastor Burchfield rushed in behind me and took charge of moving the cake to the spare refrigerator in the laundry room, where it would be safe for the night.

I looked on with my heart in my throat as the cake swayed a bit upon being moved, its delicate berries and roses shifting slightly. Ushering up a prayer for the cake's safety, I decided it would be better not to watch.

So I headed to my bedroom and grabbed the gifts, then headed out to the driveway, where I found Mason and the others standing near their vehicles talking.

It didn't make a lot of sense to ride with Mason, who had arrived in his own truck. I would need Tilly after dinner to get to Tasha's place. So, in a strange twist, I found myself alone on the way to my own rehearsal dinner.

Okay, not alone after all. Just as I got ready to back out of the driveway, Dallas asked if he could ride with me. I was thrilled to have him but a little confused.

"Where's Tasha?" I asked as he climbed into the passenger seat.

"In her car with Summer, Colt, and Gage. I needed a private chat with you."

"Sure." I started the truck, the low rumble of the engine offering a familiar, comfortable sound. I was once again reminded of Papaw, of all the times I'd ridden in this old truck seated next to him, bouncing along the country roads on our way to town.

What would he think about tonight? Would he be proud of me? Would he, like Mom, beg me not to leave my childhood home, or would he encourage me to live my dreams on that amazing property along the lake, the one he had dreamed of owning?

I felt I knew the answer.

Still wrapped up in my thoughts, I eased my way backward out of the long driveway.

When I got out to the road, I glanced my brother's way. "So, what's up?"

He seemed nervous. Weird. "I wanted to run something by you. I'm putting together a plan, but it needs your approval."

"Oh?" I turned left to head to Seven Points.

"It involves the bouquet toss. When you throw the bouquet, don't be surprised at what happens next."

"What happens next?" I straightened Tilly out on the two-lane country road. How could he possibly know what would happen next? Unless. . . I stared at him as the answer unpacked itself in my brain.

"Dallas. Do you plan to—"

"Only if you're okay with it. I don't want to take away from your big night."

The sweetest fondness for my brother rushed over me in that moment. I was thrilled for him—overjoyed that he'd fallen head over heels for the one friend who seemed to know me best and love me in spite of my quirks. And how blissful to think that he'd chosen my wedding day as the perfect time to mark the most important moment of his life.

"Are you kidding? Why would you worry about that? By the time I toss that bouquet, my big night will be mostly behind me. But how can you be sure she'll catch it?" I did my best to pick up speed as a vehicle drew close behind us.

"Well, that's where you come in. I was hoping, at the very last minute, you could tell the bridesmaids to stand down."

"Well, considering they're all married but Tasha and Summer, I won't have many to tell." I glanced in my rearview mirror then slightly eased my way to the right to let the impatient driver pass me. Turned out it was Tasha. Go figure. She honked and gave us a funny little wave, then buzzed right on by.

"That girl." I laughed. "If she had any idea what we were talking about right now—"

"She can't know." He gave me a serious look. "This has to be a total surprise."

"Oh, I have a feeling it will be. But what about the other single ladies in the crowd? There's no way I can let them know without giving it all away. Right?"

"Yeah." He paused, and I had a feeling he was thinking things through. "Put the single bridesmaids up front with Tasha in the center, then aim it right at her."

I laughed. "No pressure."

Hopefully it would all work out. But even if it didn't, I had a feeling Dallas would figure out a way to get his proposal in.

Proposal.

Mom would probably start flipping bedrooms all over again. But she would still have Gage in the house, anyway.

Maybe not for long, but I wouldn't fret over that just yet.

"I've been waiting until I had saved up enough money for a ring," Dallas said, oblivious to my thoughts. "Want to see it? I have pictures."

Did I ever!

I pulled up to an intersection in Seven Points and came to a stop. After checking the rearview mirror to make sure no one else was behind me, I turned on the overhead light. He reached for his phone and opened it to a picture of a gorgeous solitaire.

My breath caught in my throat as I took in the exquisite diamond, gleaming against the perfect delicate silver background. It shimmered, the facets picking up on the light in the picture.

"Dallas, this is amazing. She's going to love that sparkle."

"Thank you. You remember that brooch that Dot brought into the store a couple months back, the one from her great-aunt?"

"Of course. I paid her two hundred dollars for it after she told me it had been in the family for over eighty years."

"I heard. Then you passed it off to Logan to be appraised because you were worried we couldn't make back the money on it."

"Right."

"He found out the diamonds were real. And he knew I was looking."

"He did?" This startled me.

"Yeah, it was actually worth a lot more. But when he told Dot, she said not to worry about it."

"Kind of like what's happening right now with the Frasier Oil sign."

He shrugged. "You'll have to fill me in on that later. But anyway, Logan sold it to me for two hundred and one dollars, significantly less than the value, obviously. And he told me where to go in Tyler to have the stones removed and the silver melted down to be turned into the ring of Tasha's dreams."

I couldn't believe all of this. "Really, Dallas? You're telling me you've been planning this for almost two months? And Logan knows?"

"Yeah." He laughed. "I knew it would take a while to have the ring made, but I had a special design in mind. I was actually snooping on the day you and Tasha were talking about your ring. Remember, she told you all about what she wanted when she saw yours?"

I did remember, of course. But the fact that he was listening in surprised me.

"You're quite the snoop," I said.

"Thanks." A nervous laugh rose up from my brother as he shoved the phone back into his pocket. "I knew I could never afford a ring like that, but once I saw that brooch, I thought I might have a fighting chance at something similar. So I took it to a jeweler in Tyler, and the rest is history."

I didn't know which made me prouder, that he'd somehow outmaneuvered Tasha by snooping, or that Logan had somehow passed that brooch off to Dallas without my knowledge for only a dollar more than I'd paid for it.

"Logan told me he found a buyer for the brooch online," I said. "I never thought to ask him how much he got for it. He takes care of most of the financial stuff, so it didn't even occur to me."

"He did list it online, so he wasn't lying. But he sold it to me in person."

"We made a whopping dollar on it." I laughed as I eased Tilly into the parking lot at the steakhouse. "And you got yourself a bride."

"Well, almost. If all goes well."

"Do her parents know?"

"Yeah." Dallas smiled. "I talked to her dad a couple weeks ago, to ask his permission to marry her."

"Good boy."

"I didn't know what kind of life I could offer her when we first started dating, but now that I've got a steady job at the restaurant, I'm doing okay."

"Where will you live?" I pulled into a parking spot.

He shrugged. "I guess we'll cross that bridge when we come to it. But I have some ideas."

"Not at the house with the rest of the family?"

He shook his head. "No. We'll need our space."

I turned the vehicle off and leaned back in my seat, deep in thought. "Mom's going to flip."

"Yeah. Let's keep it on the down-low for now."

"Absolutely." I definitely agreed with that. "I don't want anything to ruin my rehearsal dinner, after all."

"Exactly. This night is all about you. And tomorrow, especially, so let me know if you change your mind. The last thing I want to do is take away from your big day."

"You will only add to it, I promise." I rested my hand on his. "And in case I haven't already said it, I'm so proud of you, Dallas—for the new job, your relationship with Tasha, all of it. You're all grown up. It's..."

"Weird?"

"Yeah, but sweet. You're not that rotten little kid who lied about setting off sparklers and almost burning down the barn."

He groaned. "Sorry about that, by the way."

"Nah, I'm sorry I brought it up." The flash of a car's headlights hit us straight on, and I realized Mason had pulled into the spot across from us. "Just thinking about the fire the other day stirred it up, I guess."

"Speaking of which, I had a text from Shawn earlier. He said they've taken Buck Adler in for questioning."

I nodded. "I had a text from him right before the rehearsal. But nothing since."

"Well, he probably realizes you're busy tonight."

"Yeah."

I watched as Mason got out of his truck and took decisive steps in our direction. Before I could even reach for the door handle Mason was on the other side, opening the door for me in a sweeping grand gesture. He bowed low as I emerged from the truck, and I couldn't help but smile.

"That's twice you've done that," I said. "Is this what I have to look forward to for the rest of my life?"

"Well, I'm not sure about the bowing, but I hope I always remember to be a gentleman," he said with great flair.

I had no doubt he would.

CHAPTER TWENTY-SEVEN

Dallas headed off to meet up with Tasha, who pulled in a couple of spots away. Mason and I walked inside the restaurant hand in hand to discover the servers were waiting for us with great anticipation and fanfare. I already felt special just hearing them gush over us.

We had reserved a fabulous party room at the back of the building, just on the edge of the lake, which was brightly lit in twinkling white Christmas lights. I was thrilled when I learned that Nadine had come ahead of us and fully decorated the room with lovely, wintry decor. I would have to remember to thank her later. Tonight, I needed food.

Guests were given the option of steak or chicken, but I already knew what I wanted—sirloin. This girl was hungry. No, make that hangry—the Texas version of hungry.

The next two hours were a lovely blur. The exquisite food. The laugh-a-minute stories. The tender speeches from my parents and Aunt Bessie Mae. The kind words from our friends. I couldn't have imagined the night going any better. It was completely magical.

Sometime around eight thirty we passed out gifts to everyone in attendance. I had purchased bracelets for the girls to wear tomorrow, and

Mason had given the guys cuff links. We had lockets made for Mom and Bessie Mae and the perfect sage-green tie for Dad.

The room once again erupted in lively chatter as folks looked over their gifts.

I reached for Mason's hand under the table to give it a squeeze, just to make sure I wasn't dreaming all of this. Tomorrow night at this same time, I would be his bride. We would head to our new home and spend our wedding night together.

A shiver ran up my spine as I thought it through.

Or maybe it was just a blast of cold air coming from the door leading to the large deck, which the server opened to usher us outside for a fireworks display they had arranged just for us. We stepped out onto the wooden slats, and I could make out the waters of Cedar Creek Lake off in the distance under the twinkling lights.

Before long, the fireworks began. Now the lake was in full view, dancing opposite the flashes of light as fireworks lit the night sky above us.

Mason held me tight, which was good, because I found myself shivering in spite of my jacket. Off in the distance the fireworks popped and crackled against the cold night air. Before long, a faint hint of gunpowder settled over me. In that moment I had a flashback to the ash on the day of the fire. Just as quickly I pushed that image away.

Out of the corner of my eye I caught a glimpse of someone clearing the tables inside the restaurant. I peered through the large glass window, wondering if I was seeing things.

"Mason, look!" I nudged him with my elbow and he turned to look as well.

Aaron Bradford. Clearing our table, head bowed low.

Gage must have seen him too. He slipped away from the group and headed into the restaurant. The fireworks continued overhead, but I had a feeling there were more going on inside. Through the window I could see the two of them in an intense conversation. I did my best not to let it distract me too much.

Now I was shivering in earnest. Mason took off his coat and draped it over my shoulders, my attention once again on the sparkling lights in the dark sky above.

I glanced around at the various couples. Mom and Dad rested easily against each other, eyes shifted upward. Jake and Carrie enjoyed a similar embrace, comfortable with each other. Logan and Meghan were more focused on each other than the fireworks. Hushed words traveled between them. And Tasha and Dallas were similarly preoccupied, exchanging tender glances under the night sky, the hint of a smile on my friend's face still visible with every firework that sparkled.

My favorite couple to watch? Bessie Mae and Bob. She leaned her head against his shoulder as he held her in a protective embrace. Oh, how I loved seeing the two of them together.

As the fireworks display came to an end, we stood for a moment, staring at the night sky.

"This is just the best night ever," I said after a moment of silence.

"Amen to that," Mom agreed.

After lingering a bit longer, we eventually made our way back inside and Mason settled the tab. The rehearsal dinner was on him, a thank-you to our family and friends for all they had done for us. I knew better than to argue.

While he took care of the check, I managed to get a moment with Gage, who looked troubled after his conversation with Aaron.

"Well?" I asked. "How did it go?"

"I guess he's working here now. They hired him on as a busboy."

"Big step down from his job at the fire department."

"Yeah." Gage released a slow breath. "I asked him about the fire. Told him the rumors going around. I had to confront him about being at Purtis Creek."

"And?"

"He was definitely camping there. I asked why he didn't just come talk to me, and he said he was embarrassed about losing his job and needed to clear his head. But when he saw me tonight he knew he couldn't avoid me."

"Do you think he had anything to do with setting the fire?"

"No, and he's got an alibi. When he left Purtis Creek he went straight to Tyler to meet with his new AA sponsor. The guy's already talked to the police and confirmed they were together."

"Well, that's good." I paused to think that through. "Did Aaron understand why you suspected him?"

"Yeah. But it didn't make the conversation any easier. I think he could see how shook up I was over that fire coming so close to our property."

"Me too," I acknowledged. "It takes a lot to shake me, but I was pretty rattled. I don't know when I've ever prayed that hard. Or that fast." A nervous laugh wriggled out.

"Same. It would've wrecked me to know my best friend was involved. So I'm glad he wasn't, if for no other reason than my own peace of mind."

I stifled a yawn, suddenly feeling like I couldn't keep my eyes open much longer. Probably all of that food.

"Looks like the bride needs her beauty sleep."

"This bride is beautiful enough already." These words came from Mason, who had walked up behind us.

"Well, just regular sleep, then." Gage's face lit into a smile. "And in case I haven't said it before, I'm really happy for both of you. You're so blessed to have each other." He paused. "And I'm only slightly jealous of the fact that you're going to be in that big house on the lake."

"You can come fishing whenever you like," Mason said.

"Really?" My brother's eyes lit up.

"Well, call first." I laughed. "But otherwise, yes."

"There's some good fishing on that corner of the lake," he said.

Warm feelings washed over me as I responded, "I know. Papaw used to take me there when I was a kid."

Gage glanced over at Summer, who was deep in conversation with Meghan about something. "Better go say good night. You ladies don't stay up too late."

"Oh, trust me, we won't," I replied.

As my family and friends began to drift from the room, Mason pulled me aside and wrapped me in his arms.

"The next time I see you, you'll be dressed in white."

"And you'll be wearing a honey-brown suit with a sage-green tie."

"I will."

"And we'll stand in the field."

"Facing south." He winked. "Hoping Delilah doesn't settle on that moment to deliver."

"She's already in the barn. And I suppose we'll put Riley there too."

"No way. She was great at the rehearsal today. I say we leave her to her own devices. She'll be fine."

I happened to glance over at Dallas and Tasha then looked back at Mason. "Hey, there's something I need to tell you."

His gaze shifted to my brother and best friend, and then he whispered,

"About Dallas popping the question?"

"You knew?"

"Only since last night. Dallas pulled me aside to ask my opinion. I'm great with it, but I told him to run it by you."

"I love the idea."

"I think he was a little worried it would draw attention away from us, but I told him it would be the icing on the cake." He paused and then laughed. "Icing on the cake."

"Well, I'm all in. But I'm a little nervous about throwing the bouquet. My aim's not that great."

"I remember when you were on the girls' softball team. You're not lying about your aim."

Oh no he didn't! "Well, I aimed my heart at you and landed right on the mark. So I'd say I got what I wanted."

"No, I got what I wanted. And I can't wait to spend the rest of my life with you." He gave me the sweetest kiss then gazed into my eyes. "Oh, one last thing."

"What's that?"

"You know how your dad's been joking about thermal blankets for the guests?"

"Yes. I could've used one tonight. Dad probably would've done it too, if I hadn't stopped him."

"Well. . ." Mason paused, and his gaze shifted down then back up again. "He didn't. . .but I did."

"What?"

"I bought sixty sage-green throws, one for each hay bale. Nadine was the one who suggested it. And she even told me about a place I could have them embroidered. In honey brown. I picked them up this morning."

I slugged him on the arm. "Are you serious right now?"

He rubbed at his arm in overly dramatic fashion, as if I'd hurt him. "I am. We want our guests to be comfortable. And they—well, at least sixty of them—can take them home as a memento. They're good quality and the embroidery came out great."

"I can't believe you did this, Mason."

"I didn't want you to panic if you saw a blanket folded on each bale."

"So, what did you have embroidered on them?"

"Our names and the date. But I figured I've dropped enough surprises on you already. Didn't want you to be too caught off guard with this one in case you didn't like the color or something."

"Do you happen to have a picture?"

"Of course. I knew you would ask."

He reached for his phone and pulled up a picture. I had to gasp when I saw the gorgeous throw. He had the right shade of sage—the pale version, and a soft medium brown appliqué with our names and tomorrow's date. I was so moved by this act of kindness and generosity that I almost burst into tears.

Tasha appeared at my side just as the tears sprang up.

"Oh no you don't!" She waggled her finger in my face. "We can't afford tears tonight. You don't want to walk down the aisle tomorrow with puffy eyes." Her gaze shifted to Mason's phone. "Oooh, pretty! What is this?"

"Thermal blankets for the guests," he explained.

She sighed. "You're a great fiancé. Must be nice to have a great fiancé like that." Just as quickly she tugged me by the arm. "C'mon, we've got to get back to my place."

I gave Mason one last sweet kiss and we headed out to the parking lot to leave.

Meghan asked if she could ride with me over to Tasha's house, and I was happy to have the company.

We settled into my truck and she gushed with praise over how beautiful the day had been.

"I couldn't have done any of it without you ladies," I countered. "You have no idea how blessed I feel to have you as part of this, Meghan."

"Thank you. I'm honored." She grew silent for a moment, so I glanced her way.

"If I'm being honest, I've been worried about you."

"Why is that?" she asked.

"I'm hoping you're not feeling slighted because we're doing a big fancy wedding and you guys eloped."

Meghan shrugged. "I mean, there are times when I wish we'd done a church wedding."

"You still can, you know. You can renew your vows—at the church, or home, or wherever you like."

"I'll think about it." She cleared her throat and shifted her position in the seat. "But it's not the most pressing thing on my mind right now, trust me."

The way she said that made me uneasy.

Just as quickly, she asked if I could pull the car off the road.

So I did. She leaped out and, seconds later, was doubled over on the side of the road, emptying her stomach of its contents. I rushed to stand next to her, my hand on her back.

"You haven't been well since last weekend," I said. "Are you okay?" I raced to get a napkin from my glove box then shoved it into her hand.

"I will be." She swiped at her mouth then looked my way, her lips curling up in a grin. "In about seven and a half months."

"Oh, Meghan!" I clamped my hand over my mouth as the realization set in. Then I brought it back down again, almost unable to speak. "Are—are—are you saying you're. . ."

"Mm-hmm." She laughed and then rested her hand on her stomach. "We definitely didn't plan it this early, but apparently the Lord had other ideas. Not that I'm totally blaming Him, mind you. But no one was more shocked than I was when I took that test Wednesday morning." She dabbed at her mouth again and rested against the truck.

"Wait. . .Wednesday morning?"

"Yep. Merry Christmas Eve!" She laughed again. "I wish you could've seen Logan's face when I showed it to him. I've never seen your very practical brother more shocked. Or emotional. So, if we seemed strange at the family gathering on Christmas Day, that's why. We were just. . . processing. And that's why I crashed out on the sofa."

"Who else knows?" I asked.

"No one. You're the first person I've told."

"Whoa." I helped her back into the passenger seat, then closed the door and went around to my side.

As I got settled in the driver's seat once more, Meghan pulled down the visor and stared at her reflection in the mirror under the glow of the tiny bulb above it. "I probably should've just told you last night when we had our little heart-to-heart, but I wasn't ready just yet."

"It's okay." My heart flooded with joy as I thought this through. "Oh, man. I just realized how hard you were working on the day of the fire. And you breathed in all of that smoke." I put the truck back in gear and eased my way back out onto the road.

"I was nauseous that day and again at Tasha's place, but I don't think it had as much to do with the smoke as we thought. Clearly."

My thoughts shifted to my upcoming marriage to Mason. We'd talked about kids, of course. I wanted them. He wanted them. But we planned to give ourselves a year or two of settling in before bringing any little ones into the world.

Unless God had other ideas, of course.

And maybe that's what had happened with Meghan too.

"So I guess I'd better let Bessie Mae off the hook." Meghan giggled.

"What do you mean?"

"She was worried it was her cake that made me sick. Now we know it definitely wasn't. I've had morning sickness every day this week, which is why I finally broke down and bought the test. I couldn't take it anymore."

"And I'm sure the chaos of this week hasn't helped, starting with the fire and ending with a huge Christmas celebration and a wedding."

"Probably not, but it was a lot of fun." She paused. "Well, not the fire part but the Christmas festivities. I grew up an only child, and my parents weren't always very attentive. So things look a lot different at the Hadley house than they did at mine." She sighed. "I want that for my children—to be surrounded by family and loved ones, not just on Christmas Day but birthdays and so on. This really is one of the most remarkable families I've ever had the privilege of knowing. I honestly can't believe I'm a part of it. It almost seems too good to be true."

I had to agree. I'd grown up in the Hadley clan and hadn't even realized how fortunate I was. Hearing Meghan's perspective helped me realize just how blessed I'd always been.

And would continue to be.

Still, my thoughts were reeling.

Bessie Mae was a honeymooner.

Mom and Dad were getting a fresh start.

Jake and Carrie had the sweetest baby girl on the planet.

Dallas was about to propose to my best friend.

Logan and Meghan were expecting.

Gage was falling head over heels for Summer.

And me? Oh, right. I was the one getting married.

Tomorrow.

CHAPTER TWENTY-EIGHT

Meghan and I arrived at Tasha's house to discover another party in full bloom. Apparently, Nadine was hard at work in her role as hostess, judging from the way she greeted us at the door, all smiles.

"How was the rehearsal, y'all?" she crooned as she ushered me inside the beautiful home.

"Perfection!" I said, and then paused to sniff the air. In spite of my very full stomach, something was calling out to me from the kitchen. Something sweet.

We followed on her heels to discover a lovely setup of desserts, teas, and coffees. The whole place looked—and smelled—magical. I could hardly believe we still had more celebration festivities in front of us, but here we were.

Tasha thanked Nadine for her help and asked if she wanted to spend the night.

"No, ma'am." Nadine reached for her purse. "My sister is staying over at my new place. We're planning to watch a romantic comedy and then have our own slumber party. But y'all have the time of your lives." She gave me a serious look. "And even if you're tempted to do so, don't stay up late, young lady. You have a big day tomorrow."

I did, indeed.

I thanked her for working so hard on my behalf this week, including the decor at the rehearsal dinner, and her eyes misted over.

"Honey, you're like family to me. You all are."

These words were followed by hugs all around.

After she left we began the arduous task of emptying all our things into the various bedrooms. Tasha offered to help me with my stuff and reached for my wedding gown with great flair. She then led the way into the master, which was decorated with flower petals and chocolates on the pillow. I could always tell Nadine's handiwork.

"You're staying in the master bedroom, RaeLyn." Tasha hung my wedding gown in the closet and shook the bag out to make sure nothing inside would get crinkled. "And the rest of us are sharing the other bedrooms."

"Wait. I'm all alone?" I set my makeup bag on the bed. "No way! One of you has to stay in here with me." I shot her a quick glance. Tasha was the logical choice. She'd been with me through thick and thin for years now. We'd shared every celebration, every grief, every pain, every joy.

She quickly agreed and the other ladies adjusted their plans. Before we knew it, we were all gathered in the front parlor sipping hot tea and nibbling on those delicious cookies Nadine had left behind. I rested my head on the sofa and closed my eyes as the ladies all chattered around me.

"You okay over there?" Summer asked.

I opened one eye and saw the concern on her face. "Yep. Just reliving the day."

"It was pretty amazing."

"It certainly was."

"And tomorrow is going to be even better." Tasha clasped her hands together. "What time do we have to be at the salon?"

"Lorelai said to come around ten. She's closing down the shop to all of her customers to take care of us. Hair, makeup, the works."

"Lorelai's a little over the top with the makeup." Creases formed between Summer's eyes. "Are we sure she can be trusted not to overdo?"

I'd already given that a lot of thought and had Lorelai's word that she would proceed carefully.

"Mom took Dallas and Gage to Lorelai every summer to have their heads shaved down. I'll never forget the time they came back with

Mohawks." The memory flooded over me, and I couldn't help but laugh.

"Those boys were something else when they were young." Tasha shook her head. "If you'd told me I would end up dating one of them, I never would have believed you. They were rotten."

"Yep, as boys are sometimes prone to be," Summer chimed in.

Thinking about my brothers as boys reminded me of Kenner and Karter. I still needed to wrap up that article for my editor, but I had some concerns about publishing the story with so many unanswered questions about the fire's origin. I would have to give that some more thought. And pray about it. The Lord would surely show me what to do.

We finally settled into bed around midnight. Tasha chattered nonstop as she changed into her pj's and climbed under the covers. I crawled into bed, laptop in hand, knowing I must complete my article before I fell asleep if I really planned to turn it in. It shouldn't take long, if inspiration hit just right.

"Tell me you're not working." Tasha reached for her bedside lamp to turn it off.

"I promised my editor I'd have this turned in before I left town."

"RaeLyn, seriously? You're working on your wedding day?" She pointed to the clock, which read 12:06 a.m.

"The article is mostly written. I just have to tidy it up and press the SEND button. Could you give me your Wi-Fi code, please?"

With a grunt she shared the code, then rolled over in bed. "Promise you'll get plenty of sleep."

"I promise."

I stared at the blinking cursor on the screen and read back through the words I'd already penned but couldn't figure out how to wrap things up. Should I update with the information about Buck? I didn't really have details, did I? And without details, I couldn't really conclude the story accurately.

I did have the word of the boys and their mother, but perhaps I should focus more on the human angle, the faith angle, and leave the whodunit part out completely. Yes, that's what I would do. This article would drive home the point that God would be with us through the fire, the flood, and the storm. And I would home in on the part about swimming in the lake—how those wet clothes had saved them in the end.

It seemed rather ironic that their disobedience had been the very thing to spare them, but God could definitely use anything He wanted to get us through the messes in our lives. And I drove the point home as best I could.

The words flowed for a couple of minutes and then dried up.

Tasha rolled over, and I sensed her staring at me.

"Am I keeping you awake?" I asked.

"No, I can't sleep."

"Because of my typing?"

She sat up in the bed and rested against the pillows. "No. To be honest, I'm fretting."

"About?"

"I'm a little worried that the vacation rental hasn't had a steady flow of renters this winter. I know it could just be a fluke. Maybe all of the local rentals are having trouble. I don't know. But it's kind of scary, moving from month to month not knowing who will come, or for how long."

"Here's a thought." I paused and chose my words carefully. "I know you're worried about the mortgage and all, but what if you just kept the house?"

"You mean, live here permanently?" Creases formed between her eyes. "Instead of renting it out?"

"I know you have a mortgage, but you've just been promoted at the restaurant and you said yourself that comes with a raise."

"Yeah, but it's a lot to think about. I'm just one person. You know?"

I did. But I also knew a little more than that.

"Just pray about it," I said.

She leaned back against her pillows. "I will." A little sigh escaped. "Wouldn't that be the life?"

It would, indeed.

And if anyone on the planet deserved an amazing life, it was my precious bestie. My support. My confidante. A spiritual powerhouse.

Before long, Tasha's gentle snores served as a backdrop for the work I still needed to accomplish. I put my earbuds in and read back over everything I'd already written.

Then, just to clarify some things in my mind, I rewatched the FaceTime video with the twins. Something about it felt off, but I couldn't put my finger on it. My thoughts shifted to Buck, to the story he'd told. Then I thought about Aaron's expression tonight in the restaurant, how down in the dumps he looked. Had the police really dismissed him as a suspect?

I scribbled a few more lines of text into my article but wasn't ready to press the SEND button just yet. I couldn't let go of the feeling that something didn't add up.

Falling asleep turned out to be much easier than I thought it might be. Within minutes I was out like a light. And when I awoke the next morning, it took me a moment to realize where I was. . .until Tasha and the others showed up with breakfast in bed. Then I had no doubt—the pampering was now fully underway.

I stared down at the breakfast tray, complete with fruit, toast, bacon, and an omelet. "You went all out!"

"It's important to get some nutrition, girl," Tasha countered. "You won't be eating again until after the wedding. So fill up!"

She didn't have to ask twice. I dove right in, especially enjoying that delicious omelet, which was stuffed full of all the things I loved—ham, cheese, onions, peppers, and mushrooms. Yum.

My excitement continued on as we prepared for the day. I showered and dressed in casual clothes and we headed off to Curl Up & Dye. We had agreed to go Dutch for the hair, makeup, and mani-pedi but were stunned when Lorelai told us that someone had already covered the bill on our behalf.

I was shocked to learn Logan had taken care of all of it.

The boy had earned his calculator socks.

Lorelai got me settled into a salon chair, and she went to work on me while a couple of the other stylists started on Meghan and Tasha. Summer and Carrie took a couple of seats in the waiting area and reached for style magazines.

Which, it turned out, were six years old. Go figure.

Not that any of us needed to be reading today. We were all too busy laughing and visiting. Lorelai asked a thousand questions about my wedding as she worked, and I answered as best I could. Before long, my hair was shampooed and up in rollers. A short while later, she set me under one of the big dryers. I felt like a chicken going into the roasting pan.

Mom arrived a couple of minutes after that, apologizing for her tardiness. "It took us a little longer to put the quilts on the hay bales than expected," she explained. "And then we had a little problem with my car. Something to do with a leaky hose. But your dad dropped us off in his truck, RaeLyn. Can we ride with you to Tasha's after this?"

It would take some juggling of passengers to make the vehicle situation work, but I didn't mind a bit. In fact, I looked forward to spending time alone with them.

Bessie Mae stepped into the salon behind Mom, face beaming. "We have T-minus six hours to perfect these curls, ladies!"

My aunt kept talking, but I found myself distracted by her clip-on hairpiece, which was truly one of the strangest things I'd ever seen in my life. The dark brown hair piece didn't even come close to matching her silver hair. And it stuck up in the air in chaotic fashion. Not that I would call it fashion.

"What do you think, ladies? I bought it on the internet!" Bessie Mae turned to show it off and nearly toppled in the process.

Mom caught her before she fell, thank goodness, but the hairpiece flew off my aunt's head and shot across the room, hitting Lorelai upside the head and then falling to the floor.

Poor Lorelai let out a shrill cry, then looked down at the hairpiece on the ground. "What in the world do you have here, Bessie Mae? A squirrel?"

"No, silly. It's my hair."

"Definitely not *your* hair." Lorelai picked it up with her fingertips and tossed it back at her. "In fact, it's not real hair at all. It's synthetic."

Bessie Mae caught it like a pro. "Dot calls hers 'spare hair.' But I guess I'll stick with my natural 'do." She took a seat in one of the empty chairs in the waiting area. "It was just a joke, anyway. Thought you might get a kick out of it, RaeLyn. A little wedding day humor." Bessie Mae waved her spare hair in my general direction and then shoved it into her oversized purse.

"Oh, I definitely did." Leave it to my crazy aunt to bring smiles to our faces on such a crazy day.

Before long, my hair was dry and it was time to remove the curlers. Mom was clearly a nervous wreck as she looked on. As the stylists worked on my hair she kept a careful watch.

"That's a bit too much curl." Her nose wrinkled in concern as she pointed out the stylist's presumed error.

"It will loosen as the day goes on," Lorelai explained. "I rolled it tight on purpose."

I glanced over just as a young stylist named Finney completed the curling process for Meghan's hair. She looked my way wide-eyed, and I could see concern registering in her eyes as her long hair was teased and curled in a way that made it look about three times its normal size.

"Looks like we're going full Dolly Parton," Mom whispered. "Do we trust the process or say something?"

"Trust the process," Lorelai called out. "We won't let you down."

I hoped so, but this was all a bit much.

So was the makeup, which started going on moments later. I'd always had a more natural look—Mason loved that about me—but these folks had a different plan. They pulled out a makeup bag so full it would've made a stage actress nervous.

"Hang on, y'all!" Lorelai snapped a photo. "This one's too good to pass up. I've got to put this on our social media account so other incoming brides will know what we have to offer."

Should I panic now or wait till later?

"We're calling this our Bouffants & Blessings bridal package," Lorelai explained. "Folks will come from all over."

Hopefully for the right reasons.

I reached to pat her hand. "Remember, I'm really going for a more natural look. Nothing over the top—with hair or makeup. Just. . . simple."

Her bright smile faded a bit, but she eventually nodded. "Sure, honey. I'm sure it all seems a bit much right now, but I can assure you, the end product will be just what you're hoping for. Trust me."

So I did my best to place my trust in her. She'd never let me down in all the years I'd known her.

While she worked, Lorelai asked me about the honeymoon, and I told her we were flying out to Playa Del Carmen tomorrow morning after spending tonight at our new house.

Tonight.

Tonight, I would become Mrs. Mason Fredericks. I'd spend the night in my new home.

Spend the night.

My cheeks flushed warm.

"Well, I'll put enough hair spray in this 'do that you'll wake up looking just like you did when you got into the bed," Lorelai said.

"Don't you dare!" Bessie Mae glanced my way, hand raised. "What's the point of a weddin' night if you're not gonna muss your hair?"

Okay, now my face was really on fire.

Lorelai got a little slaphappy with the hair spray anyway, and Tasha found it all amusing.

"Don't get too close to the candles tonight, RaeLyn. You'll go up in flames."

Oh boy. I sure hoped not.

Up above us, a mounted television played the news at noon from Henderson County. It was muted, but I could see the captions. My heart skipped a beat as Karter's and Kenner's faces came into view. Had someone beat me to the punch on the local angle?

"Lorelai, can you turn that up, please?" I pointed to the TV.

"Well, sure, honey." She grabbed the remote, and before long we were all listening to the animated tale the boys were telling.

Sure enough, a reporter at Tyler's KLTV drilled the kids and asked them to tell their story in the order it happened.

Only, the story they told didn't exactly match what they'd told me on FaceTime.

Close, but not exactly. They didn't mention their swim in the lake.

No one else at the salon seemed to pick up on it, but it troubled me, the answers they'd given her. And it made me question, well. . .absolutely everything.

Not that I had a minute to question anything—except, perhaps, my aunt's spare hair. On that, I felt sure we could all agree.

CHAPTER TWENTY-NINE

Before I could give the situation with the boys any more thought, Lorelai finished up my hair and makeup. I suspected she'd done a lovely job, based on the tears in Mom's eyes, but when Lorelai swung my chair around so that I could face the mirror, I almost burst into tears.

My makeup was soft and ethereal. Almost radiant. I leaned forward to give my face a closer look. She had highlighted my cheeks and added a hint of color to my lips.

And my hair! Those beautiful soft curls framed my face in a way that took my breath away. The whole thing was just what I was going for—romantic and effortless. And definitely not over the top.

"Trust the process," Lorelai whispered.

I would never doubt her again.

And the other ladies? They were equally as lovely, each one looking like a fashion model, in the best sense of the words.

We gushed with great fanfare over the lovely job Lorelai and her team had done; then Bessie Mae left them a lovely tip—above and beyond whatever my brother planned to pay.

My beautiful bridesmaids headed back to Tasha's place in her vehicle, while Mom and Bessie Mae climbed into Tilly with me. My little red truck zipped along the country roads, pointed toward Tasha's house. Pointed toward the best afternoon of my life.

With bright, sunny skies overhead and temps in the low sixties, the day was practically perfect.

As we neared Tasha's place, Bessie Mae carried on about her perfectly coiffed hair, which she examined in her compact mirror. "This is so much fun! I haven't worn my hair like this since 1982."

She looked beautiful, and I told her so.

Nothing could spoil our mood.

Well, until Mom mentioned Buck Adler by name. "I heard they took him in for questioning last night," she said as she examined her reflection in the visor mirror. "I can't wrap my head around it."

Oh dear. In all the chaos, I hadn't told my family about my suspicions of Buck or my back-and-forth messages with Deputy Warren. So I filled them in as best I could. From the back seat, I could tell that Bessie Mae wasn't buying the story. . .but why?

"The man has been falsely accused." Her words were tight. Stern.

"What do you mean, Bessie Mae?" I put on my turn signal and eased my car to a stop at a four-way intersection.

"This is all because of that Frasier Oil business, right?" she quizzed.

"Yes." I nodded and then turned right.

"Well, I could fill your ears with stories about that company, and none of them would be good. Your papaw was nearly blindsided by them several times over the years. If he had lived to see this, he'd have plenty to say about it. Frasier Oil ripped him off. They ripped us all off."

"There was some sort of speculation that Buck doesn't own his property like everyone thought," I explained as I picked up speed on the country road. "From what I heard, another family member is the rightful owner."

"A cousin who's got connections to Frasier." Bessie Mae's voice grew tight. "He was bought and paid for."

"What?"

"Buck owns that land, fair and square. I've known that family since Buck was a child. Frasier coerced that spiteful cousin of his to lay a false claim, but it's a lie and everyone knows it."

I couldn't help but gasp. "Why didn't you tell us all of this days ago, Bessie Mae?"

"I had no idea anyone suspected Buck Adler of starting that fire. Last

I heard, it was a lightning strike. Or maybe that friend of Gage's who was mad at the fire department. But, Buck Adler?" She made a loud *psst* sound and then grew quiet.

True enough, she and Bob had missed the conversation about Buck on Monday. They came in after the fact. Had my suspicions caused the wrong man to be questioned?

"What did you mean when you said that Frasier Oil ripped him off?" I asked.

"Well, first of all, he's sitting on gold over there, and Frasier knows it. That's why they want that piece of property for themselves."

I released a slow sigh. "Sounds like they might end up with it. He's behind on his property taxes."

"Then we'll have a fundraiser. All of us. We'll raise the money and give it to him to cover those taxes."

"I don't think we'll have to do that." Not if Dad split the proceeds of the sign with him.

How ironic, to think a Frasier Oil sign might cover the cost of Buck's debt and save his property.

"One of the things that your papaw discovered years ago was a discrepancy in the amount of royalties they were paying," Bessie Mae added. "We weren't paid our full share, any of us. Buck and your papaw hired an attorney together to get to the bottom of it. I'm telling you, those folks are as crooked as a dog's hind leg. But they've got high-dollar lawyers and get away with everything."

"Maybe not this time."

Maybe God had set all of this up in advance, to win Buck back to Him and to cover all of his costs.

"If I had known you were fretting over all of this, I would have told you sooner, RaeLyn. We have a long history with Frasier, and I wouldn't trust 'em as far as I could throw 'em."

A ball formed in my stomach as I thought this through. I was the one who had caused this to happen to Buck, so the blame was on me. I eased my way up the street and saw Tasha's place ahead. The other ladies had beaten us here and were already exiting their vehicles.

"All of us old folks knew what was going on."

"So he's been cheated out of money by Frasier all this time?" I pulled into the driveway and shut off the truck.

"Absolutely. Then they involved his cousin to try to get control of the land. Sounds like they were almost successful."

"He ended up almost losing everything." These words came from Mom, who looked more than a little troubled by all of this.

But was that enough to cause him to burn it all down in retribution? That was the question I wasn't yet able to answer. And right now, I couldn't shift my thoughts in that direction to try to figure it out. I had other things to do. . .like meet my groom at the altar.

Mom and Bessie Mae got out of the truck, but I lingered to send a text to Shawn Warren. My heart wriggled its way up to my throat as I typed: "I might have been wrong about Buck Adler. He might be innocent. His family member has ties to Frasier, and they want his land."

To which Shawn responded: "Aren't you supposed to be getting married today?"

I managed a quick, "Yeah."

He came back with, "We're on it. Rest easy. Will catch you up when I can. Go get married, RaeLyn. See you in a few."

I shoved the phone in my purse, content that he was on the job, then bolted into the house, ready to get this show on the road. A quick glance at the clock caused my heart to leap: 1:47 p.m. Annie would be here shortly to start taking photos.

We buzzed upstairs and began the process of dressing for the wedding.

When my mother and aunt showed off their gowns, I couldn't help but gasp. They were both stunning in that fabulous sage green. And the beautiful hair and makeup job sent the whole thing over the top. My dad was going to flip. Bob too, though he might not recognize Bessie Mae.

My bridesmaids dressed quickly, chattering a mile a minute as they did, their nervous energy contagious. I watched as Mom helped Meghan zip up her dress, which fit perfectly.

"Thanks for letting it out, Flora!" Meghan threw her arms around my mother's neck. "It's perfect."

"You look like a million bucks, sweetheart." Mom leaned in close and whispered, "I'd say you're practically beaming."

That comment went over the heads of everyone else in the room but didn't escape my notice.

Meghan flashed her a warm smile and reached to grip her hand.

Annie showed up as I prepared to get into my gown. She followed us through the process, asking me to stop from time to time so that she could snap photos.

And then the real magic happened, the moment I'd waited for, for so long. I eased my way into that wintry white wedding gown with its fitted bodice and tulle skirt, and everyone gasped.

With Annie snapping photos, Mama zipped up the back, revealing the pearl buttons that ran the full length of the upper half of the dress. But what really took my breath away was that sweetheart neckline and Irish lace cascading down the bodice.

I ran my hands along the tulle skirt and noticed how it caught the light coming through the French doors to my right. I could almost imagine it underneath the glow of the afternoon sun on that field. That perfect, holy field where I would take my vows.

The moment my veil went on, Mom had a complete meltdown. She couldn't seem to contain her emotions. I almost joined in, but Tasha hollered, "Don't do it! Don't cry!"

"You don't want anything to ruin that makeup, honey," Annie said as she snapped a close-up of my face. "Trust me. I've seen this far too often."

It was too late to start over with my makeup, so I did my best to dry my tears. But the idea that I was finally going to marry Mason Fredericks was almost too much for my tender heart to handle.

Annie distracted me by suggesting we move out to the back deck so that she could get photos of me with the lake in the background. I'd never been one for posing, but I did my best. Then she added the bridesmaids to the mix. Next came the best pictures of all, the ones with Mom and Bessie Mae. We had so much fun we almost forgot we had to leave soon.

Afterward, Annie decided to grab a couple of photos in front of those beautiful Christmas trees in the parlor. Then another on the chaise lounge.

Finally, the moment came. We had to get home and have ourselves a wedding.

Only one thing I hadn't taken into account. Who would drive Tilly? With me in a wedding gown, I was hardly the best candidate, but none of the others were familiar with the old girl. Bessie Mae offered, but I almost lost my breath thinking through what might happen.

So, in the end, I drove myself to my own wedding. Mom held tight to my gown as I climbed into the driver's seat; then Annie took the opportunity to snap several pictures of me behind the wheel.

"Your papaw would've loved this." Bessie Mae's eyes brimmed with tears. "Oh, how I wish he was here to see you on your wedding day."

Tears immediately sprang to my eyes as well, and I did what I could to will them away.

Mom and Bessie Mae climbed into the truck next to me, and we made our way up the road toward home and toward my happily ever after.

Poor old Tilly still sputtered a bit, but I patted the steering wheel and begged her to keep up with Tasha, who led the way in her vehicle ahead of me.

When we pulled into the driveway, Dad was there to meet us with Pastor Burchfield standing next to him. He looked so handsome in his new suit.

My father took one look at me in my gown and put his hand to his heart. Before I could even climb out of the vehicle, he was there, arms extended, ready to offer the sweetest hug ever. Thank goodness Annie pulled up in time to capture the images.

Soon enough, the bridesmaids joined us for a couple of pictures with my father, and he had us all laughing.

"Now, before you mention that spreadsheet, RaeLyn, I want you to know we're right on target. Vendors are all here. Food has arrived. Quilts are on the bales of hay. Weather has agreed to cooperate. Enrique is teaching us all Spanish. We just have to dress Tilly for her big entrance."

"Thank you, Dad." I gave him a kiss on the cheek. "Where are the guys?"

"Still at your new house getting ready, I think. Gage texted me, but I told him they weren't allowed to come home until you gals were settled inside."

We had some things to take care of first. Like getting Tilly ready. But Dad was already on the job. He and Pastor Burchfield took over with Tilly, placing a Christmas wreath on the grill and loading up the bed with a Christmas tree on its side, covered in battery-operated twinkling white lights. And adding a bale of hay for the bride to ride on.

I would have stayed to watch their work, but we still had a few things to take care of inside. As we approached the back door, I gazed out to the field, where those bales of hay sat ready. Even from here I could see the quilts had been added. God bless my family and friends for their hard work. How I would make all of this up to them, I had no idea.

When I got inside I found Dot hard at work in the kitchen, finalizing the bouquets and corsages. I had to gasp when I saw my bouquet. It far surpassed anything I could have imagined: Those gorgeous white roses along with frosted red berries and evergreen simply took my breath away.

After an adequate amount of gushing, she finally pulled me aside for a little chat.

"I did just what you asked for, honey. One of those white roses is a special English rose to honor Mason's mom. And we tied your grandfather's old key to Tilly into the ribbons."

She showed me and I almost wept. I could sense my grandfather's presence, even now.

Bessie Mae carried on about how much my papaw would have loved all of this, and I found myself misty-eyed all over again.

"Speaking of Tilly. . ." Dot glanced up at the clock. "I've got to get outside and add the poinsettias and evergreens to the back."

"Dad's already putting the Christmas tree and hay bale in place."

"It's going to look like a Christmas postcard, honey. I can't wait to see your vision come together."

Neither could I.

"Oh!" Bessie Mae stopped cold. "We've got to get that cake out to the tent."

"The guys are going to do it when they get here," I said. It was on the spreadsheet. Jake and Logan knew to take care of it. "Where's the topper?"

She walked over to a cabinet on the far side of the room and reached inside, then came out with the topper I'd chosen—a vintage red truck with a bride and groom inside. On a day this special, nothing else would do.

CHAPTER THIRTY

At four thirty, with guests assembled and all the players in place, I slipped on that gorgeous white fur stole and walked with my father to the driveway to board my ride to the wedding field. And there, in the driveway, I saw my Tilly, my beautiful, perfect Tilly, all decked out with her wintry decor.

Dad placed a step stool at the back to help me up into the bed of the truck, where I took my spot on a bale of hay perched next to the tipped-over tree. He snapped several pictures of me. Then, with my father behind the wheel, we made our way across the field to make our big entrance.

I did my best not to fall out of the truck this time around.

Running behind us all the way. . .Riley. Tail wagging, always panting, eyes on me. My girl. And I wouldn't have it any other way.

By the time we arrived, the last of the couples had made their way up the aisle and were standing in perfect formation at the front, awaiting my arrival. Annie captured it all, snapshot after snapshot, as the crowd let out gasps and even a round of applause at my dramatic entrance.

Even from here, at the back of the crowd, I could make out my groom's face. And I couldn't wait to get to him.

Dad parked Tilly and came around to help me down. Then, as we took our places at the back of the aisle, the wedding march began.

"You ready for this, kiddo?" my father whispered.

I pressed down the lump in my throat and nodded. Then we began our walk arm in arm down the aisle. I kept my gaze on the man at the front, the one who had held me spellbound from the time I first laid eyes on him in school.

My Mason. The one God had hand-delivered. The one who held my heart and would now share his life with me.

I glanced toward the guests and had to stifle the gasp as I saw how fabulous they all looked seated on those hay bales with those sage-green thermal blankets spread across their laps. Perfection.

I shifted my focus to Mason, feeling a little blissful myself.

Up at the front Annie stood off to the side, click-click-clicking away. I noticed she snapped a picture of something behind me and glanced back to see that Riley had joined us as we made our way down the aisle. Mom clucked her tongue at her and she rested in front of her bale of hay, where Colt and baby Annalisa still sat in the red wagon.

Annie snapped a picture of that too.

Before I knew it, my father was officially giving me away—lifting my veil and pressing a kiss onto my cheek, then placing my hand in Mason's.

The look on my groom's face told me all I needed to know about how I looked in my wedding gown. His eyes huge, Mason mouthed the word "Wow!"

I could've said the same thing about him. My sweetheart looked like something out of a romance movie in that amazing honey-brown suit, white shirt, and sage-green tie.

Hand in hand we turned to face Pastor Burchfield, who was all smiles. He pointed to the clear sky above and said, "The Lord did it, y'all. We prayed for sunshine, and He most certainly delivered, didn't He?"

From behind me, I heard my father offer a rousing "Amen!"

"It's practically a Christmas miracle," Pastor Burchfield said. "And if I know anyone who deserves the perfect wedding day, it's these two."

We started the ceremony with a special candle-lighting ceremony to honor those who were no longer with us. We invited my father and Bessie Mae up to light a candle in memory of Papaw. Then Mason and I lit a candle for his parents. Out of the corner of my eye, I caught a glimpse of Mason's aunt Lucy, who had tears in her eyes.

Pastor Burchfield read the little note Mason and I had written:

Today RaeLyn and Mason honor the memory of those loved ones who helped shape them into the people they have become: Papaw Hadley and Mason's beloved parents, who are no longer with us but who look on from heaven, cheering this special day.

For a mere second, I felt heavyhearted that our loved ones were missing out on this grand day. Just as quickly, that pain left as I gazed into the eyes of the man who held my future in his hands.

What happened after that was kind of a blur. I remembered the vows. I definitely remembered slipping the rings on our fingers. And that kiss at the end, after Pastor Burchfield pronounced us man and wife? Wow! There were enough sparks there to relive for a lifetime.

The little bits that glued it all together, however? I missed most of that. My heart was thumping so loudly that it echoed in my ears and made me a little dizzy. But I did happen to catch the part where we were standing directly under the mistletoe on the arbor when that kiss took place.

Somehow, we made it to the back of the aisle. Riley came bounding our way and tried to leap up on us as Mason swept me into his arms, but my husband—my *husband*—managed to get her under control. Not before Annie got a photo, though.

We greeted our guests as they flooded down the aisle toward us, all smiles. I'd never heard the word "Congratulations!" more in my life.

At Pastor Burchfield's bidding, our friends made their way to the reception tent, where the music was already playing. Hopefully our guests wouldn't mind nibbling on appetizers while we took some gorgeous sunset photos.

I gazed off to the west and gasped when I saw the sunset.

"Oh, Mason! Look!"

It was nothing short of magical. The Lord had painted the skies in brilliant pinks and oranges, sweeping in shades of deep purple and amber. The sun was a golden orb in the distance, casting an ethereal hue over the whole field and giving everything—absolutely everything—a heavenly glow, like you saw in those old religious paintings in museums.

Mason turned and his eyes widened as he took it all in. "Whoa. How did you arrange that?"

"Easy," I said. "It was on my spreadsheet."

"Well, keep it up with the spreadsheets, then. That's all I've got to say."

Over the next half hour, Annie staged us in all sorts of positions—some serious and traditional, others quirky and fun.

Dad pulled Tilly up to the front, next to the Christmas trees, and Mason and I scooted up onto the tailgate and rested my bouquet between us. Annie captured us in all sorts of poses and angles, even including Riley in a couple of them. Then she asked the rest of the wedding party to join us.

We took several with my parents with Tilly as our backdrop. Then Annie took several more that included Bessie Mae and Bob. I had no doubt Papaw would have loved every single one. Finally, we got one with his aunt Lucy, who was happy to pose with her husband on either side of Mason and me.

Just about the time the sun slipped off beyond the horizon, we wrapped up the photo session and headed into the tent. Landon did a fabulous job deejaying as we made our grand entrance, and Annie snagged photos right and left.

My breath caught in my throat when I saw that gorgeous tiered wedding cake—all decked out with white roses, evergreen, and berries—in the center of the room on that grand table with its wooden base. The best part? That red truck topper with the little bride and groom. I just couldn't get enough of it!

My gaze shifted to the food area, where I took in all the things that Iva and Eva had prepared. And Enrique. That churro bar was one of the loveliest surprises of the night. He and Dot had spared no expense.

We took our seats with the rest of the bridal party at the table up front, and food was served. Well, most of the guests served themselves. That was the joy of the finger food plan. But Iva and Eva brought our plates to us first so that we wouldn't miss out.

"Promise you'll eat something," Iva said. "I've been to many a wedding where the bride and groom skipped out on the food and regretted it later."

As I gazed down at all the luscious foods on my plate, I realized she wouldn't have to ask me twice. I started off with a nibble of the brisket slider. Heavens to Betsy, was it good. The perfect smoky Texas flavors. Then I reached for the green bean bundle wrapped in bacon.

Annie happened by with the camera as green beans dangled from my fingers. She snapped a photo, and I had to laugh at how that one would turn out.

Probably about as funny as the one she took of Mason shoveling a deviled egg into his mouth.

Or the one of me wiping jalapeño honey butter off my face after downing one of the most delicious corn bread bites I'd ever eaten.

Man, these ladies could cook.

I saved the best for last—the chicken-fried steak bites. Unfortunately, after only one bite, Landon announced it was time for the festivities to begin.

Before I knew it, music was playing and we were out on the dance floor having our first dance while Dolly crooned "I Will Always Love You." Then came the moment I'd been both dreading and looking forward to—the dance with my dad. This time I couldn't stop the tears from flowing as he held me in his arms and whisked me around the dance floor while "I Loved Her First" played.

"He's a good man, RaeLyn." My father nodded in Mason's direction.

"He is," I agreed. "And he's going to be a great husband."

We finished and my dad gave a big bow, garnering applause from the crowd. Which was, of course, exactly what he was looking for.

Afterward, Mason asked his aunt to join him for the mother-groom dance. She wiped away tears and took his hand. As they took a spin around the floor, I looked around the room, my heart full as I watched our guests celebrating.

Off in the distance I saw Enrique gabbing with Iva and Eva. They were all laughing and having a wonderful time.

Guests gravitated toward the churro bar, and before long, a line had formed. I found myself craving one of those sugary treats. I didn't have to wait long. Enrique showed up with plates for Mason and me, complete with melted chocolate and dulce de leche. Yum.

I took one bite and practically swooned.

"Enrique!"

He said something in Spanish that I couldn't quite make out, then made a beeline back to his station to wait on the guests.

Moments later the floor was opened to all our guests and the real celebration began. I couldn't help but feel overcome as I watched all my brothers with the women they loved. And how sweet to see little Colt steal his mom away from my brother. I was so glad Annie caught that moment on film.

As the guests continued to celebrate, we headed off to cut the cake.

This was the part I was dreading. Southern tradition called for smashing cake into your loved one's face, something I didn't care for. So we opted for sweet, tidy bites instead, entertaining the crowd with a big kiss while we still had sugar on our lips.

Next came the toasts. Dallas and Tasha—in their roles of best man and maid of honor—offered sweet, fun words of encouragement.

When Dallas looked my way, he gave me a little wink.

And that's when I remembered the big event yet to come.

The bouquet toss.

No one knew it was coming, of course. I'd almost forgotten myself. But clearly Dallas had not. He patted his jacket pocket and gave me a look that said, *Are we almost ready?*

I put my finger up, asking for a moment.

Then I made my way to Meghan and filled her in. She gasped and then told Summer. Who told Carrie. And between them all, they formulated a plan to clear a path for Tasha to be front and center so that she could catch that bouquet.

Moments later, Landon announced the tossing of the bridal bouquet.

Poor Dallas looked so nervous I thought he might give himself away.

Several single ladies pushed their way to the front, but I watched as Summer, Meghan, and Carrie did their work, creating a chasm down the middle. Hopefully I would surpass my softball skills with this next move.

When I gripped the bouquet in hand and prepared to toss it over my shoulder, I whispered up a prayer that it would land in the right hands.

Then I let her fly.

My breath caught in my throat as I turned and saw Tasha, triumphant, with the bouquet in hand. It took her a moment to realize that Dallas was already down on one knee. A gasp went up from the crowd, but the loudest one came from Tasha, who looked like she might pass out.

It took some time for the crowd to settle down, but when they did, he gazed up at her, love radiating from his eyes. "Tasha, I fell in love with you before you even knew I existed."

"I knew you existed!" she countered.

He laughed. "I didn't think you were ever going to give me the time of day, but now I'm asking you if you'll give me the *rest* of your days. Will you marry me, Tasha?"

I watched as my best friend shoved the bouquet into Summer's hands and said, "*Will* I? Of course I will!" Then stuck out her left hand in playful fashion.

He slipped the ring onto her finger and then rose to lift her into the air with a celebratory shout.

The audience went nuts at this point. And Landon immediately started playing a familiar upbeat song: "Celebration." Before long, everyone was singing along.

"Mason, look!" I pointed up to the chandelier above my brother and best friend. "They're standing under the mistletoe! Who else can say they got engaged under the mistletoe?"

"No one I know. But we just got married under the mistletoe, so there is that."

Mom came rushing my way and pulled me away from the crowd. "RaeLyn, did you know that was going to happen?"

"Just found out last night. Dallas asked if I would be okay with it."

"I can't believe he pulled that off. I never saw it coming."

Maybe she didn't want to see it coming?

"Know what else I didn't see?" Mom shifted her gaze to Meghan and Logan, who were dancing in the center of the dance floor. "My new daughter-in-law is a really good person."

"I suspected as much."

"We had a quiet little heart-to-heart at the hair salon, and she told me their news." Mom's eyes sparkled with delight. "I'm going to be a grandma. . .again! Can you believe it?"

"Logan's going to make a great dad, and Meghan's going to make a terrific mom."

"She's nervous, but I told her not to worry. She can come to me and ask anything she likes. We're going to have so much fun shopping for that new baby. When you get back from your honeymoon, we'll have to talk about a baby shower for her."

"Of course. I'd love that."

Mom paused and gave me a tender smile. "Do you know why I've been so heartbroken about you leaving, RaeLyn?"

"It's a big change."

"It's not just that." She reached to give my hand a squeeze. "I've had the privilege of raising you, of watching you blossom from a precocious little girl into a woman that I'm incredibly proud of."

I felt the sting of tears in my eyes as she continued.

"I don't know if I've ever told you just how blessed I am to be your mom." She pulled me into an embrace, and I felt a lump grow in my throat as she kissed my forehead. "You've held your own in this houseful of rowdy boys."

"Probably because I'm such a tomboy myself."

"You sure don't look like one tonight. But regardless, you're a strong woman of God, and I'm blessed to call you not just my daughter but my friend."

"Aw, man." I felt tears slip down my cheeks.

"That's why I'll miss you so much. It's not that I need to mother you so much. I'm just losing my best friend."

"No you're not, Mom. I promise I'll be close by."

"In that fabulous house on the lake."

"Where we'll host barbecues and swim parties and. . ."

"More baby showers?" She quirked a brow.

"Hey now, let's don't get the cart ahead of the horse." I laughed and released myself from her grip. "But yes, maybe someday. When the time is right. And you'll see me several days a week at the shop, so. . ."

"I know." She sighed. "And for the record, I've already been looking at new bedding for the new master bedroom. Want to see it?"

"Seriously? You went shopping without your best friend?" I gave her a pretend scowl.

"Didn't buy anything. But I've been looking, and I can't wait to show you what I've found. Your old mom's ventured into the twenty-first century."

"Wow." Progress.

"Tell me the truth. . .what do you think of this?" She pulled up her phone and opened her shopping cart on Amazon. I had to laugh when I saw the wild tropical bedding set with its shocking pink-and-gold features. And those palm trees. Wow.

"Your father's going to love the flamingos, don't you think?"

"Mom. . .seriously?"

"No." She laughed and shoved her phone into her purse. "Just wanted to see your reaction. It was all your dad's idea, to convince you how much I need you."

"And I need both of you. I always will. But right now. . ." My gaze shifted to Mason, who was deep in conversation with Dot. His gaze shifted my way, and the loveliest smile lit his face. "Right now, I think I see someone who needs me even more."

CHAPTER THIRTY-ONE

We kept the party going for quite some time. But somewhere around eight thirty Mason and I were both showing signs of fatigue. We had completed all the things on my spreadsheet—and were ready to head home.

Home.

I could barely think of the word without a smile crossing my face.

Home, where we would spend our first night together as man and wife.

The very idea made me so happy I wanted to cry.

I'm not sure how or when it happened, but the groomsmen had cleared out the bed of my beloved truck and decorated her with the usual Just Married paraphernalia dangling from the tailgate.

When we climbed in the cab of the truck to head off to the house, the crowd followed along behind us, cheering and carrying on with great joy. I caught a glimpse of Mom's face as she stood off in the distance. My dad slipped his arm around her waist and whispered something in her ear that made her smile. Seeing them together like that brought me great comfort.

With the whole crowd looking on, we drove off to our new home to begin our happily ever after.

The drive went by in a flash. Before I knew it, he was lifting me over the threshold and ushering me into our new home. The one where all my dreams were about to come true.

~

No matter what I'd drummed up in my imagination, it didn't even come close to the feelings that swept over me as my husband and I shared that blissful first night together. I would have to adopt Iva and Eva's favorite word—*ooh-la-la!*

Mason and I woke early, just as the sun rose, and made our way out to the deck to have our first cup of coffee as husband and wife.

I eased my way down into the Adirondack chair overlooking the water and took a little sip of the steaming hot coffee. Off in the distance, a fisherman buzzed by in his small motorboat. I waved, and he waved back.

Mason took the chair across from me. He looked my way with a smile. "This has been quite the week for you, Mrs. Fredericks."

"Hasn't it, though?" I laughed.

"You moved Bessie Mae, battled a fire, hosted a brunch, dealt with a flood, planned a wedding, got the shock of your life with Dot's marriage, got married, and watched your brother and best friend get engaged. I'd say that's a pretty full week."

"You were pretty busy yourself, pulling off the surprise of the century with our new house." I reached over to grab his hand. "Have I thanked you for our new house?"

"Only thirty times. But thirty-one is the magic number."

I gave his hand another squeeze. "This is the start of a great new life together."

"One thing's for sure—it's not going to be boring."

"You can say that twice and mean it."

"It's not going to be boring," he repeated. . .and then laughed. "Not if this week is any indicator."

"I think we can safely assume it will be very. . .lively. I'm a Hadley, after all."

"You're a Fredericks."

"Oh, that's right." RaeLyn Fredericks did have a nice ring to it.

"At any rate, I'm hoping our honeymoon will be quiet, peaceful, and drama-free."

"Amen to that."

While Mason showered, I settled onto the bed in the master bedroom, laptop in hand, to see if I could possibly salvage the article I'd written about Karter and Kenner. Something about it still felt off. I went back through all the info one last time, and that's when the niggling issue hit me squarely in the face.

I made a quick call to Gage, and he answered right away.

"Aren't you supposed to be on a honeymoon or something?"

"Gage, were the boys wet?"

"I beg your pardon?"

"Karter and Kenner. When you found them at Buck's place, were their clothes wet?"

"I don't think so. Why?"

I groaned. "Because they told me they were in the lake when the fire started. They made it through the flames to the highway because they were damp from the water."

"Right. That's what they told us too."

"But they weren't wet."

"It's all kind of a blur, but you're right. I don't remember their clothes being wet. So, what are you saying?"

I shifted the phone to my other ear. "I'm saying boys will be boys. Sometimes they lie. Sometimes they *say* they saved the day when, in reality, they caused the problem in the first place."

"You think that they—"

"We've been saying all along that this was a biblical miracle. But maybe there's another reason they didn't smell like smoke or have any burns. You know? Maybe that whole running-through-the-fire-to-safety story was made up because—"

"They set the fire."

"Right."

He paused. "What are you thinking, RaeLyn?"

"I'm thinking they're boys. And boys sometimes do mischievous things."

"Like set off fireworks in a barn and almost burn the ranch down."

I shifted my position on the bed. "And then blame it on their sister because they don't want to get into trouble."

"Then wait fifteen years to come clean." He paused. "I'll call the chief and ask him to reach out to them."

"Promise you'll get back to me when you know something?"

"Yes. But, RaeLyn?"

"Yeah?"

"Go on your honeymoon."

I looked up as Mason came out of the shower dressed in nothing but a towel. My heart rate quickened.

"Um, okay." I ended the call with Gage and looked up with a smile.

"Better get a move on, Mrs. Fredericks," my husband said. "We've got a plane to catch."

"Absolutely." I shoved the laptop aside and dove into action.

Half an hour later we were dressed and headed to Dallas in Mason's truck.

And twenty minutes after that, Dad texted a picture of the most beautiful little filly I'd ever seen. I decided to name her Honey.

As we approached the entrance to the DFW airport, my phone rang. I glanced down to discover Mom's name on the screen.

"You okay if I take this?" I asked. "It's my mom."

"Don't mind a bit." Mason turned on the signal and changed lanes while I answered the call. I could tell he was distracted with his GPS, so I opted not to put the call on speakerphone.

"Hey, Mom. What's up?"

"RaeLyn, I'm sorry to bother you, but you're never going to believe what's happened!"

"After this week?" I chuckled. "Try me."

"Your dad and I are headed south to Galveston."

"Galveston? In December?"

"Yes!" A playful laugh followed. "Apparently, Dot talked him into taking me on a second honeymoon. A cruise! We're leaving out of Galveston tomorrow morning for six days in the Caribbean."

"No way."

"I think it was the all-you-can-eat buffets that won him over. Apparently, he got the tickets deeply discounted at the last minute. I had no idea your father was so..." She giggled. "Impulsive."

"Well now." I laughed. "See there, Mom? Maybe this next season of your life will be a lot more exciting than you dared to dream."

"We're going on the *Allure of the Seas*, same ship Dot took. Doesn't that sound...alluring?" Another giggle followed.

All righty then. Maybe my dad still had a few surprises left in him.

Mom went on and on about the stops they would be making in Cozumel and Roatán, but she lost me when Mason glanced my way.

"My parents are going on a Caribbean cruise," I explained after I ended the call with Mom.

"Please tell me they're not coming to Playa Del Carmen."

I laughed. "No. Cozumel and Roatan. But I wouldn't put it past her to ask the captain to divert the *Allure of the Seas* to Playa Del Carmen."

He laughed. "*Allure of the Seas*?"

"I know. You should've heard the way she said it." I couldn't help but grin. "It was very—"

"Alluring?"

"Yeah."

"Well, I'm glad for your mother. She needs something special right now."

"Agreed. She's been through a lot."

"We all have."

Mason finally located the right parking garage, and minutes later we were unloading our luggage from his truck.

And that's when the text came through from Gage. Just three words: "The boys confessed."

"Whoa." I nearly lost my grip on my phone.

Looked like I wouldn't be turning in that article after all.

"What is it?" Mason asked as he hefted my bag from the back of the truck.

"Oh. . ." I shoved my phone back into my purse. "Nothing that can't wait until we're back from our honeymoon."

"Great!" A relaxed smile lit his handsome face. "Because I've got a thousand things planned for us while we're in Playa Del Carmen. How do you feel about a massage in a private cabana on the beach with the ocean waves pounding the shore in the background?"

"Well, it sounds terrific." I bit back a smile as I reached for my suitcase. "But that's just not possible, I'm afraid."

"Not possible?" Mason's smile faded as he set the suitcase down. "Why is that?"

"Because, silly. . ." I said with a playful wink. "It's simply not on the spreadsheet."

Classic Churros

INGREDIENTS

For the Dough:

1 cup water

2½ tablespoons butter

1 tablespoon sugar

½ teaspoon salt

1 cup flour

2 large eggs

1 teaspoon vanilla

For Frying:

Neutral oil (like vegetable or canola)

For Coating:

½ cup sugar
1 teaspoon ground cinnamon

Optional Dipping Sauce:

Melted chocolate, caramel, or dulce de leche

INSTRUCTIONS

Whisk together cinnamon and sugar in a small bowl. Combine water, butter, sugar, and salt in medium saucepan and bring to simmer. Reduce heat and add flour; then stir vigorously until a smooth dough forms (about 1 to 2 minutes). Remove from heat and let the dough cool for 5 minutes.

Place eggs and vanilla in mixing bowl and beat until combined. Slowly work in dough, beating until it becomes smooth. Transfer dough to piping bag fitted with large star tip (Wilton 1M works great).

Heat oil in deep pot or fryer (about 2 inches of oil heated to 350 degrees). Pipe 6-inch strips of dough directly into the hot oil, cutting the dough with scissors as it drops in. Fry in batches to avoid overcrowding.

Fry for 2 to 3 minutes per side or until golden brown and crisp. Use slotted spoon to transfer to paper towel–lined plate to drain. Roll in cinnamon-sugar mixture. Serve with melted caramel, chocolate sauce, or dulce de leche if desired.

A Note from the Author

Dear Readers:

In the mid-nineties, as I drove up to the Mabank area from Houston (where I lived), I saw smoke off in the distance. The closer we got to my mother and stepfather's acreage (sixty-three gorgeous acres of cattle land), the thicker the smoke got.

When we arrived on Mom's street, the reality of what faced us was unavoidable. The property across the road, to our left, was in a roaring blaze, flames moving so fast my car couldn't keep up with them on the narrow country road.

My children and I made it to Mom's driveway and went inside. In that moment, a decision was made to gather in a circle and pray. We offered up a passionate plea for the Lord's protection then rushed outside to grab hoses to help water everything down.

Just as you read in this story, firefighters got that massive blaze stopped right at the edge of her property. And I can tell you as a firsthand witness that not a spark landed on any of us.

As I sat to write this story, I was faced with another real-life situation, this one happening in California, where folks weren't so fortunate. I watched the news daily, my heart heavy as I saw the devastation near a home where our family once lived.

From those ashes, I'm sure California will rise. And, I can assure you, we as a family never forgot the mercy and grace of God as we faced our

Isaiah 43 moment. No doubt you've been through a few fires too. Fear not. The Lord is right there, ready to carry you through.

Blessings on you all,
Janice Thompson

JANICE THOMPSON, who lives in the Houston area, writes novels, nonfiction, magazine articles, and musical comedies for the stage. The mother of four married daughters, she is quickly adding grandchildren to the family mix.

The Little Red Truck Mysteries

The Hadley family opens Trinkets and Treasures antique store in their old barn. Soon the ranchers turned antique dealers must become sleuths to solve a string of mysteries.

Tracking Tilly
Book 1
by Janice Thompson

The Hadley family ranch is struggling, so RaeLyn, her parents, and her brothers decide to turn the old barn into an antique store. The only thing missing to go with the store is Grandpa's old red truck, Tilly, that was sold several years ago. Now coming back up on the auction block, Tilly will need a lot of work, but RaeLyn is sure it will be worth it—if only she can beat out other bidders and then find out who has stolen Tilly after the auction ends. RaeLyn finds herself in the role of amateur sleuth, and the outcome could make or break the new family venture.

Paperback / 978-1-63609-908-8